THE CRITICS RAVE ABOUT
NIGHTWATCHER!

"A natural born storyteller, Wilson possesses a marvelous gift for pulse-pounding narrative drive."
—*The Clarion Ledger*

"Tautly suspenseful."   —*The Commercial Appeal*

"First rate...suspenseful. It's told at a breakneck pace that doesn't allow the reader to pause for breath."
—*Mostly Murder*

"One of the best!"
—*Richmond Times-Dispatch*

"Wilson sustains the suspense to the very end of the story."
—*Houston Home Journal*

"As an inventor of a plot, Wilson is something."
—*Los Angeles Times*

NIGHTWATCHER

CHARLES WILSON

LEISURE BOOKS   NEW YORK CITY

A LEISURE BOOK®

July 1997

Published by

Dorchester Publishing Co., Inc.
276 Fifth Avenue
New York, NY 10001

Printed in the United States of America.

To my family: Linda, Charles, Cassie, and Destin;
with a special thanks to Shirley, Cas, and Ladye;
to Lynn Clark who helped me "English it up";
and to Tommy Furby, without whose encouragement I
would have never written this in the first place.

CHAPTER

1

It was an unsettled night at the John H. Douglas State Hospital for the Insane, the smell of an impending storm in the air. Staff nurse Judith Salter, hurrying along the sidewalk between patient dormitories at the forty acre complex, wondered if she would complete her evening medication deliveries before the rain began.

Suddenly the horizon erupted with the flashing of a dozen nearly simultaneous lightning bolts, the sky behind the jagged streaks of energy turning a bright yellow, the rain clouds bleaching to a soft fluffy blue. She smiled at the beauty of the scene.

Then, as the night became dark and forbidding again, her smile quickly faded at the reminder of how her life had deteriorated: quick, bright, beautiful moments she enjoyed so much and couldn't resist now always ended in a black, fearful darkness.

She did not know when she had lost control of the game or how, only that she had. Now, no matter what a man appeared to be when she started an affair, no matter what he promised, the ending was the same— he trying to force her into going farther than she enjoyed, past fantasy into real danger.

She shook her head as she hurried up the steps to resident unit R-14 and pushed the admittance buzzer. It would be different in New Orleans. She would start her life over there, find a good church-going father for the twins and not take any chances this time; she'd keep her marriage normal from the very beginning.

She pushed the admittance buzzer again. After waiting another minute she began repeatedly jabbing her finger against the button.

The door finally opened.

A lanky, pencil-mustachioed security guard stepped back to let her enter. He had a fixed smile on his narrow face and was clumsily affecting a nonchalant attitude—his head tilted slightly to the side, most of his weight on one foot.

"Evening," he said.

Irritated at how long she had been kept waiting, she didn't return the greeting, walking on past him to the cabinet at the side of the short entrance hall.

Opening her carrying case she began removing bottles of medicine from it, arranging them on the cabinet's shelves. When she finished and turned toward the guard, her face still reflected her irritation.

"Dr. Adams wants me to look in on Ben Rodgers," she said.

The guard nodded and stepped to the glass-paneled door leading to the patient quarters, unlocking it.

"Sorry I took so long," he finally said. "I was inside checking on a patient."

"Where's Jerry?"

The guard grinned but didn't answer.

She snapped her case shut. "Dammit, am I the only one around here who doesn't goof off?" She shook her head as she came around the desk. "You skipped out last night."

The man's mouth gaped open, as if astonished she had said such a thing. "No, I didn't. I ran to get a pack of smokes. When I got back Jerry told me you had just left."

"Bull. Just keep it up. One of these nights a patient's going to teach you why there's supposed to be two of you on duty."

He smiled and patted the mace and billy club which hung from his belt, then touched the handle of his holstered revolver. "No problem."

Judith frowned. She didn't like his flippant reply. She didn't like his cocky smile. And she especially didn't like patient security being entrusted to the type of guards the hospital employed: mental cowboys in wrinkled uniforms who probably couldn't find a job doing anything else.

She looked at the big, chrome-plated revolver he wore at his side. She knew patients at the hospital she would better trust with the responsibility of carrying such a weapon.

"And you're not supposed to take a gun inside around the patients," she said, and strode into the living quarters.

The guard quickly locked the door and hurried after her. "Would you rather I leave it in the office, so one of 'em can sashay in and swipe it while we're gone?"

She stopped and turned to face him. "It would be smarter if . . ." She could smell the liquor on his breath. Worse were the dilated pupils. "Never mind," she said, disgust crossing her face. "Which room is Rodgers in?"

The guard pointed down the hall past a group of milling patients. "Room 12."

Judith glanced at her watch, then shook her head. "It's nearly ten-thirty. I'm never going to finish packing."

"Still gonna leave, huh? I been hearing Dr. Salter's gonna let the kids come back."

"Court order," she said.

"When you taking off?"

"First thing in the morning. I've had enough of this place."

"I hate that you're leaving. I'll sorta miss you around here."

His tone was sincere and Judith caught herself giving him a smile.

"Where you headed?" he asked.

"New Orleans, stay with Daddy awhile. Haven't made up my mind whether I'll work in a hospital down there or not. Well, let me go see about Rodgers."

As she turned and moved down the hall the guard stared after her, the tip of his tongue moistening his lips. To the side of the hall a pair of R-14's patients stood in the doorway to their room, their eyes also following the young nurse's tightly uniformed figure.

Judith quickly determined there was nothing wrong with Ben Rodgers. If you considered chronic depression and delusions of persecution as nothing wrong, she thought. But that was why he was here in the first place. At least he wasn't physically sick, and that was what Dr. Adams had wanted her to check. Glancing at her watch she shook her head and walked from the room, moving back down the hall.

The security guard stepped from the linen room at

the end of the hallway and hurried to let her out. His pupils were even larger now.

"What do you expect," she mumbled to herself, shaking her head.

"What?"

"Nothing." Quid pro quo. The hospital pays the guards next to nothing—it gets what it pays for. The patients might as well be guarding themselves. One of these days something terrible was going to occur. It was just a matter of time.

It wasn't her problem, though. Nothing to do with the hospital was her problem anymore. And her other problems would be behind her, too, after tomorrow. Screw men, and screw their threats, too.

Hurrying through the night's shadows once again, she was back at the pharmacy in ten minutes.

Glancing at her watch she noted her check-out time on the duty roster, forty-five minutes after her shift was supposed to have ended.

"Bet when fat-face Johansen okays my check she'll screw me out of the overtime," she said to the pharmacist. "Well, bye. You were one of my few favorite people here—very few."

"Good luck, Judith. I'll miss you."

At the curb she paused in the dim light from the street lamp, staring at her antique MG—a present from her father, Brandon Richards. Daddy, she thought, maybe it's your fault I expect so much from men. You shouldn't have spoiled me so.

The rain had begun to fall as she stopped her MG beside the guardhouse at the hospital's main gate. The security guard waved her through without stepping outside.

A hundred feet down the highway she turned onto the blacktop road which circled back alongside the hospital perimeter fence. A few hundred yards farther she drove into the cluster of rent-subsidized staff cottages adjoining the hospital complex.

She spent a frenetic half-hour finishing her packing, leaving out only what she would be wearing during the drive to New Orleans. She then moved to the kitchen and used white icing to cover the cake she had baked that morning. Selecting blue icing, she scrawled a happy message on top of the white, then stepped back and smiled down at her work.

After putting the cake in the refrigerator she hurried toward her bedroom, unbuttoning her uniform as she walked.

Fifteen minutes later she was through with her bath. Using a towel to rub her hair briskly, she stepped naked from the bathroom back into her bedroom.

She sensed the figure who moved from the wall behind her rather than heard it. Too late to run, her scream was cut off by the gloved hand covering her mouth.

Hard blows chopped repeatedly into the side of her neck and she went limp; her form slid down the intruder's body to the floor.

The figure stood a moment, breathing heavily. Then it stooped and gathered her in its arms, carrying her across the room and roughly depositing her backward onto the bed.

Reaching into its right pocket it removed a small dark vial which it placed on the bedside table. Fumbling in its left pocket it produced a contraceptive packet. Undressing quickly, the figure stripped naked except for its socks. Finally, it tore open the contraceptive packet and prepared itself.

Climbing onto the bed, it moved astride Judith's waist. Its knees sunk into the mattress on each side of her body, the figure's thighs hugged her ribs as it sat back on Judith's soft abdomen, resting a moment, staring with cold eyes. Then it moved its fingers to her heavy breasts, able to feel their warmth even through the thin surgical gloves covering its hands.

Judith moaned, her eyes slowly opening.

"Hello, bitch."

Even in her dazed condition she recognized the figure; her shock registered in the terrified expression which contorted her face. She tried to raise her arms to protect herself, but they were pinned against her sides by the clasping legs.

"No," she softly begged, tears starting to seep from her eyes. "Please, no. Please don't do this. Please."

The figure raised a clenched fist—

"No!"

—and slammed it hard into the side of Judith's face.

"Bitch!"

Another blow.

"Dirty bitch!"

Another blow.

"Dirty *damn bitch!*"

Then another, and another, and another, and . . .

CHAPTER

2

The sun had just begun to rise when Brandon Richards turned his Cadillac onto the blacktop road leading to the staff cottages. Ever since leaving his Lake Pontchartrain home he had alternated between driving at a reckless pace and then slowing back to the speed limit—the Davis County Mississippi Sheriff's Department had said there was no need to risk driving fast; she was already dead.

He shuddered involuntarily, his hands trembling against the steering wheel, tears starting down his cheeks again. His neck felt constricted and he loosened his tie farther, spread the neck of his white shirt wider. Maybe, please God, they were wrong.

Approaching Judith's cottage he saw the police vehicles parked at its front—a white van with a crime lab insignia on its side, and a couple automobiles. As big a hurry as he had been in to get there, now he didn't want to arrive.

"Please, no, God," he begged one last time as he turned off the key.

"I'm sorry, sir. This is a restricted crime scene area. You'll have to leave."

Richards looked up. He hadn't noticed the highway patrol officer until he heard the voice.

"Sir, are you all right?" The officer's tone was softer this time.

"I'm her father." Richards realized how he must look, and brushed the hair back from his forehead.

"Excuse me, sir, but wait right there a minute." The gray-uniformed patrolman turned and strode toward the cottage.

Stepping from his automobile, Richards watched the patrolman move onto the porch and stop next to a man standing at the cottage door. Dressed in a dark business suit and appearing to be in his late forties, the man was nodding his head at the officer's words. Then the two stepped off the porch and came across the lawn.

"Mr. Richards. I'm Sheriff Tidmore. I'm very sorry."

The sheriff's voice was exceptionally soft for a man so big. He was at least two inches taller than Richards's six feet, and much more heavily built—well over two hundred pounds. Richards relinquished the support of the side of his Cadillac and held his hand out.

Staring intently at Richards's face, the sheriff took a moment to notice the proffered hand, then he was clumsy in his grasp. "I'm sorry," he said again.

"Are the children here yet? Judith's children, they

were taken away . . . by her husband. The court ordered him to have them back this morning."

"Yes, sir, I know. I wouldn't worry about that right now. Would you like to sit down?"

Richards self-consciously smoothed his hair back again, and in doing so felt the oily stickiness of perspiration against his palm. He felt a drop roll off his nose. He knew the color had drained from his face; he could feel it, and he felt dizzy. He looked toward the cottage. "Where is she?" His voice had a strange hoarseness and he cleared his throat.

"You won't be able to see her today," the sheriff said softly. "She'll be at the funeral home tomorrow. I can have one of my deputies drive you to a motel."

Guessing why he couldn't see her now increased the perspiration on Richards's back, and the lump in his throat forced him to stand silent a moment. "It happened in there?"

"Yes, sir. She was getting ready for bed."

"Can I go in?"

"I don't think that would do you any good. You've had a long drive, and with this on your mind the whole time. I really think you ought to let one of my deputies—"

"I'd like to go inside." He could feel his lip tremble.

"It's vivid, Mr. Richards. I'm afraid you . . . Something like that could bother you for a long time . . . too long."

The highway patrol officer tried to be helpful. "It's a crime scene, sir. We have to keep it sealed up." His tone was compassionate.

"I can handle it, Sheriff. I won't touch anything."

The sheriff had been elected by the rural inhabitants of Davis County not because of his knowledge of criminology—he had been a dairy farmer before he won the election—but because he was thought of as an honest, God-fearing man. "Okay. I really don't think you should, but I'll take you through. The lab people are about finished, but they might need to come back. It won't do us any good if you disturb anything."

Richards nodded and started toward the house. The front door was standing open and he didn't have to touch anything when he walked inside.

Two men in white laboratory coats were kneeling in the living room-kitchen combination, their gloved hands busy at a spot on the hardwood floor. They didn't look up. He walked into the bedroom.

My God, no! He couldn't handle it.

The police had removed the sheets from Judith's bed, but a large bloody circle on the mattress showed where the beating had begun. The headboard was covered with red stains now turning black. There was even a spot on the wall above the headboard. The killer had beaten and torn at his daughter until her body was running red, and then continued to hit her, splashing her lifeblood into the air.

He stood rigid, staring in shock, his heart racing. His vision began to blur, his knees became rubbery. Turning away, he hurried back toward the front door. Barely outside, he vomited on the porch.

It was a few minutes before he trusted his voice again. Inhaling through his mouth in an attempt to avoid the stench of blood in his nostrils, he took a deep breath, then turned to the sheriff. "How did it happen?"

"Patients at one of the dorms killed their security guard. They pried up the bottom of the perimeter fence and crawled under it. It's only a boundary fence, not meant to prevent anyone from getting out. One of them broke in on her."

"So you don't know which one is responsible?"

"There were twenty-two patients in the building. A dozen escaped. Nine were found wandering around on the grounds, three are gone. They were from unit R-14. It's where the hospital keeps the difficult cases, the ones who occasionally get out of hand. But they weren't considered dangerous. Something like this . . ." The sheriff glanced back toward the cottage door. "It's hard to believe one of them was capable of this. But we'll find out which one did it."

"There was only the one guard?"

"Supposed to have been two. We don't know where the second one is. Thought they might have taken him hostage. He was signed in on the duty roster. But when my deputies called his home his wife said not to worry, she knew where he was. She said she would see he got down here right away. He hasn't showed yet. We're certainly going to be talking to him when he does.

"There were also two orderlies," the sheriff continued. "They say they were in the linen room folding laundry and didn't hear anything. When they finished they noticed the patients missing and the guard lying in the hall with a broken neck. The rules say the orderlies are supposed to check each patient's room every fifteen minutes. They claim they weren't in the linen room over five or ten minutes."

Richards felt his cheeks flush, realized his anger was apparent in his voice, and didn't care. "They discovered the escape five or ten minutes after it happened, and nobody warned the people living in the cottages?"

The sheriff's voice remained soft. "We found drugs in the linen room. No telling how long they had really been in there. Everyone was notified as soon as they reported it. That's when security discovered your daughter."

Richards didn't say anything, only turned and

stepped back into the house. The sheriff followed, shaking his head.

This time Richards didn't enter Judith's room. Instead he walked on through the living area and down the short hallway to the children's bedroom.

It was undisturbed, the twin beds neatly made, the toys arranged carefully on the shelves.

Across the hall the small bathroom appeared untouched.

He walked back toward the living area, stopping when he noticed the faint scuff marks on the hardwood floor. There were four of them, spaced evenly between the door to Judith's bedroom and the hall.

The sheriff's eyes moved to the marks. "The patient took off his shoes in the bedroom, probably to keep from being heard. She must have been taking a bath at the time. She had brought a towel into the bedroom with her, and all the clothes she had been wearing were in the bathroom.

"Anyway, he definitely was in his stocking feet when he was in the bedroom. There're sock prints next to the bed where he stepped in some blood. He must have gotten some on one of his shoes when he was slipping them back on. When he came out here he left these scuff marks. Probably was disoriented. There's no way out down the hall except for the children's bedroom windows, and they're locked." The sheriff glanced toward the kitchen door. "That door leads to the side of the yard. That's where he went out. There was blood on the doorknob and some drops across the kitchen floor. He evidently came in that way, too. The front door was bolted from the inside."

Richards walked to the kitchen door and looked through its glass panes. The side yard was separated from the next cottage by a thick hedgerow. He couldn't see through it. Neither could the neighbors, if they had happened to glance toward her cottage during the night.

He couldn't shake one troubling thought. "Sheriff, was . . . was there anything else done to her? Was she molested?"

The sheriff looked into Richards's eyes a long moment, then gave a slight nod. "Lab says she was raped, at least penetrated. Whoever raped her, he didn't ejaculate."

Richards moved to the kitchen counter and leaned back against it. He took a deep breath and let it out slowly. His gaze fell on the refrigerator.

The thought which suddenly entered his mind was irrational, but he couldn't make it go away. The corner of his mouth twitched. A single tear started down his right cheek.

"Mr. Richards," the sheriff said softly, "let's go back outside."

Richards shook his head. "I can't help it, I don't want the food to rot."

The sheriff's expression was one of puzzlement.

"I don't want her food to rot. I don't want it to lie there . . . and just . . . rot."

The sheriff glanced toward the refrigerator. "I'll take care of it," he said, his voice low and gentle. "Is there any particular place . . . ?"

"Give it to somebody. I don't want it to rot." He could feel tears running down both his cheeks and he was ashamed, and he wanted his daughter, and he didn't want the food to rot, and he knew he had to go back outside into the fresh air again.

"I'll carry it to my house," the sheriff said. "Let's see how much there is." He pulled a handkerchief from his pocket. Draping it over his hand, he pulled on the refrigerator door from its top corner rather than the handle, swinging it open.

There wasn't much inside. Lunchmeat, bacon, eggs, a half-empty gallon of milk, and a quart of orange juice. And a large white, thickly frosted cake. In a blue icing scrawl Judith had spelled out, WELCOME HOME KIDS.

CHAPTER

3

Richards had to travel the full twenty miles into Jackson to find a presentable hotel, an old Holiday Inn. He ordered a hamburger and a glass of tea from room service, yet managed only two bites before pushing the plate aside. Continuing to sit at the room's table, he stared out the window, tears slowly seeping from his eyes. The ice in his tea had disappeared before he moved again.

He didn't eat again that day, only remained silently sitting until well into the night. Finally, he decided he would try to rest.

Slipping between the sheets of the big double bed, he lay there quietly, waiting for sleep to come. It didn't. At two A.M. he threw off the covers and stepped out of the bed. Thirty minutes later he was once again turning onto the road which led to the staff cottages.

As he drove down the blacktop he looked through the Cadillac's passenger window, staring past the eight-foot cyclone fence which ran alongside the road and separated the hospital complex from the staff quarters. Most of the old buildings within the grounds were shrouded in darkness. He could distinguish a few of the hundred-year-old oaks which dotted the area. Beautiful in any other setting, the huge trees, their lower limbs draped in Spanish moss which drooped toward the ground, only added to the forbidding air of the complex.

His eyes narrowed when he glimpsed a figure walking along one of the dimly lit sidewalks. *To walk down a sidewalk in such a place and see a figure walking toward you . . .* He shook his head. Why in God's name had she ever chosen to work here, with a better job offer in New Orleans before she had even graduated?

The street in front of his daughter's home was now empty, but the lights in the cottage had been left burning.

Walking across the small front yard, he paused to look once again toward the hospital grounds. From where he stood it was no more than a couple hundred feet to the perimeter fence. There was no security floodlight focused on the part of the barrier directly across from Judith's, but a floodlight a hundred yards away radiated enough illumination to outline the eight-foot cyclone wire.

His eyes narrowed when he noticed the dim glow of light at the top of a building just inside the fence. As his eyes adjusted to the dark, he saw the light was from a barred window on the building's top floor. Then he noticed another dim light, and movement.

There was a second window. Someone had been standing there, their body blocking the light from that opening.

Squinting, his eyes continuing to adjust, he saw that the building was three stories, its only distinguishable feature the two barred windows on the third floor.

He saw movement again at the second window, a shadowy form once more cutting off most of the glow from the opening. And then whoever it was moved away from the window.

Richards stood staring a moment longer, then turned and stepped onto the cottage porch. Before entering the home, he stopped and took several deep breaths of air in through his mouth. Then he stepped through the door and moved toward Judith's bedroom.

The image he retained from earlier in the day was not exaggerated. He felt the nausea returning. It looked like a bottle of blood had exploded in the bedroom—a big bottle.

Steeling himself, he moved farther into the room. On the floor to the far side of the bed he saw a wide circle of dried blood. The sheriff had said that sometime during the attack Judith had either fallen or been thrown off the bed.

Then he noticed the second dried puddle. It was next to the base of the bedside table and connected to the first by a long thin smear.

His eyes moved from the circle to the dark smudges up the side of the table. He shook his head in dismay. His hands clenched into fists. He stepped closer.

The police had set the telephone back on the nightstand, but the bloody handprint on the receiver was the final confirmation of what he feared. Judith hadn't been knocked mercifully unconscious, going to her death without pain. Sometime after the horrible beating she had regained consciousness. He hadn't wanted to know that.

He shook his head helplessly. The agony she must have been in as she pulled herself to her last hope for help—a telephone the sheriff said the killer had already disabled in the living room.

Perspiration was breaking out on his body. He brought a trembling hand up to loosen the tie which he then remembered he had left in the motel room.

"I'll find out which one of them did this to you, sweetheart. I promise you I will. I won't let you down again."

He tried to clear his mind. He had to think. He had come back to the cottage to think, to think of something no one else had thought of, to notice something only a father would notice. . . .

Yet nothing made any sense. An insane patient, lucid enough to disable the telephones before the attack? And the sheriff said there were no fingerprints. The investigators thought the patient had worn surgical gloves. All the dorm supply rooms stored gloves for the orderlies' protection. For a patient to have stolen a pair before escaping, though, meant he was already planning the attack—didn't it?

There should have been more bloodstains outside the bedroom. There were, however, only the scuff marks, a smear on the doorknob, and three drops on the kitchen floor. Not enough, considering the patient had to be covered in Judith's blood—had even walked in it.

He stared at the five prints made by the killer's bloody socks, and then he knelt and examined them.

Three were from a right foot, two from a left. The trail ended halfway toward the bathroom. Though the prints were left by socks, fuzzy imprints of the actual feet could be made out, where the weight of the balls and heels made a darker imprint than the archs. Even some of the individual toes were discernible.

The three steps from the right foot were clearer than those of the left; the ball, heel, and toe imprints were more distinct. The first of the two prints from the left foot was without any detail at all, smudged as the killer rotated off the foot, stepping away from the bed. The second one was slightly more distinguishable as to the ball and heel, but only the big toe and the two toes to the outside of the foot left an impression.

The sheriff said the lab estimated the killer wore from a ten and a half to a twelve shoe. Did all three of the escaped patients have sizes within that range? He had not thought to ask.

Rising to his feet, his eyes moved to the hole in the ceiling, to where the police had gouged the .22 slug loose. Four spent casings and her automatic had been found lying on the floor next to the bed. The sheriff was sure one of the patients was carrying the missing three slugs in his body. Again, why no trail of blood outside the bedroom?

Moving into the small bathroom, his eyes carefully swept every item. A bar of soap sat in its plastic container next to the single sink. A silver-plated tray on the dressing table contained perfumes, bath oils, and various powders. Faint traces of blue powder marked where the police had searched for fingerprints. A towel lay on the floor. He stared for a long moment at the towel.

He moved back into the bedroom. Earlier in the day there had been a towel on the bedroom floor, a bloody one lying next to the bed. The police must have taken it. And now the one in the bathroom. Judith didn't normally use two towels.

He had spent a weekend with his daughter. Not needlessly soiling laundry was one of the ways she saved money, she had said. Her rule to the twins was one towel per week, per person. The idea had at first seemed to him as . . . well, not good hygiene. Why, she had asked? After a good soaping and rinsing, all the towel was used for was to dry off clean bodies.

So the children had only one towel each on the rack in their bathroom, and she did the same in hers.

He shut his eyes. So much blood. Judith's attacker had to be soaked in it. Was the second towel one he had used? Had he cleaned himself in the bathroom before he left? There wasn't any blood on the towel to indicate . . .

After a good soaping and rinsing, all the towel was used for was to dry off clean bodies!

My God!

He moved back into the bathroom and to the tub, staring down into it.

Had the patient, crazily, insanely, sat calmly in the tub taking a bath after his horrible deed?

There was a bar of soap lying at the bottom of the tub. He leaned over and touched it. It was firm. He turned his palm up and stared at the finger he had touched to the soap.

Had the patient held the bar in his hands, his prints there one second and washed away the next? No, he wore gloves. There would be no prints on the fixtures either.

Footprints! His stare moved to his own feet. Any footprints inside the tub would be washed away as the tub drained—but not those which the patient might have left behind when he stepped in and out of the tub.

Gingerly, he moved backward, stepping as far as he could, hoping he hadn't already destroyed any prints which might have been left next to the tub.

Standing outside the bathroom door he looked back

inside for a long moment. If it turned out there were no footprints, what was there? Psychological profiles —surely the psychiatrists had done them. Shouldn't such records give a clue as to which of the three patients could have committed such a heinous attack, yet at the same time have been so clever? The perpetrator had been careful to leave no fingerprints, had disabled the telephones, and now there was the possibility he had cleaned the evidence of the attack from his body before he left the cottage. Couldn't *something* be read in the lack of evidence?

Turning, his gaze fell on the bare mattress of Judith's bed. He moved to it and reached out a hand. The black stains were dry to the touch. He stared at them a long moment, then suddenly reached down and pressed his palms hard against the mattress, shut his eyes, and waited. He felt only the caked blood under his palms and a growing sense of revulsion. He straightened, shook his head. His lips grew tight. What was he doing? This wasn't like him. He was logical, always had been. Yet now he was allowing himself to be reduced to base emotions—a dying patient desperately clutching a magic mail-order amulet to his chest; a drowning swimmer frantically grabbing for the support of a floating straw; a spiritualist trying to conjure a sense of what happened from a bare mattress. *God help him, what could he do?* His lip trembled. Exhaling audibly, he left the bedroom. He would call the sheriff when it became daylight; maybe there were footprints.

At the center of the living room-kitchen combination, he stopped to stare at the scuff marks on the hardwood floor. It was then that the icemaker clicked, dumping cubes into the plastic tray in the refrigerator, startling him.

Glancing toward the sound, he remembered Judith's food and how the thought of it spoiling had affected him. Covering his hand with his handkerchief he walked to the refrigerator and opened it.

The sheriff had done as he said he would. All the food was gone except for the cake—it was understandable why the man had not wanted to carry such a reminder home with him.

Someone had removed a piece from it.

He lifted the cake from the refrigerator and set it on the countertop. The missing piece appeared to have been scooped or dug out.

His brow wrinkled questioningly. He looked down to the floor at the front of the refrigerator. He ran his eyes across the rest of the kitchen tile. Then he went through the house once again. This time his eyes carefully searched the hardwood floor.

At the edge of the hallway he saw the crumbs, not much bigger than dust particles. Kneeling, he touched them with the tips of his fingers.

Still in a crouch, he ran his eyes farther down the hall. Ten feet away was another crumb, big enough that it should have been noticed earlier. He moved to where it lay.

Lifting it, he mashed it between his fingers. It was still moist. He glanced to the left, into the children's bedroom, and then back to his right, into the small hall bathroom. Then his eyes moved to the ceiling above him, to the string hanging from the trapdoor to the attic.

Rising to his feet, he pulled on the string; he watched the trapdoor come down. The attic was a dark hole above him. He glanced to each side of the hall but saw no light switch.

Out at his automobile he opened the glove compartment and took out the snub-nosed .38 revolver. He was unable to find the flashlight he thought was in the trunk.

Back in the kitchen, he rummaged through the cabinet drawers. In one he found a butane cigarette lighter.

At the bottom of the steps leading to the attic, his foot resting on the first rung, he looked up into the dark opening and hesitated again. He shook his head. Couldn't be, he thought. The killer would have to be crazy to hide in the attic . . . *really crazy.*

Turning, he went back into the living room and lifted the telephone receiver. It was dead. Maybe it had been connected through the hospital switchboard . . . with no need for it to be connected anymore.

Back in the hallway he once again looked up into the dark hole. He knew he couldn't leave to find a pay telephone. By the time he returned he'd never know if someone had left while he was gone or not. He had told Judith her .22 was adequate, and it wasn't. He should have told her she needed a bigger pistol, but he didn't. I can't let her down again. You have a gun. Go on, dammit.

The steps creaked as he moved up them, adding to his nervousness. And then he was in the attic. The short flame from the nearly empty butane lighter casting a circle of dim light; beyond the circle total blackness surrounded him. His hand felt clammy against the handle of the revolver and he clasped it tighter, fearing it might slip.

The attic was floored and he first knelt and studied the wooden planks around the entrance. Rising to his feet he moved slowly toward the back.

Two large cardboard boxes sat where the planking ended, a smaller one on their top.

Then he heard the barely audible sound behind him. A cold chill swept his body, tingling down his back and across his buttocks.

He whirled around, the butane lighter going out at

his movement. He flicked it on again just as an enormous rat passed through the periphery of the lighter's glow. The rat hurdled a small cardboard box and disappeared into the darkness, its scampering feet making the same kind of barely audible noise he had first heard.

"Come on," he said out loud to himself. "Okay?" The sound of his voice reassured him. He shivered at the thought of somebody answering him—and smiled at himself.

He could smell the rats now, the stench so strong in his nostrils he wondered why he was only then noticing it.

He moved the small box aside to look into the bigger ones underneath. On the first, the cardboard flaps covering the opening were jointed together and he had to exert an effort to pop them loose, a cloud of dust rising at their separation. He sneezed, and after doing so heard another scampering across the floor.

The box was empty, and the other one held a single sweater, rather what was left of a sweater. The rats had reassembled the garment into a nest. He turned and moved back across the planking toward the front of the attic.

The butane lighter went out again.

Several flicks failed to light it. Shaking it, agitating the gas, he finally succeeded in getting it to flame once more. He hurried on to the front of the attic.

Several more large boxes sat there. Then he saw the foot sticking out from between two of the boxes. At that moment the lighter went out again.

Hurried repeated flicks did no good. He stopped and listened, his body in a partial crouch, the hand pointing the revolver beginning to shake. Perspiration began running down his face, dripping off his chin.

To back up and move away seemed more frightening than to remain as he was, not making a sound, listening. His breathing grew louder and he tried to muffle it.

For a long time he remained in his partial crouch, straining to hear. Then he cocked the .38 and slowly sank to his knees.

"I have a gun," he announced.

Silence.

He dropped the useless lighter and slowly reached ahead into the darkness. He felt nothing.

Shuffling slowly forward on his knees, he reached out again, moving his hand in a circle, feeling. Nothing, except the dusty wooden planking.

He shuffled a little closer.

Jesus! His hand recoiled from the shoe he had touched.

Steeling his nerves, he reached again.

A shoe, a sock. His fingers worked up to the fabric of the trousers. Rough material. He circled his hand around the ankle, clasped it tightly, and pulled.

Boxes moved as the body slid toward him. He nearly fired his revolver in fright though it was his effort which had caused the movement.

He shut his eyes—he couldn't see anyway—and steadied himself.

Slowly, he reached out again. He found the ankle, ran his fingers up past the socks to the inside of the trouser leg. The skin was cold.

Inching forward again, he reached out and touched the neck, then the face. Cold.

Stone cold dead.

CHAPTER

4

Red and blue flashing lights from the Sheriff's Department vehicles mingled with the blue-green rotating lights of the highway patrol, creating a discotheque effect on the cottage front.

Richards watched as the ambulance attendants wheeled out the white-draped body of Eddie Hopper. Sheriff Tidmore was standing a few feet away, speaking to the deputy who had brought him a brown manilla envelope. The sheriff pulled something from the envelope, looked at it a moment, and then replaced it.

The coroner followed the stretcher from the cottage and walked to where the sheriff stood. Richards moved to where he could hear the small spectacled man's words.

"The hole in the forehead looks rough," the coroner said in his high-pitched voice, nervously fidgeting with the side of his glasses as he spoke. "Yet the angle at which it was fired caused it to follow the cranium around and exit the scalp through the top of the head. It definitely gave him a concussion. He was probably unconscious for a good while. That didn't lead to his expiration, though, no, sir." He shook his head for emphasis.

"The shot in the stomach was causing some bleeding," he continued. "Probably pretty painful. Hell, maybe the poor man thought he was having hunger pains and came down to find something to eat; he was crazy, wasn't he?" He nodded as if answering his own question. "What killed him was right here." The coroner jabbed his neck, just under his jaw, and then nodded his head again.

"Yes, sir, shell grazed the jugular, took part of it away as clean as if you used a scalpel, left only a thin membrane holding the blood back. All his moving around, it finally burst, same as an aneurysm rupturing. When it did, he was dead in minutes. As best I can tell now, I'll be placing his time of death at two or three hours ago. Well, I'll be at the office if you should need me for anything else." He turned and with short, quick steps moved off the porch. He nodded twice as he crossed the lawn on the way to his green Toyota.

Richards stared after the coroner for a moment, then faced the sheriff. "Couldn't have knocked him out, could it? Not with him being the one who beat her. She would have had to shoot him when he first attacked her, and then she'd run while he was unconscious. After the beating she . . . she wouldn't have been able to shoot him after the beating; so he couldn't have done it."

"To dwell on these things doesn't help, Mr. Richards."

Jesus Christ, Richards thought. "Dammit, I'm trying to understand." He was sorry for his tone even before he had finished speaking.

Tidmore nodded, his only trace of irritation the slight narrowing of his eyes. "Okay. Hopper didn't kill her."

"I didn't mean to raise my voice, Sheriff, but I knew it. Another reason I knew he didn't do it was there wasn't enough blood on him, was there? He had some on the front of his pants, on the left side of the front of his shirt, and on his left hand. There was only a little on the heel of his right hand. It's not enough to have been Judith's. It's his own blood. He didn't beat her. She shot him and knocked him out, like the coroner said, but somebody else was with him. I'm trying to picture . . ."

The sheriff opened the manilla envelope the deputy had delivered and slid out a picture, handing it to Richards.

"That's a picture of Jack Graff. He's one of the two still loose. We want to keep this confidential until after he's picked up, but he's the one."

Richards glanced at the picture, a head shot of a man dressed in a work shirt. *He's the one what?* "Are you saying . . . ?"

The sheriff nodded. "He's had a history of physical attacks, and he wears a ten and a half shoe. Hospital records say he's also got AB blood. That's the clincher. Those little drops in the kitchen? Lab typed them as AB. Wish they could have given us more than that, but just wasn't enough blood. In this case it's not gonna make any difference, though. AB is rare, only three percent of the population have it. Graff's the only one who lived in R-14 that does.

"Your daughter was A. Lab boys also found Type O on the floor in the bedroom. There was enough of it to break it down. It'll end up being about as good as a fingerprint. But we don't really need it. Hopper and Randy Edginton—that's the other one that's loose—they're both O. Hopper being here pretty well tells us where that came from.

"My guess is she heard them come in, had time to grab her gun and shoot Hopper. Graff got the gun away from her. Maybe he got scratched or cut in the struggle. When he finished, he ran, dripped the three drops of blood when he crossed the kitchen floor. Whenever Hopper woke up he hid in the attic."

Richards was nodding his head in excited agreement. "Edginton could have been here, too, couldn't he? All three of them could have been involved."

"It's possible."

Looking past the sheriff's head, Richards's eyes fell on the hospital perimeter fence. Remembering the form he had seen in the window, his eyes narrowed. Stepping from the porch, he walked out into the yard, and looked back toward the hospital grounds once more.

"Sheriff, would you come here for a moment?"

Tidmore moved out into the yard, glanced in the direction Richards was staring.

"Up there. See the two windows?"

"That's the maximum-security unit," the sheriff said. "The window on the left is Marcus Minnefield's cell. He's probably the most famous . . . infamous . . . they've got locked up in there."

"Sheriff, that fence is no more than a hundred and fifty to two hundred feet from here, the building maybe fifty feet farther. If he—"

A dark figure moved to the window on the left.

"There he is again," Richards said. "He was standing there when I first came up tonight. If he was standing there when the patients escaped . . ." Richards could feel his excitement mounting. He moved toward the side of the yard.

There was enough illumination from the security light a hundred yards down the fence so that it would have been impossible for the three patients to have escaped without being in clear view of the man in the window—if he had been watching. If he was, he could know whether it was just the two or all three of the patients who had entered Judith's cottage.

"Sheriff, can we talk to that patient?"

Tidmore continued to stare across the fence for a moment, then turned back to face Richards. "We?" he said, and then laughed. "Sure. Why not? You're turning out to be the best investigator we've got." A big smile spread across the sheriff's face. "Don't need a job, do you?"

Richards smiled. Though it quickly left his face it was the first real smile he had managed since the original call from the Sheriff's Department had awakened him at his home in Lake Pontchartrain. It felt good being able to smile, and suddenly he felt guilty at having done so.

"I'll have one of my deputies call Dr. Thornburg and set us up a meeting over at the hospital. In the meantime I'd like for you to join me for breakfast."

Richards couldn't remember when he last ate. He needed to. Not just then, though. "I appreciate it, but I think I'll go back to the motel and change clothes, then go by the funeral home when it opens. I haven't seen her yet."

A gentle smile came to the sheriff's face. "Okay," he said softly. "When I get the appointment set up at the hospital, I'll come by the funeral home and pick you up. I'll give you plenty of time."

CHAPTER

5

During the drive back to the Holiday Inn, Richards couldn't keep his thoughts off Judith, and didn't try.

"Hello, Daddy," she would say. "Don't look so sad." She always said he was sad if he wasn't smiling. She smiled all the time, enjoyed life, perhaps too much.

Her grades in college were never very good—too much partying. He tried to make her cut that out and study more. It was hard to make the proper decision each time. He had raised her ever since her mother died when Judith was ten years old, balancing that task with fifty and sixty-hour work weeks spent trying to build a law practice in a small town in Mississippi, then, later, in New Orleans.

He had cut back on Judith's money and she cut back on eating—spent the same amount partying. She did finish nursing school, though. Then she went to work at the mental hospital.

Not long after taking the job she had eloped with Dr. Martin Salter, a psychiatrist at the hospital. Richards remembered being pleased at the union, for he had begun to seriously worry about Judith's single lifestyle. "Enjoying the good life," as she called it.

Only a month prior to Judith's meeting Martin, Richards had driven up from New Orleans to find two men staying in her cottage. He hadn't asked, but she had explained they were only old college friends on their way through the area. They might have been, but both were sleeping in her bedroom, with the guest bedroom empty.

His joy with her marriage was short-lived. A month after Judith became pregnant she had called him to say that her husband was being unfaithful. Richards remembered not knowing what to advise her.

After the twins were born, the relationship seemed to improve. As far as he had known everything was going well. When they visited each other, she seemed completely happy. Then everything fell apart at once.

He had called to wish the twins a happy fifth birthday and Judith had started crying. She didn't want to worry him, she said, but her husband had continued to be unfaithful through the years. And now things were worse. Martin's latest lover was another man.

He had insisted she leave and come to New Orleans, but she said no. She still wanted to try and make a go of her marriage.

Finally Martin didn't come home one night, and she didn't know where he was until she received a call from him a week later. He had decided to move back to the coast, he said. He wanted Judith and the twins to join him there, him and his friend. She filed for divorce.

A few weeks later Martin came back while she was at work. The baby sitter hadn't known any better. All she knew was that the children's father had said he was going to take his kids to the Dairy Queen. He didn't bring them back.

Judith hired a local detective named John Winstead, and he helped in gathering the information which led to the court ordering Martin to return the children.

After the court order Martin had called and threatened her; said he would kill her before he gave up his children. After receiving the call from the Sheriff's Department, Richards's first thought had been that the threat had been carried out, a threat to which he had advised his daughter not to pay any attention. If it had been Martin who had killed her, he didn't know if he could live with himself.

Randy Edginton, twice-convicted child molester and recent escapee from the John H. Douglas State Hospital for the Insane, sat on a park bench at the edge of a playground outside of Mobile, Alabama. His squat upper body scooted all the way back on the bench, his short legs were not quite long enough to allow his feet to touch the ground. He was enjoying watching the children play.

He was particularly enjoying the antics of one chubby blond-haired boy who had an especially virile look about him—to Edginton's way of thinking.

Edginton had picked out one other promising candidate earlier. On the other side of the park a stout little black boy had been practicing his tennis serve by himself. Only minutes after Edginton had started retrieving balls for the boy, however, the child's mother had walked up. Thanking him, she had taken over collecting the tennis balls.

Edginton scooted forward and stood when the chubby blond came running toward him. The boy had finished the candy bar Edginton had given him earlier and showed proper upbringing by depositing its wrapper in the refuse barrel sitting next to the bench.

Edginton smiled sweetly.

"How did I look, Mr. Jones?" The boy had been displaying his moves for the nice man and now he wanted an opinion.

"You're going to be a splendid football player," Edginton said. He reached out and patted the little boy's head, stroking the soft blond hair for a moment.

The boy smiled. "You really think so?"

"Well, look at you now—eight years old and such big shoulders . . . and hips . . . and legs. What do you weigh already?" Edginton gripped each side of the boy's shoulders, as if measuring how wide they were, then trailed his fingertips across the boy's chest.

"A hundred and five." The boy smiled proudly, stretching himself to the very limit of his five-foot frame. He was only a couple inches shorter than Edginton.

"Wow. That's big, real big, and I can tell you have superior speed. You'll be a professional football player, you wait and see. I know what I'm speaking of. . . . Would you like me to show you some things professional players do?"

The boy beamed. "Yeah. I already know how to catch a football. I can run over people better than anybody."

"Oh, there's a lot more to it than that. There's so many things I don't know where to start. Let's see. Let's start with exercises and go through everything they do before a game. Then I'll show you what they do in a game."

Edginton's voice was beginning to change into a higher pitched nasal twang which always occurred when he reached this point. The boy didn't seem to notice.

"Okay," the boy said. "I can touch my toes. See?" He almost could, but his stomach interfered a little too much.

"No," Edginton said, "on second thought I think we need to start at the very beginning." He moved an index finger to his chin as he thought. "First we'll do as they do in the locker room. Everything. I surely wish I had some tape." There was a longing, reflective look on Edginton's face.

"What for?"

"They always use a lot of tape . . . then they put on their supporters." Edginton quivered in delight. "They do some special warmups . . . which I'm going to show you . . . when they're in the locker room."

Edginton noticed that the two little boys who had been playing with the blond were leaving the park. No one else was in sight.

"Let's go over there," he said. "We'll use that for our locker room. It will do nicely." Edginton pointed to the concrete block restroom sitting on the other side of the slides and swings.

Inside a small viewing room at the Dantone Brothers Funeral Home, Richards stood with his hand resting on Judith's own crossed hands.

"Sweetheart, I can't do anything about the twins. They're his now. But whatever else he is, he loves them. That's why he stole them away the first time. They will be okay.

"But I promise you, the one who did this to you . . ." He couldn't bring himself to say Jack Graff's name. It seemed like a sacrilege with her lying there. ". . . he will die. I'm going to see to it that he does, I swear. And if anybody helped him, I'll kill him, too. I swear to God. I won't rest until you can."

A tear trickled down his cheek.

"Stella, it's your turn to take care of her now until I come and we're all together again. I love you both."

"Mr. Richards. Sheriff Tidmore is on the phone."

It was the manager of the funeral home. He showed Richards to the telephone in the waiting room.

"Hello."

"Mr. Richards." Tidmore's voice was low, solemn. "We have a problem. Jack Graff never escaped. Hospital security found him hiding in the dorm's attic. Evidently he got scared when the guard was killed and has been hiding there ever since. The AB blood doesn't make any sense now. Neither do the footprints. Edginton's the only one still on the loose and he wears a seven."

Annie Harrell had been keeping her eye on the little white man ever since she had found him retrieving tennis balls for her son. When she saw him walk the fat blond-haired boy into the playground restroom she knew her suspicions had been correct.

"Ermon," she said to her son. "You stay right here on this court and don't you go anywhere else. Now I mean it. Don't go anywhere. I'll be right back."

Ermon nodded a perfunctory okay and blasted another ball over the top of the restraining fence.

Annie made certain to pick up her purse before she strode toward the restroom.

The building had no windows, so she stood for a minute beside it, thinking.

Windows would have been perfect. Now, with no way to officially observe the man in the act, she would have to make sure her timing was right.

It bothered her somewhat, to wait until something such as *that* had started. To wait somehow seemed as if she were being heartless and cruel, as if an arrest with compromising evidence was more important to her than protecting the child. Such was not the case.

If she stepped inside before the man made any advances, he would deny having any intention of doing anything other than relieving himself in the restroom. There would be nothing she could do. A week from now, maybe tomorrow, even later this afternoon, he would be right back to his old tricks again. How many more times would a child's mind be damaged before the man was caught?

She didn't want it to go too far, though, and she certainly didn't want the child hurt. She moved to the door to the restroom and leaned back against the wall, cocking her ear, trying to hear. As she waited she opened her purse and curled her fingers around the .38 Special she carried inside.

Then she thought of Ermon. How would she like it if he were in there alone with the man while a police officer stood outside doing nothing? "Crap!" she whispered bitterly. She stepped around the door into the restroom.

The boy saw her first, when he turned back around from laying his trousers on the wooden bench. Edginton had his back to her and dropped to his knees, unaware he was being observed.

"Good," he said, his voice high and thin. "Very good . . . honey. Now after they take their old pants off, they arrange their underwear into a thang they call a supporter. Do you know what a supporter is for?"

The man's thick-fingered hands moved to the waist-band of the little boy's underwear. Even from where she stood, Annie could see the man's hands were trembling, and his head moved toward the boy.

"I'm goin' to show you sumthin' speshul now."

"That's it! Stop!"

Edginton jumped up, whirling around. "Leave, bitch." His tone was harsh and cold now, all trace of his speech impediment gone.

"Don't believe there's anything you know that the little white boy needs to learn. But I'm getting ready to teach you a big lesson."

"I told you to leave, bitch!"

Edginton reached into his pocket.

Annie jerked the .38 from her handbag and dropped into a crouch, cocking it.

"Don't move. I'm a police officer. You are under arrest. Don't take your hand out of your pocket. You have a right to—"

Edginton pulled a knife from his pocket.

Annie's concern was that the man might grab the child as a shield. She scooted a step forward, and then another, still in a crouch, both hands clasping the butt of the revolver.

"Drop the knife, shorty. I'm not joking. Kid, get on out of here. Now!"

The blond-haired boy's forehead crinkled in puzzlement.

"NOW!"

The boy grabbed his trousers from the wooden bench and ran past her.

"NOW DROP THE DAMN KNIFE!"

Edginton screamed, raised the knife above his head and charged.

The roar of her revolver within the small restroom momentarily deafened Annie.

CHAPTER

6

Two wire fences spaced ten feet apart circled the Maximum-Security Building for the Criminally Insane. At the top of each was a coil of razor wire. Signs spaced every twenty feet along the inner fence warned of high voltage. Brandon Richards and Sheriff Raymond Tidmore stood waiting as the fences' remote-controlled gates slowly opened.

The two were quiet, having not said much during the drive from the funeral home. What was there to say? Richards wondered. He had been correct about the blood on Hopper. The lab had reported that none of it was Judith's. So Hopper wasn't the killer. Graff had never left his dorm. Edginton was the only suspect left, but he didn't have AB blood, and his feet were too small to have left the sock prints.

The sheriff had said to not be discouraged, Edginton could have been there, could have been the one who raped and killed Judith; whoever was there with him could have left both the blood and sockprints. Who? Only two had escaped. The confusing uncertainty scared Richards, actually left a cold ache in his stomach.

He had to know who killed his daughter; he couldn't live with never knowing. He glanced up to the side of the building, to the two openings on the third floor. Please God, let the man have been standing there at the time.

After passing through the fences they were made to wait at the front of the building under the scrutiny of television cameras. Another wait occurred inside a short hallway while the steel entrance door clanged shut behind them. Then the door at the end of the hallway opened and they emerged into a small, sparsely furnished office.

The guard who had been operating the remote controls sat at a desk in front of a bank of television monitors. Two other officers were engaged in conversation in the middle of the room. One of them, a massive man in a brown uniform and Sam Browne belt with a pistol, can of mace, and billy club hanging from his waist, stepped forward. He had brass captain's bars pinned atop his tunic shoulders. "Raymond," he said, holding out his hand to the sheriff.

"Alan. Nice to see you again. This is Mr. Brandon Richards. Brandon, this is Alan Molpus. He's the security captain here."

The captain nodded. "Dr. Thornburg said I was to take you gentlemen up to Minnefield's cell. Stay between the yellow lines in the center of the hallway, Mr. Richards, and none of 'em can reach you there. I tell you, we have some who are apt to try if you give 'em a chance."

Alan removed his weapons and laid them on one of the desks. The guard sitting there opened a drawer and deposited them inside it.

"Mr. Richards, it's better if you don't be answering one of 'em if they talk to you," Alan said. "If you say the wrong thing it'll only get 'em going. Wrong to them is not always like what's wrong to you and me."

"Especially Ronnie," the guard who was seated said, then chuckled. "Cap'n, don't forget to show him Ronnie. Better'n a day at the zoo. He's a real piece of work."

The captain smiled, then pointed toward the door at the far end of the office. The guard reached up to push a button on a wall panel mounted behind the desk. The metallic clang of sliding bolts indicated the door was now unlocked.

"Come along."

They walked through the door into a wide hallway, cells on each side of its two-hundred-foot length. The cells had typical jaillike barred fronts, except that the bars ended at a six foot height, embedding into a concrete overhang which continued to rise to the ceiling. The walls of each cell were solid steel. To keep the patients from being able to reach each other, Richards decided.

He could not tell how many of the cells were occupied, for the concrete overhang and steel walls also acted as shades, cutting off much of the light from the already dim hallway, casting the back of each cell in darkness.

Halfway down the hall, Alan nodded to the side, then spoke in a low voice. "That's him. Ronnie."

Richards glanced to his left to see only a darkened cell. He thought he saw a movement near its rear.

Swiveling his head, he kept his eyes on the front of the enclosure as he passed by, but never could distinguish the man.

"He usually puts on a show when somebody new comes in," Alan said. "I've seen officers turn pale when he screamed at 'em. Those bars start looking pretty flimsy when he starts pulling on 'em."

Richards glanced back over his shoulder a last time.

The cells on the second floor were of an entirely different type. They had steel-plated fronts as well as sides, with only a narrow peephole in their doors, the type of cells he had imagined he would see inside a ward for the criminally insane. He wondered if they were padded.

Moving up the staircase to the third floor, he began to notice the smell of human waste. When he emerged into the hallway the stench was nearly overpowering. Other than the odor, and that the cells had bars rather than steel partitions separating them, the third floor was much the same as the first. Each cell was furnished in an identical manner: a bed to the right side; a small wooden table sitting against the back wall, bolted to the floor; a chair bolted in place in front of the table; and a commode—in full view of the other cells—sitting against the wall opposite the bed.

Marcus Minnefield was leaning against the front of his cell, his forearms resting on a cross bar, his hands protruding limply out into the hallway. Though he was of otherwise normal stature, his forearms were massive and matted with thick black hair. He was dressed in flowered pajamas and wearing soft blue house slippers.

"Captain," he said as they approached the cell. "Sheriff Tidmore, sir."

Richards noted the patient's pecking order greeting, diplomatically giving recognition to the security cap-

·tain first, the only one who would remain when the rest of them left. He doubted the order was a coincidence, further reminding himself that insanity in and of itself did not denote a lack of intelligence.

"Marcus," the sheriff said, "this is Mr. Brandon Richards. He's the father of the nurse who was murdered night before last."

Minnefield nodded politely. "You have my sincerest sympathy," he said, the seeming genuineness of his tone more than the words surprising Richards.

"Thank you."

The old gaunt-faced man lying on his bed in the cell to the right of Minnefield's coughed, raised the back of a frail hand to wipe the string of wetness from his mouth, then dropped the hand back to his chest without ever opening his eyes. Richards noted the sketch taped to the back wall of the man's cell. Drawn in chalk on regular lined notebook paper, it was a well-done caricature of the man's own angular face. A pair of horns protruded from the forehead. A tiny angel, with horns, hovered off the left ear.

"Marcus," the sheriff said, "you have a pretty fair view of his daughter's cottage from your window. We were wondering if you might have noticed anything unusual the night of the murder?"

Richards looked at the opening at the back of the cell. It was heavily barred, gaps of only three to four inches between the lengths of steel. The gossamer fabric covering the bars served as a window screen, he decided. He caught himself wondering how cold was kept out during the winter, and brought his mind back to the important matter at hand.

Minnefield glanced over his shoulder at the opening. "It would surprise you what all I see. There is something playing outside my opening all the time."

"What played night before last, Marcus?"

"Are you making fun of me, Sheriff?" A smirk moved to Minnefield's face, and he cocked his head as if questioning a naughty child. But Richards also saw the tautness of the neck and the tightening of the forearm muscles. Despite his teasing expression the man was affected deeply by what he took as patronization.

"Never mind," Minnefield said, dropping his stare from the sheriff, "never mind. Everyone makes fun of me. When I use the term *playing,* it is because of what the psychiatrists have reduced me to. They will not allow me a television. The opening is all I have, so I sometimes refer to it as more than it actually is."

"Can you help us, Marcus?" the sheriff asked, impatience noticeable in his tone.

Minnefield seemed to ignore that it was the sheriff who had asked the question, instead directing his reply to Richards.

"You know . . . Brandon . . . it played. Yet my watching it would not help you. An insane individual is barred from testifying in court, and I am certified." Only then did his forearms finally relax and the bulging neck muscles retreat.

"Marcus," the sheriff said, "we're not talking about court. You tell us what you saw and you've done your part."

As Minnefield answered, his eyes never left Richards's face. "What is your part?"

"What do you mean?" the sheriff asked.

"You ask me to assist you," Minnefield said. He finally changed his gaze to the sheriff, shifting only his eyes as he did so. "That is my part. What can you do for me? I am sure you grasp my meaning."

Richards knew he had just been studied. He wondered what the man had learned, or thought he had learned. And Richards had learned something also. It would be impossible to explain, but after the few seconds of eye contact there was no doubt in his mind as to the depths of Minnefield's insanity.

"Marcus," the sheriff said, "I would appreciate it if you would just tell us what you saw."

"I believe my statement was that it played. I did not contend I was watching at the time . . . nor do I say I was not."

"What do you want, Marcus?" the sheriff asked, not bothering to hide an exasperated tone.

"You have observed me, Sheriff, and are at this moment."

Minnefield stepped back from the bars and dropped his hands, palms out, as if displaying himself better. "Maybe you will agree to testify as to my improvement during my next sanity hearing. And, Sheriff, until the hearing, I would also appreciate being allowed a television. I have grown bored with the aspects of introversion. A television would allow me a more varied perspective. Oh, yes, one other request. I would appreciate it if you could persuade the guards to change the setting on the thermostat. They maintain much too warm an environment within the building. I suspect they do so in an attempt to keep the patients listless." Minnefield moved his eyes to the security captain and smiled. Alan smiled back.

Richards looked to the sheriff, waiting for his response.

"Marcus, if you give us information that proves helpful, then I'll talk to the doctors about a TV, see what they think about it."

"Not good enough." Minnefield turned his back to them and crossed his arms.

"I don't want to mislead you, Marcus." The sheriff glanced at Richards a moment and back to the cell. "I'll do what I can for you. But you know I'd be lying if

I told you my appearing at your sanity hearing would do you any good."

Jesus, Richards thought, tell him whatever he wants to hear.

Minnefield responded, his voice directed toward the back of his cell. "I can live without your help. I have done so until now. I do not have very much longer to endure this place, with or without your help."

"Marcus, you help us, and I swear I'll try to help you. But you know you're not going to get out of here. If you did—"

"I do not wish to hear lies!" Minnefield's sudden, sharp tone unnerved Richards.

"If you did, if they declared you sane, you've got half a dozen murders you would have to stand trial for. You know that as well as I do."

"I will not deal with people who lie," Minnefield said, his voice level once more, his tone monotonous, final. "I have nothing more to say to you, Sheriff." He walked to the back of his cell and peered out through the barred opening, never unfolding his arms.

"Marcus," the sheriff said, "will you try to be reasonable? We need your help and I'll do what I can for you, if you give it to us. Okay? Marcus . . . ?"

The patient's head was moving slightly as his eyes followed something outside the opening.

The old man in the adjacent cell coughed again, and his eyes opened. Other than that he remained motionless, seemingly oblivious to the strained conversation taking place a few feet from him.

"Marcus," the sheriff tried again, "will you talk to us, help Mr. Richards out?"

Minnefield stepped closer to the opening and looked down toward the ground. Then he unfolded his arms and yawned, turned around and walked to the bed at the side of his cell. Sitting, he slipped off his cotton house shoes, turned, and lay back on his pillow.

Richards stared at the massive forearms folded behind the man's head, saw the matted hair on them quivering as the muscles underneath twitched spasmodically. Jesus!

The security captain shook his head, beckoned, and turned, and they started back down the hall.

CHAPTER

7

As the sheriff guided his Lincoln Continental away from the maximum security building, Richards sat silently in the passenger seat, his mind swirling with his thoughts. He couldn't help but feel that Minnefield had seen something the night Judith was murdered, but what? And, if he had, what would he ultimately demand in return for divulging what he knew? Richards feared the answer.

"You thinking about Minnefield?" the sheriff asked.

"I'm sorry, what did you say?"

"Don't let his attitude bother you, Mr. Richards. I don't know if he saw anything or not, but he'll end up telling us; no reason not to. He'll come up with something reasonable to trade for. I could get the psychiatrists to set a TV in that empty cell next to his. Whatever I do for him, though, he's going to play with us for a little while, keep us coming back."

The sheriff paused as he reached inside his coat to his vest pocket. Pulling out a pair of cigars, he offered one to Richards.

"No, thank you."

Slipping one of the cigars back into his pocket, Tidmore stripped the cellophane from the other as he held it at the top of the steering wheel. Sticking the narrower end in his mouth, he lit it with a gold-plated lighter he produced from inside his coat. Satisfied, he continued with what he had been saying.

"Course, part of the reason he'll keep us coming back is that he enjoys having company. You would, too, in his situation. Mainly though, it's just the way his mind works. The psychiatrists say among other things he has a need to dominate; I mean a really out-of-whack need. He has to control people, call the shots—drives him off the deep end when he can't. Where he's at now, he's obviously not controlling much. We're going to have to kiss his butt good to get him to help us, let him know how important he is to us. That'll really be more of a key than what we can do for him—the TV, whatever. I'm telling you, these people's minds work real strangely."

Another smile moved to his face. He shook his head, then leaned towards Richards.

"This is on the Q.T., but talking about the ways their minds work, hospital security has been running polygraphs on the patients in R-14. Won't be able to use the information . . . you know, legally. They're just hoping to get a lead they can develop. It's not just your daughter, security still doesn't have the slightest idea who killed the guard. All the patients are saying is that he was just lying there with the front door open.

"Well, you'd have to see the polygraph results to believe 'em. The examiner thought the machine was screwing up at first. They got one patient, everything he says registers as a lie, even when they know he's telling the truth."

The sheriff's hand moved to a switch on the side of the driver's door, cracking the Lincoln's window and letting some of the thick cigar smoke escape. He leaned back towards Richards again.

"One character can make it register he's lying when he wants it to or telling the truth when he wants it to. He got to making the machine register back and forth, a lie one time, truth the next. Even when they ask him the same question two times in a row, the machine indicates two different skin responses. These are strange people, Mr. Richards." The sheriff shook his head, then reached for the window switch as he stopped the Lincoln beside the guardhouse at the hospital's main gate.

The guard smiled and waved them through.

Richards didn't want to have to wait to know if Minnefield had seen anything. "Why not offer whatever you can, but base it on him telling us now?"

Tidmore shook his head. "We'd get an answer, but we wouldn't know if he's telling the truth or not. Then when he wanted us back he'd just remember something else. Minnefield's not dumb. He's got his ways, but he's able to reason. That window he's got in his cell, that's a deal he worked out with Alan. He talked Alan into putting the patients that can't take care of themselves on the third floor. Everyday the orderlies lock the door to the floor and let Minnefield out of his cell. He cleans up the crap in the cells . . . literally. Once a week he gives the patients a good washing; does a lot of things Alan was having a hard time getting the orderlies to do. He gets a cell with a view for a reward."

Richards had never thought of a criminally insane lockup having trustees.

"And remember what I said about him needing to be the one that does the domineering," the sheriff continued. "If we press him he could get upset, might put him in a mood to not do any more housework. Alan wouldn't like that." Tidmore paused a moment, a reflective expression coming to his face. "John Winstead might be able to help us out with Minnefield. He's the detective your daughter hired after Salter carried the twins off."

Richards nodded. "Judith was pleased with him. Wanted me to meet the man, but I never was in the area afterwards."

"Yeah, Winstead's good at whatever he does. He's sort of a legend around this area. Before he went private he was the one who arrested Minnefield. For some reason Minnefield really respects J.J.—that's what everybody calls Winstead around these parts. Minnefield might talk to him. He's always bragging on J.J., says he's the best cop in the country."

"Maybe," Richards said, "because it helps Minnefield to feel important if he thinks it took the best cop to catch him."

The sheriff smiled. "Hell, an investigator, and now a psychiatrist. You sure you don't need a job?"

Richards politely returned the smile. "How did he catch him?"

"It was about seven years ago now. Minnefield contracted to bring a big load of cocaine in from Mexico. Delivered it to some of the Dixie Mafia in Biloxi. They decided it wasn't up to snuff and cut his price, told him that was all he was getting, that they were running the show. Well, no one was going to make a fool out of him. That's what he told the psychiatrists later, that the thugs in Biloxi had tried to make a fool out of him. Anyway, he blew his stack, came back later the same night with a couple of his followers.

"They gutted one of the guys right in the guy's home. You ever seen anybody gut a cow? They did it just like that, just dropped everything right out on the floor. You should see the pictures." The sheriff shook his head.

"The second guy they went after lived in an apartment. After they explained what they were going to do to him, he jerked loose. I believe I could have, too. Anyway, this guy ran through a plate-glass door out onto a balcony and right on through the balcony rail, steady hollering, his legs still churning when he hit the pavement. As luck would have it, a couple of cops had pulled their cars into the parking lot to sneak some shuteye.

"When they called Minnefield out, the two followers came out instead, waving knives and hollering some crap about Satan and took some double-ought in the chest.

"Minnefield went out the side with the guy's girlfriend as a hostage. Got in her car and backed out into the street before one of the police cruisers rammed it. It was a stand off—him sitting in the car with a pistol to the gal's head and the cops hiding behind buildings and trees keeping their guns on him.

"That's where J.J. came into the picture. He was a special investigator for the Attorney General's office then, before he retired and went private. I don't remember what he was down there for. Anyway, he must have not had much excitement going on in his life right then. He decided he would walk right out there and trade himself for the gal." The sheriff chuckled. "Crazy bastard."

"Anyway, took off his gun and shirt, walked out and made the offer. Said the cops didn't care about the gal, they'd shoot when Minnefield tried to pull off, but they wouldn't take a chance on hitting a fellow law enforcement officer. Minnefield must've thought he was facing a fellow lunatic, and he said he was going to take them both. J.J. said, nope, me or her, he wasn't going to climb in the car with Minnefield unless he turned the girl loose first. Minnefield said he'd just shoot him then. J.J. said, you do that, you damn sure going to get shot. If you take me, the cops aren't going to shoot. Damn if Minnefield didn't go for it." He shook his head and laughed, then turned toward his window and exhaled a cloud of smoke before leaning back again.

"J.J. told the other cops to get the hell out and got in the car and they drove off. End of story: J.J. grabbed Minnefield's gun hand, the car hit a tree, and the other cops got there before Minnefield broke J.J.'s neck. Took damn near every cop in Biloxi to hold that nut down and cuff him. They still couldn't move him until they strapped a straight jacket on him and roped him to a stretcher."

Tidmore's brow furrowed in thought. "Something about being crazy must make you some kind of strong," he said. "Alan didn't tell you to stay inside those yellow lines just to be talking. One of them gets hold of you it's like a snapping turtle."

Richards's curiosity was unsatisfied. "You were speaking about his followers, and them yelling something about Satan?"

"Minnefield's business was shipping cocaine out of Mexico, but his real love was a satanic cult he put together. They had a big spread out in the desert country south of Neuvo Laredo. Authorities dug up a flatbed truckload of bones around there. His followers say he's the Prince of Darkness. He's got it mixed up a little bit, though. He thinks he's supposed to stay up and rule all night, never sleeps after dark. He catches what shuteye he gets after the sun comes up. The guards used to call him 'The Vampire' until the psychiatrists told them maybe they shouldn't be giving him any ideas." Tidmore chuckled.

"Even with him behind bars that shut the guards up quick. Anyway, his staying up nights is why I think there is a good chance he could've seen something the night your daughter was killed."

At the mention of the night, a thought occurred to Richards. "Sheriff, is it possible Graff did go to Judith's, then came back to his dorm?"

"Not a scratch on him. No sign of any kind of struggle. He was in his pajamas and they didn't have a drop of blood on 'em. They checked under his fingernails, everywhere. Edginton has to be the one who killed and raped her. Beats me where the AB came from. Maybe when we catch Edginton he'll be able to tell us something."

"Maybe the hospital records are wrong," Richards said. "Or maybe the lab made a mistake in the typing."

"Sheriff's office number one," a voice crackled over the radio.

Tidmore reached to the dash and moved the radio microphone to his lips. "Sheriff Tidmore, here."

"They got Edginton outside of Mobile."

Tidmore looked at Richards and smiled. "Where are they holding him?"

"The morgue. He brought a knife to a gunfight."

A faint chuckle could be heard over the radio and irritation crossed the sheriff's face.

"An officer outside of Mobile drilled him through the head. And, Sheriff, if the lab still says whoever killed the Salter gal raped her, you better start looking for another suspect. Edginton didn't have no penis."

"What?"

"He'd got fixed up to look like a woman. Mobile morgue boys say it looks realistic. He couldn't have done the job on the Salter gal, he didn't have the tool."

Another chuckle.

"Dammit, Destin, Mr. Richards is in the car with me."

"Oh, I'm sorry. Should've watched my mouth. I'm sorry, Mr. Richards."

CHAPTER

8

Private detective John J. Winstead stood in a room inside the seediest boarding house in the city.

Sitting on the bed and hurriedly slipping on his shoes was its occupant, the bartender from the Old South Bar and Grill. The man's face was flushed from his heart's nervous pumping, even the bald spot in the center of his scalp showed coloring.

"Told you, Mr. Winstead, I ain't gonna get involved."

Winstead remained motionless for a moment, his arms folded across his barrel chest, staring coldly. Then he shrugged, dropped his arms to his side, and moved toward the bed.

The bartender jumped up, one foot still bare, holding his unbuttoned pants to his waist with his hands.

"Mr. Winstead, please."

The big muscular detective continued to move forward, until the bartender's back was against the wall.

"Okay!" the bartender exclaimed. "Okay. Okay, dammit."

Winstead smiled and reached to the bedside table, turning on the radio which sat there.

The bartender turned pale. "I said *okay!*"

Winstead chuckled. "Afternoon news, Sam, like to hear the news." He looked at his watch. Then his eyes moved around the room. Spotting a waste can, he moved to it and spat a stream of tobacco juice. Digging inside his cheek with a hooked index finger, he removed a moist brown wad and dropped it into the can.

The bartender hobbled back around to the bed, hastily slipping on his other shoe, all the time keeping his eyes riveted on the big detective. "You know I'll lose my job. You know if I say somethin' like that on the stand Mr. Spadini ain't gonna keep me on. I wish—"

"I'm waiting." The radio was too loud and Winstead turned it down.

"All I know is the kid came and asked for a drink," the bartender began. "I think two drinks. Then the bouncer came up, Barton, who works the door. He told the kid he was too young and to leave."

"What did the kid do?"

"He had a smart-aleck look on his face and he told Barton—"

"I said, what did he do?"

"Nothin'. At least nothin' I saw but—"

"One *last* time."

"Nothin'."

Winstead smiled. "Good. Start lying for the thugs

who run that joint, Sam, next thing you know you'll be haulin' a little coke for 'em."

"You know better than that."

Winstead nodded, a reflective look on his face. "Yeah, a two-time loser like you, be bad."

"I'm gonna testify for the kid, Mr. Winstead. You gonna help me find another job?"

Winstead ignored the question. "Want you to realize how much your testimony means to me, Sam, personally. Never made much money as a cop, that's why I'm private now. Planning to make a lot of money. Money in my line of work depends on reputation. Attorneys pay me a hell of a fee for pulling witnesses together and getting 'em ready. How well I get 'em ready either pulls in more work or makes people not so anxious to call. Results is everything." Winstead hesitated a moment, staring into the bartender's eyes. "Getting 'em ready, Sam, is making sure they're gonna tell the truth. You understand what I'm gettin' at?"

The bartender stared a brief moment, then nodded.

"For your conscience, Sam, the kid's seventeen years old, might weigh 160 pounds soaking wet. No fat-ass bouncer has got a right beating on a kid like that, even if he did swing at him. But he didn't. Right?"

"Right."

"And you didn't hear the kid say anything, right?"

"Right."

"THIS IS A SPECIAL BULLETIN FROM WDON. WDON NEWS HAS JUST LEARNED FROM A SOURCE WITHIN THE DAVIS COUNTY SHERIFF'S DEPARTMENT THAT THERE IS NOW A POSSIBILITY THAT JOHN H. DOUGLAS STATE HOSPITAL FOR THE INSANE STAFF NURSE JUDITH SALTER WAS NOT, AS EARLIER REPORTED, MURDERED BY THE ESCAPEES FROM THE HOSPITAL. LET ME REPEAT. WDON NEWS HAS JUST LEARNED THAT THE DAVIS COUNTY SHERIFF'S DEPARTMENT NOW BELIEVES THAT

STAFF NURSE JUDITH SALTER'S MURDER WAS NOT RELATED TO
THE ESCAPE OF INMATES WHICH OCCURRED THE SAME NIGHT
AS THE MURDER. WE HAVE A MOBILE UNIT ON THE WAY TO
THE DAVIS COUNTY SHERIFF'S OFFICE AND WILL BRING YOU
AN UPDATE ON THIS STORY AS SOON AS IT BECOMES AVAIL-
ABLE TO US. WDON, ALWAYS FIRST, WITH THE NEWS IMPOR-
TANT TO YOU . . ."

"Just tell the truth," Winstead said from where he
had hurried to the door, a big forefinger pointing back
toward the bartender for emphasis. "The way you just
told it to me. Don't be doing no guessing 'bout how
the kid looked or speculating on his attitude."

The slamming of the door added extra emphasis.

The bartender flashed his middle finger at the
closed door, not daring to say it out loud, and then he
quickly dropped his finger.

CHAPTER

9

After retrieving his Cadillac from where he had left it parked at the funeral home, Richards followed the sheriff to his office.

It was surprisingly well furnished, and not only for a sheriff's office. Very few of the more successful attorneys in New Orleans had places of work so luxuriously furnished.

An antique mahogany desk and expensive leather chair sat at the back of the office. A pair of overstuffed leather chairs were placed in front of the desk, and an oversized, very expensive-looking couch sat along the front wall. The only filing cabinet in the office was actually a French Provincial buffet.

Upon entering the office, Tidmore excused himself

and walked into the small connecting bathroom. Richards seated himself on the couch. A strange set of comparisons kept passing through his mind.

It disgusted him to even think about Minnefield and Judith at the same time. The two were not even remotely similar: he a vicious mass murderer, she a person who had cried when she read about a terminally ill child. Yet it kept passing through his mind that both had traded away their pride. He traded his by cleaning commodes for a view, she traded hers for the sake of her children and her marriage, continuing to live for so long with a man of her husband's sexual proclivities. *And what of me now?* he thought. What would I trade for the name of her killer? Could something be desired so strongly as to pervert lifelong values, or did strong character in and of itself prevent a person wanting anything *that* badly? Tidmore's return from the bathroom drew Richards back from his thoughts.

The sheriff seated himself on the end of the couch. He looked noticeably haggard. Richards expected that he himself did also; plus, he was exasperated.

"Sheriff, how could the investigators overlook the fact that Edginton had undergone a sex-change operation?"

"Me, Mr. Richards. It was my doing. I only told my deputies to ask for the blood types, and if there was any record of violence, especially sex-related violence. The clerks at the hospital gave us what we asked for. I'm sure the clerks had no idea she'd been raped. We haven't released any details, except to say she was murdered."

Richards shifted on the couch to where he directly faced Tidmore. "Sheriff, this is crazy. We know Hopper didn't kill Judith. Graff never left his dorm. Edginton could have killed her, but couldn't have raped her, and he couldn't have left the sock prints. It's obvious someone else was there with Hopper, maybe there with Hopper and Edginton. The only one we can eliminate for sure is Graff. Is there anything I don't know, any evidence that might help me understand a little better?"

"That's right, you're an attorney, aren't you?"

Richards shook his head, held his hands open ·in exasperation. "Securities attorney. Syndications, offerings, that's all I've ever done. I don't know a damn thing about criminal law, investigations, anything like this, except what I learned in school. Yet the second towel meant something to me when nobody else noticed it. If there's anything you could tell me that I don't already know, maybe it would help me think of something else."

"There's nothing," the sheriff said, shaking his head for emphasis. "You know how she was killed, and that she was raped. There's the blood type—and by the way, I've had everyone who lived in R-14 retyped. The hospital records were right in every case. So there's the AB blood, the shoe size, and hopefully the lab boys lifted some footprints out of the bathroom. That's it. Nothing more. There is one other possibility. There were no semen traces. Edginton could have killed her, then he might have artificially . . ."

He paused a moment, staring into Richards's eyes. "Mr. Richards, I always feel awkward talking to you, her father . . . but Edginton could have artificially abused her, used some object. On the other hand, like I told you on the way over here, the psychiatrists are firm in their belief that he wouldn't sexually assault a woman under any circumstances. A boy, maybe, not a woman."

"Did you ever speak to the security guard who was missing?" Richards asked. He had just remembered him.

"He was with a girlfriend, and he volunteered for a polygraph. He's clean."

Richards was searching his mind, trying to remember every possibility he had imagined. "What about AB blood types on the rest of the patients at the hospital? Could anyone have slipped out of another dorm and then back without being missed?"

"Doubtful. There's a couple dozen with the right blood type. We've talked to each of them. We also questioned the orderlies at each unit as to whether it was possible for a patient to have left and returned. I just don't believe that happened."

Richards moved his hand to his head and smoothed his hair back, looked at the floor for a moment, then raised his face again. "What about the staff?"

Tidmore yawned before he answered, stretching his arms above his head. "Excuse me. Only three staff members are AB. They all volunteered for polygraphs. Nothing."

Richards took in a deep breath, letting it out audibly. "What is it, Sheriff? What are we overlooking?"

"I'm worn out, Mr. Richards. I'm surprised you haven't passed out. I don't know when you've slept. Let's hang it up for today, get some rest. We'll get everything started again in the morning."

In the morning, Richards thought. Judith's funeral was in the morning. "Okay, Sheriff. If you don't mind, I'd like to talk with you again after the funeral. I know I've—"

"Of course. I plan to be there. We'll come back here afterwards."

"What I was starting to say, Sheriff, is I know I've been a lot of trouble. I really appreciate you putting up with me like you have. And please, call me Brandon."

"On the contrary, Mr. Richards . . . Brandon. Under the same circumstances I'd have already fallen apart. But you do need some sleep. You can't keep going forever. I believe if you would ever lay your head down you would pass out, but I can get you a sleeping pill if you need one."

Richards shook his head, then kept moving it in despair. "Sheriff, the only two patients who might have been at Judith's are dead. How are we ever going to know?"

"We'll know. Don't start worrying about something like that. We'll get some sleep tonight and then start fresh in the morning. And Brandon, call me Raymond."

Richards turned his head at the knock on the door.

"Come in," the sheriff said.

A large, broad-shouldered man dressed in a noticeably cheap, three-piece polyester suit entered the office.

"J.J.," the sheriff said, standing and holding out his hand. "I was speaking to Mr. Richards about you earlier." The two men shook hands, then the sheriff turned toward Richards. "Brandon, this is John J. Winstead. J.J., Brandon Richards."

"I'm glad to meet you, Mr. Winstead," Richards said, coming to his feet. "Judith was really appreciative of the help you gave her. I am, too."

Winstead nodded, then turned back to face the sheriff, either not noticing or ignoring Richards's outstretched hand.

Richards dropped his hand to his side. Never a man impressed with dress, he still couldn't help noticing the detective's worn, zippered boots. He also noticed Winstead had a serious, almost angry expression on his face.

"Heard how the patients couldn't have done it," the detective said, his tone almost a growl. "Shit, should have known. You shouldn't been worrying about them in the first place. Should've been checking her husband out."

Richards, his eyes narrowing, raised his stare to Winstead's face.

"Now, J.J.," the sheriff said, reseating himself on the couch. "First place, we're not sure the patients didn't do it, leastways Edginton and Hopper. We've just got a little problem with a mysterious blood sample, but we'll figure it eventually."

"Look at this shit," Winstead said, handing an index card to Tidmore. "You should've been checking the staff files instead of patient records."

As he studied the index card, the half smile left the sheriff's face. "I'll be damned," he said.

Richards leaned forward. "What?"

The sheriff held the card up. It was stamped: FORMER EMPLOYEE. It was a file card on Dr. Martin Salter. Caucasian male, six foot, two inches, one-hundred eighty-five pounds, blood type—AB.

Richards felt a chill pass over him.

"Knew as soon as I heard she'd been killed," Winstead said, "that that son of a bitch did it. He's mean enough. He had motives; didn't want to give up the kids; and he's AB. You all reporting the patients done it just threw my thinkin' off."

"And the doctor just decided to go by the hospital and pick up Hopper for company?" was the sheriff's remark.

"Haven't worked all that out yet," Winstead said. His eyes moved around the room.

The sheriff pointed.

The big detective moved to the wastebasket in the corner of the room and spit a brown stream into it. Using a crooked forefinger he dug the chew from his mouth and deposited it into the basket.

"Several angles come to mind," he continued as he walked back to the couch. "One, Salter wanted to make it look like someone else done it. Blaming loonies is a pretty good idea. Who's gonna believe 'em when they claim they didn't?"

Richards caught himself nodding.

"Big thing is Salter had to put 'em at Judith's cottage at the same time she was," Winstead continued. "He could've got inside the complex under the fence, same way the nuts escaped. Wouldn't had no trouble getting into R-14. Guard was working there when Salter was, knew him well; wouldn't thought nothin' about letting him in . . . at least cracking the door. Salter didn't care the guard saw him 'cause the guard wasn't gonna be around to be telling nobody.

"Besides letting the patients out, Salter could've carried Hopper with him to make sure he was found at the scene—shot him with Judith's gun. Shots knocked Hopper cold and when Salter left, Hopper woke up and hid out in the attic."

"Remember," the sheriff said, moving to the edge of the couch, "you're talking about a doctor. He would have known whether Hopper was dead or not."

Richards's head was moving back and forth as if he were watching a tennis match.

"Not a guaranteed fact. If a bastard just killed a couple people, maybe three, he would be thinkin' more about getting the hell out rather than checking pulses. There's been more than one killer fled from the scene with a victim still kicking.

"Another possibility," Winstead continued. "The escape might be a coincidence. You thought of that? I'm not stating it as an ironclad fact that Salter had anything to do with the escape. Maybe Hopper just wandered up at a bad time. Perimeter fence is only a hundred, hundred-fifty feet from Judith's. Maybe

Salter was leaving and thought Hopper spotted him. Carried Hopper back to the cottage to get rid of him. Whether Salter planned a coverup or not, he was mighty capable of figuring it out after being put in the position of needin' to dispose of Hopper."

Richards was impressed with Winstead's possibilities, but had a nagging doubt which the detective had not yet addressed. "Why would Salter take the time to rape her, Mr. Winstead, someone he hated enough to kill? It doesn't make sense."

Richards noticed the big detective's irritated look. It clearly stated he didn't appreciate an amateur butting in. Richards had grown so used to the sheriff's mild manner that he had forgotten he was an amateur and a stranger among the law enforcement professionals.

The sheriff must have also noticed, for it was he who answered the question. "Rape is usually an act of aggression, rather than lust. Quit worrying about the why. Let me tell you the reason you don't ever worry about the why. The first thing most anyone investigating a murder finds out is that they can't think like a killer does. Think about it, for whatever the reason . . . and I'm talking about a premeditated murder now, not a family dispute or barroom brawl that gets out of hand. Anybody capable of planning and carrying out a murder is nuts, has a screw loose somewhere. How do you think like someone who is crazy if you're not crazy? What you or I or any sane person would do just doesn't matter in figuring out why a killer did something. The important thing is what was done. Use your time thinking about that, not why."

Winstead nodded his head. "Raymond's right. And what was done is that your daughter was killed by a person with a ten and a half to a twelve shoe size and AB blood. Salter has both. He bought his shoes at

Kahns. He wears an eleven. Who had motive to do it? Again, our good doctor."

"J.J.," the sheriff said, "there's three hundred thousand people living in a fifty-mile radius around the city. Three percent have AB blood. That gives you nine thousand suspects. I'm sure a damn good percentage of them have shoe sizes between a ten and a half and a twelve. I'm not saying the doctor is not a prime suspect. He is. First thing in the morning, I'm going to be finding out where he was night before last. But right now we don't have a legitimate reason to suspect him more than anybody else. I think it only fair to Brandon for him to know that you can't stand the doctor."

Richards glanced toward the detective.

"Don't like the son of a bitch," Winstead said. "Never did. You're right about that. But you wait and see, he done it."

Richards noted the extreme bitterness in the detective's tone. His feelings were much deeper than simple dislike. Anything he said about Salter would have to be taken cautiously.

"J.J. didn't tell you he's being sued by the doctor," the sheriff said to Richards, "did he? When J.J. was working for your daughter Salter tried to get violation of privacy and civil-rights charges filed against him; ended up filing a lawsuit. It'll cost him a hell of a lot more than what your daughter paid him to get his butt out of the crack it's in now."

"Mr. Winstead," Richards said, taking care to make sure his tone was properly polite, "if you were on this case what would you do?"

The expression on Winstead's face softened as he was asked his expert opinion, and Richards knew the detective would be no problem to handle.

"Like the sheriff said, I'd check out his alibi first.

But you can bet your ass he's gonna have one. So I'd bust it."

"How . . . Mr. Winstead?" Richards didn't have to act to have a look of keen interest in what the big detective was saying.

"If it's a bullshit alibi, whoever he's claiming as his alibi had to be somewhere else. I'd try to find out where that somewhere else was. Meantime I'd also check with the highway patrol. A guy commits a murder, no matter how much balls he's got, he's gonna be nervous, maybe driving erratically, maybe speeding. He might have his name on a ticket between here and his home. Airports keep a record of private planes going and coming. I'd check every place he could have filled up with gas between here and there, show 'em a photograph. There's lots of ways. The police will check the same things, but there's a few things they won't do that I will."

The sheriff laughed. "More than a few, J.J."

"Mr. Winstead, I would like to hire you. I want to know who killed my daughter and I want to know for absolute sure. I don't care how long it takes or how much it costs or how you do it."

Winstead smiled.

CHAPTER

10

The pickup truck's horn snapped Richards awake. For a moment he didn't realize where he was, then he guided his Cadillac back into the proper lane. He shook his head and lowered his window, angling his face toward the cool wind.

As the pickup passed, he smiled and waved his thanks.

"Get the hell off the road, you damn drunk!"

He couldn't help but smile.

After pulling to a stop in the motel parking lot, he briefly debated whether to eat or go straight to bed. The idea of rest won out; he had eaten most of a sandwich earlier.

Entering his room, he swung the door shut behind

him and flopped down on the bed without bothering to undress. Seeing the blinking red message light, he reached for the telephone.

"This is Brandon Richards, room three hundred sixty-seven. My message light is on."

"You have a request to return a phone call. No name."

After the motel operator gave Richards the number, he punched it in. He heard two rings, then a click, then a message: "We all knows how these things work, so speak. *Beep.*"

"This is Brandon Richards at the Holiday Inn, returning a call which was left for me. I'm in my room now. Three hundred sixty-seven. In the morning I—"

"Mr. Richards! Mr. Richards!"

"Yes."

"Mr. Richards, I was afraid you'd hang up. I'm an RN at the state hospital. I was a friend of your daughter's."

He lay back into his pillow, nodding his head, appreciative of the call.

"Your daughter and I were real close. She told me some things which might or might not be important, but I thought I needed to tell you."

Not the condolences he expected. "Important?"

"About some men she was having trouble with, Mr. Richards. I think she was scared of a couple of them. It's probably nothing . . ."

Swinging his feet to the floor, he sat upright on the edge of the bed. "What do you mean, 'having trouble?' Who was she having trouble with?" His eyes were searching for the pencil which went with the white pad next to the telephone. "Excuse me, can you hang on a moment?"

He found the pencil on the floor under the bed.

"Okay, I'm sorry. Go on. What men are you speaking about? What kind of trouble?"

"Mr. Richards, I really liked Judith. I want them to catch whoever did it. I would have called the police and told them what I know. I was scared, though. There were two different men who she said threatened her. She told me one of them had killed somebody and she was really afraid of him. I mean, he did it legal, he's some kind of police officer. Judith said that he was in police work."

He felt a sudden unnerving sensation.

"I didn't ask anymore. I didn't care at the time. She said the man had killed somebody and had reminded her of that when he threatened her. That's why I was afraid to call the police, Mr. Richards. I had to call, but I don't want you to use my name, okay?"

"Of course not. Why was the man threatening her? Who . . . ? Do you have any idea who he might have been?"

"No, sir. I talked to my husband about it. That was him on the answering machine. He works on the grounds crew out at the hospital. He liked her, too. He . . . he said . . ."

"What?"

"Nothing. He said he didn't have any idea either."

He shook his head in exasperation. "Ma'am, I really appreciate your calling, and I'm not going to tell anybody who you are. What did your husband say?"

"Mr. Richards, Judith had a rough time with Dr. Salter and she was lonely when he left. She was susceptible to any man who was nice to her, even if he was married. My husband said with her dating married men like she was, no telling who might have done it. You know, even a jealous wife, maybe. Mr. Richards, I don't mean Judith was a bad girl."

He exhaled slowly and shook his head again, but kept his voice polite.

"Ma'am, I'm not being rude, but I don't care how many married men she dated. I only want to know who they were. I mean the ones who threatened her. You have to help me find out who they are. Something she said, something which might give me an idea, a hint. You have to think hard. You said one was a policeman or in some kind of police work. Did she say what kind of work the other one was in?"

"No, only that both of them were married. That's all I know. I can sort of ask around, though I don't believe she would have told anybody anything she didn't tell me. I was her best friend. You can't tell the police I'm doing it, though. Don't tell anybody."

"I won't. Thank you. Call me if you hear anything or think of anything. No, call me anyway. What is your name?"

"I'll call you. My name is Atlene. Atlene Johnson."

He scribbled the name on the notepad. "Atlene, did you know her husband?"

"Yes."

"You know he had kidnapped the twins. Do you think he's the type of man who might have done something like this?"

"Mr. Richards, I'm not much for prejudices, you know, being black myself. Judith said she had told you about him, isn't that right? You know, him going out with other men."

"Yes."

"I don't want to sound like that's why I didn't like him. You wouldn't know he was any different by being around him. He's not effeminate. He was a real man. He was a real tough man. Mr. Richards, he could be pretty mean, too. . . . Yes, he might have done it. When I first heard about it, I thought about him. Mr.

Richards, I'm real sorry about Judith, real sorry. I have to go now. I'll be at the funeral tomorrow. I'll see you there."

After Richards replaced the telephone receiver he lay back on his pillow for a moment, thinking. Without meaning to, he fell asleep.

CHAPTER

11

The sky was gray above the cemetery, dark clouds rolling in from the south. Rain was in the forecast. Several of those attending the graveside services carried umbrellas.

Richards was pleased with the number of people present. They were there for Judith, not him. He doubted any of them remembered him, except maybe one or two, vaguely, as her father. He had moved from the area more than sixteen years before, just after burying Stella in the grave next to the one Judith would now occupy. He raised his eyes toward the sky. It had been cloudy that day, too, started raining at the end of the service.

There were half a dozen blacks among the assembled. None of them were in a nurse's uniform and he wasn't sure which one was Atlene Johnson. Probably the one who kept glancing at him.

He caught a whiff of fragrance from the flowers surrounding the coffin. It was a clean natural fragrance. Not the overpowering sickly sweet smell of too many flowers in too small a room as had been present when he sat with Judith in the funeral home. Then Reverend Gilder started reciting the final prayer.

Richards bowed his head and clasped his hands at his waist. He was standing rather than sitting under the small tent erected over the grave site. He had specifically asked that there be no row of folding chairs present for the family. There was no family, only him. The third plot of ground on the other side of Stella would be where he would come back someday.

He raised his head slightly. Staring at the coffin he spoke his thoughts silently to Judith. He realized he might be committing a sacrilege, but if so it was his transgression, not hers. She would be avenged. He had told her this before, when he had sat with her in the funeral home, but that had been when he first saw her and hurt so bad. He wanted to reassure her now that his promise had not come from the initial shock. He meant it. He intended on killing her murderer. That he was so deeply sure he would, and didn't find the thought disturbing, surprised him, he who was always lifting drowning bugs from his swimming pool. He had never been more sure of anything before.

The prayer was over, Reverend Gilder moving toward him to clasp his hands.

"She's with the Lord now, Mr. Richards."

"Thank you."

And it was over.

When he turned from the grave, those who had been assembled were already walking away, their backs to him—except for the young black woman who was looking past him toward the coffin. She was dabbing her eyes with a handkerchief. He walked to her.

"Mrs. Johnson?"

"Mr. Richards, I feel so bad."

He caught himself patting her shoulder, comforting her.

"What are we going to do?" she asked.

"The only thing for us to do," he said, "is make sure whoever did this is caught."

Atlene nodded, wiping her watery eyes again, then placed the handkerchief back in her coat pocket.

"I've been asking around, Mr. Richards. Yet, like I told you, I don't think she would have told anyone anything she didn't tell me."

"Keep trying, please."

"I will."

"I'm going back to the staff cottages this afternoon," he said. "Maybe one of her neighbors knows something about who she was dating. I attached an answering machine to the phone in my motel room. If you think of anything, anything at all, please be sure and leave it on the machine. Every time I'm back at the room I'll check it."

"Brandon." The sheriff was holding out his hand.

Richards clasped Tidmore's hand and shook it slowly.

"I was thinking you might like to come out to my place to eat," Tidmore said, a friendly smile coming to his face. "We have a gal named Ruby who cooks for us. She's the best in the state."

Richards smiled his appreciation. "Thank you, but I told Winstead I'd meet him back at the motel."

"J.J.'s been busy," the sheriff said. "Was waiting at my office when I got there this morning; had me flash my badge a little for him. If you're meeting with him

I'll let him tell you about it. What about afterwards then? After you get through with him, just call me and I'll come by and pick you up."

After he checked with Winstead, and after he checked with Judith's neighbors, it would be him alone again in the motel room, Richards knew, and he didn't like the idea. "Okay," he said. "It might be as late as four or five o'clock."

"Perfect. I'll pick you up at five-thirty, right after I leave the office. You can eat dinner with us and then I'll show you around my operation. It's not just a dairy farm. I made the front cover of *Top Farmer* with my breeding operation. I'm sort of proud of it."

Richards smiled and nodded. "I'd like that." He noticed Atlene had silently slipped away.

Looking back toward the road, he saw she had already reached the small white Ford she drove, glancing back over her shoulder at him as she climbed inside.

He understood. A man in police work was all Judith had told her. He glanced at the sheriff and then back to Atlene.

CHAPTER

12

Winstead was waiting in the Holiday Inn lobby when Richards returned from the funeral. The big detective said he had to eat lunch; he had missed breakfast. Richards surprised himself by also filling his plate from the buffet.

The sheriff had been correct, Winstead had been busy. Richards found himself becoming steadily more impressed with the detective.

"Knew I'd have a fat chance of getting anything out of Salter," Winstead said. "So first thing this morning I had Raymond call. Our good doctor had enough sense to know it was coming. He patched his attorney in on the line and the attorney did most of the talking. He said Salter received a call from a patient at twelve forty-five that night and called in a prescription to a druggist who'll vouch for him."

"I don't guess he could have called long distance," was the way Richards decided to question the detective.

Winstead forked a piece of country-fried steak into his mouth, moving it to a bulge in his cheek before answering. "Would already have got the phone records, but the patient is a problem case, started raising hell down at the drug store. Salter ran down there to calm him down at one o'clock. Pharmacist and a couple of others will all vouch for him being there. We're gonna have to say he was at his home 'round twelve forty-five.

"Coroner puts her time of death between ten-thirty and two. We can do better than that. She checked out of the hospital at ten fifty-two—let's say got to her house around eleven. Escape was reported at twelve-thirty and security found her at twelve forty-seven. So instead of from ten-thirty until two, we've got from eleven until she was found, something under two hours.

"It's a hundred and ten miles one way to Salter's home. At a little over sixty miles an hour he could've been at the cottage at eleven and back home by twelve forty-five. At ninety he could've left as late as eleven-thirty and still made it. But he's got another alibi witness, a personal friend who was supposed to have been with him from eight until ten-fifteen."

Richards had been juggling the numbers in his head. "He couldn't have done it then. If he didn't leave his home until ten-fifteen, he would have had to make a two hundred-twenty-mile round trip in a little over two hours."

"If you're thinking he drove," Winstead said, speaking past another bulge in his cheek. "There's always flying. And where was the doctor and his alibi friend when they were together until ten-fifteen? If they were here in the city it would be easy to leave at ten-fifteen, get to your daughter's at eleven, and back home at twelve forty-five."

"You don't know where they were?"

Winstead shook his head, swallowing. "Attorney said it was personal, didn't want to divulge the name, but would if they had to. They're gonna have to. Raymond's fixin' that now. But I might know who it is anyway. Salter's been seeing a male hooker here. It was going on before he left the area, every Wednesday night, like a ritual.

"I got the hooker to give us a sworn statement your daughter used against Salter to get the children back. Made Salter mad, but in a month they were seeing each other again. Salter works Saturday through Wednesday, takes off Thursday and Friday. Wednesday nights are his time to get laid. I already checked, but the hooker's not home. Really need to have someone wait at the apartment until he shows up."

"I'll pay for it."

Winstead nodded. "If the hooker is Salter's alibi, that's all the better; proves he was in the area and at the right time. Oh yeah, for what it's worth, Salter's gonna take a polygraph. Don't put any stock in such as that. He says he doesn't trust cops. According to him cops don't like people of his particular persuasion. His attorney's getting an independent examiner to give the test. You can guess what the results are gonna show. Well, guess I need to start back to work. Appreciate the lunch."

"Mr. Winstead."

"J.J.," Winstead said.

"J.J., I want everything covered, every possibility, not only Dr. Salter. Don't rule out anybody, not until we know it's him for sure."

The big detective nodded his thanks to the waitress who refilled his tea glass. "Keeping everything in mind," he said, "but if it's not him we don't have much to go on. We have some sock prints, ten and a half to a twelve size; AB bloodtype; know the time frame the attack took place in. That's about it."

"And the footprints in the bathroom," Richards said.

"Sheriff said they didn't turn out. Lifted some which were clearly your daughter's. Bigger ones, though, what there was of 'em, were too smudged to tell anything, anything at all."

Richards felt the first meal he had felt like eating turn to a cold lump in his stomach.

The sheriff had told him the prints would be as accurate as fingerprints. They were going to be the final clinching evidence when the killer was captured. He had dreamed during the night of the prosecutor presenting Martin Salter's footprints in court and laying them next to the ones lifted off the bathroom floor. He looked at the last few bites of food on his plate and laid his fork down. The phrase, "a man in police work" passed through his mind and he raised his face to Winstead's.

"J.J., how long have you been in police work?"

Winstead finished emptying his tea glass before he answered. "All my life—since I was twenty, anyway. A beat cop, made it to detective, was an investigator for the Attorney General's office, and now private, making less money than when I was official. Retired from being official 'cause I wasn't making enough money." He laughed sarcastically.

"Did you ever have to shoot at anybody?"

Winstead laughed again. "Shot at and been shot at."

"Did you ever kill anybody?"

Winstead nodded. "Yeah, I have."

Richards shook the nervousness from his mind. So had hundreds of other cops. But as they pushed back their chairs and rose to leave, the nervousness returned and wouldn't go away. Even after paying the bill at the cashier's desk and walking to where the detective was using one of the pay telephones in the motel lobby, the uneasy feeling persisted.

Winstead replaced the receiver and turned around. After he used a thumb and forefinger to place a chew inside his cheek, he nodded. "All set. I got a man on his way to check on Salter's Wednesday night friend. We'll keep a watch until the hooker shows back up at his apartment."

Richards nodded. "Good. I'm going over to the staff cottages and talk to some of Judith's neighbors. I'll be returning in a couple hours if you need me."

"Deputies already talked to the neighbors."

"I know."

Winstead stared a moment, then shrugged.

Richards looked down at his feet, as if studying them, and then back up to Winstead. "You're correct about not having much to go on with the evidence we have. I'm an average-sized person and wear a ten, almost big enough to fit within the range the lab says the killer wore. Shouldn't they have been able to narrow it down more?"

Winstead nodded. "Lab boys are trying to protect themselves; always do. Narrow it down too much and the killer turns out to have a size that don't fit, then

the defense attorney's gonna harp on that. I examined
the prints pretty good; no question but they're Salter's
size. I wear an eleven and a half and my shoe fits the
prints nearly perfect."

CHAPTER

13

The blacktop road into the staff cottages dead-ended in an L-shaped cul-de-sac, Judith's home sitting at the heel of the L. Richards first stopped at the cottage directly across the street from his daughter's.

A young, red-haired nurse answered the door, cracking it only as far as its security chain would allow. She had been living there less than a week and knew nothing; had never met his daughter. She shut the door before he could thank her.

The home next to the nurse's was empty, curtainless windows and unmowed grass indicating no one had lived there for a considerable time.

He walked across the street to the cottage next to Judith's. Moving up its steps he pushed the doorbell button several times.

Waiting a full minute without response he turned to leave, but as he did he glimpsed the slight movement of the curtains in the big picture window at the center of the cottage. Recalling the nervous fear the red-haired nurse had shown he turned back to the door and pushed the doorbell again.

"This is Brandon Richards. I'm Judith Salter's father. I was wondering if I might speak with you a moment?"

He pushed the doorbell button again. "It will only take a moment," he said, speaking even louder.

Leaning back, he looked toward where he had seen the curtains move. A cat now strolled the window sill, dragging its arched back against the glass as it walked.

Richards smiled and shrugged, shaking his head. "Not seeing visitors today, huh?" he said, giving the cat a wink.

As Richards moved from the porch, a battered brown pickup stopped at the curb in front of the cottage. Its driver, a large pot-bellied man in his fifties, dressed in faded khakis, work boots, and a yellow muscle shirt, stepped out and came around the front of the truck. He had shoulder-length brown hair and wore a red sweatband around his forehead. Richards moved to meet him.

"I'm Brandon Richards, Judith Salter's father."

The man nodded without speaking, his eyes narrowing under thin eyebrows.

"I was wondering if I might ask you some questions about my daughter?"

Angling his head with the breeze, the man drew his lips back against mottled teeth and spat a stream of tobacco juice onto the lawn. Then he turned back to Richards.

"The cops already been here. My wife pulled a double shift over at the hospital and went to bed 'round eight. I watched television 'nother couple of hours and sacked out myself. We didn't hear nothin'."

Richards smiled politely. "I was hoping maybe you knew something about whom she was dating. Thought maybe she had mentioned something to you or maybe you had seen somebody come by to pick her up."

The man's forehead wrinkled, his eyes narrowing again. He glanced toward his cottage. "Cops didn't ask nothin' 'bout that."

"I know. It's something I'm trying to find out for myself."

"I wouldn't know who all she dated."

When the man's eyes locked on the front of his cottage, Richards looked that way.

An older, angular woman with stringy brown hair had stepped from the home. She clutched a flimsy nylon robe about her as she walked toward them. The cat stood in the open doorway.

"Mister," the man said, turning toward the cottage. "We really don't know nothin.' We weren't friends with your daughter."

"You were," the woman said as she passed the man to stop in front of Richards. "I wasn't."

The man stopped and turned back, his stare lowering to the ground.

The woman's beady eyes swept Richards from head to toe. When she spoke she held her head back and slightly to the side. "Judith's father, huh? You a cop, too?"

Richards smiled politely and shook his head. "No, ma'am."

"Then why're you here?"

"This is my wife Annabelle," the man said, never raising his stare.

"Glad to meet you, ma'am. I was asking your husband if he might know anything about whom Judith was dating."

The man threw an irritated stare at Richards then dropped his eyes again.

The woman gave a half chuckle, half snort, her mouth gaping open to speak. Then she hesitated a moment.

She was thinking better of whatever she had started to say, Richards guessed, and he wondered what it was. When she did speak, her tone was somewhat softer than before.

"It's a bad thing what happened to your daughter. I'm sorry 'bout that. But if the cops want to know anything 'bout who she was dating, they'd better come around and ask themselves rather than send her father." The woman's eyes narrowed. "Why ain't they here anyway, if they wanna know?" Her biting tone was back.

Richards's smile was forced now. "What is your last name, ma'am?"

"Annabelle Lee Turnage."

"Mrs. Turnage, this is something personal. I thought you might be able to help." He glanced at her husband. The man's eyes remained lowered.

"Yeah, Hal's the one you need to be looking at, ask him. Yeah . . ." She stared at her husband and then back to Richards's face. Her scowl relaxed somewhat as she nodded at whatever was now working its way through her brain.

"Yeah," she continued. "I shouldn't be holding no grudge against you. You being her father, that's blood. You gotta be feeling bad." She turned her gaze back to her husband. "Hal, you go ahead and talk to the man. All I know 'bout's you. You tell him 'bout you and Judith, then come on in the house." Pulling her robe tighter about her body she turned and strode toward her cottage, her ankles unsteady in her pink, high-heeled house slippers.

Richards faced the woman's husband.

The man continued to stare after his wife until she had gone inside and closed the door, then turned back toward Richards.

"I got to be gettin' on inside the house, mister. I didn't do nothin' with your daughter. Just was over at her house talkin' when my wife busted in. Your daughter didn't have all her clothes on, but nothin' was going on. Nothin' was fixin' to go on either."

He turned his head and spat another stream of tobacco juice before continuing. "She asked me to check out a problem she was havin' with her lawnmower. When I finished and went inside she was gettin' dressed. She wasn't the type to get embarrassed 'bout not having no shirt on. I mean she had her bra on. You couldn't see nothin'. But it was her walkin' around in that bra what set my wife off. That's all there was to it. But Annabelle wouldn't believe me if I swore on a stack of Bibles. She don't understand 'bout girls like Judith."

The man jerked his face up, his eyes level with Richards's for the first time. "Now don't be takin' that wrong, mister. Judith weren't no bad girl. This new generation, they don't think like us old heads. Nothin' wrong with it, it's just a new time."

An irritated expression swept Richards's face. He was tired of having to assume what it was people meant. First her best friend and now her neighbor. My God, Judith was twenty-six.

"Are you saying my daughter was promiscuous, wild? Say what you mean." His tone was too sharp, and his hands had involuntarily squeezed into fists.

The man's eyes moved to the fists, but he showed no fear. He was a big man. "Mister, do you wanna hear it straight?" He spat another stream of juice, this time out of the side of his mouth, never taking his eyes off Richards.

Richards nodded, making sure the sharpness was gone from his voice before he spoke. "That's what I want."

"The reason my wife went and got so all fired hot was cause Judith started havin' men over to stay the night after her husband skipped out. She didn't try to hide it none either. That kind of stuff makes other women edgy."

Especially when their husbands start looking for excuses to visit, Richards thought. He studied the man closely, noted the roll of fat protruding above the waistband of the too-tight khakis, the unwashed and stringy hair, the beads of sweat hanging from his double chin. His daughter wouldn't have sunk so low. Annabelle didn't have anything to be mad about, at least not from Judith.

"Mr. Turnage, do you know any of the men she was dating? If you don't know any of their names, do you remember what they looked like, what kind of car they drove?"

"You mean lately, like the last couple months, only the ones she's been seein' since her husband skipped . . . ?"

Richards slumped a little as he nodded.

"Well, mostly I didn't pay no attention, just cars and men. I only seen one come by that I knew. Didn't really know him, seen his picture in the newspaper. He's that detective her husband's suin'."

"John Winstead?"

"Hell, I don't remember his name. Just that big detective from the city. You know who her husband's suin', don't you?"

"When's the last time you saw him at Judith's?"

"Maybe a month ago."

Richards's muscles relaxed. "Mr. Winstead was in her employ then."

"Might've been."

"What makes you think he was dating her?"

The man didn't answer.

"Mr. Turnage, this is important to me. I need to know why you think he was dating her. Did he ever spend the night?"

The man spat another stream of tobacco juice, then wiped his chin with the back of his hand.

"Car did."

CHAPTER

14

There was a Quick Stop convenience store where the blacktop road leading from the staff cottages intersected with the highway, and Richards stopped there, using the telephone to call Atlene Johnson's home. His stomach was bothering him again and he fumbled in his pocket for the last two Maalox tablets, plopping the chalky pills into his mouth.

"Hello."

"Atlene, this is Brandon Richards. I've been questioning some of Judith's neighbors and something has come up I need to speak with you about. I need to come by."

"I go on duty in an hour."

"It'll just take a minute."

"Well, okay. I live in Sheffield Heights, 220 Richmond."

Atlene's house was one of the better-maintained ones in a modest neighborhood of old homes. Red brick with freshly painted white shutters, the small one-story structure sat in a line of similar dwellings, but was distinguishable by its landscape.

Aesthetically shaped shrubs along the front of the house and a row of flowers down each side of the short concrete driveway attested to her husband's talents as a groundskeeper, or her taste.

She was standing outside the open door of her home when he arrived. Already dressed in her uniform, she glanced at her watch as he hurried across the sidewalk to where she stood.

He smiled politely and pressed her outstretched hand. "I'm really sorry to bother you like this," he began, "but something's come up."

She smiled pleasantly and nodded, her eyebrows arching.

"Come on inside."

Entering the living room, she directed him to a yellow sofa and then sat on a similar colored chair across from him, glancing at her watch once more.

He leaned forward, his forearms resting on his thighs, his hands clasped between his knees, and came directly to the point.

"Judith's neighbor says that she had been dating John Winstead."

Her face was only attentive, the name not causing any change in her expression.

"Winstead, Atlene, he's the detective who worked with her in getting the children back."

Her widening eyes expressed her recollection even before she spoke. "Yes, I remember her mentioning him now."

"A detective, Atlene—that means he's in police work. If he was dating her, then I've employed a man who might be the very one who threatened her; hired him to help me find out who the killer is."

Her eyebrows arched again, her eyes narrowing.

"Atlene, what did Judith say about him?"

She shook her head. "I just remember her mentioning him when she was talking about trying to have her children returned."

"Nothing about dating him?"

She shook her head again. "Like I told you, all she ever said about dating anyone was that she was seeing a couple of men who had threatened her. One of them was in police work. She never used any name or said anymore about it; just that one time."

"You never said what brought it on, why they threatened her."

She took a deep breath and let it out slowly. "They were acting up, Mr. Richards; she didn't want them around anymore. She said if they didn't stay away from her she was going to tell their wives."

His eyes slitted. "What do you mean, acting up?"

She sat silently, her eyes dropping from his to the floor, her tongue moving against the inside of her cheek. She raised her face again, but her eyes never focused directly onto his.

"I really don't know anything else that would help you. I swear. If I did I'd tell you."

He knew better. He leaned farther forward, staring directly into her eyes.

"Atlene, when you first spoke to me on the telephone I could tell you were being careful with what you said. I thought it was because you were scared. I'm sure you were. But that isn't all of it, is it? I mean, after you told me about the two men and the police connection, you had said everything you would have been worried about. You were being careful with what you said about Judith, weren't you?"

Atlene continued to stare at the floor and he was now positive he was right.

"I need to know everything, Atlene, everything you know about her—her lifestyle, who her friends were. What doesn't seem important to you might be the very thing that ties all this together for me, helps me to find her killer."

Atlene continued to look at the floor, then across to the wall, everywhere but back into his eyes. Finally she turned her face to his, leveling her eyes with his.

"Mr. Richards, Judith . . ." She hesitated a long moment. "She was really a good person, kind, gentle . . ."

"I know, Atlene. Please."

She continued to stare into his eyes, and then she shook her head. "You're not going to like it."

"Please."

She dropped her stare to the floor and nodded slowly. And then, the decision made, the words flowed from her mouth.

"She enjoyed men, Mr. Richards. She enjoyed men and she enjoyed games. She was always a little like that, even before she met Dr. Salter. But after she met him it got worse.

"She originally met him, and a friend of his, in a bar one night and he got off with her. It was the first time he ever got off with a woman and that's what he had always wanted, she said. To him she was some kind of godsend, and she fell for him, too. That's when they eloped. It continued, too, for a while, just him and her. And then he got back like he was before he met her, and couldn't respond anymore. He started stepping out on her, with men. That was just before the twins were born.

"Afterwards they tried to work it out, solve his problem, and it was sorta hit and miss. Sometimes he needed another man with them, sometimes he didn't. She went along. Then they got into acting out fantasies. I think, originally, to help him. Then one day he just left. But Judith didn't stop. In fact, she went farther and farther. The fantasies started being rough. She began to like to be made to do things."

She paused, raising her face and looking into his eyes.

He smoothed the hair back from his forehead and nodded. "It's okay," he said, "go on."

"She couldn't wait to tell me each time, Mr. Richards, and I couldn't wait to hear—maybe that's how I got my thrills, vicariously; I didn't have the guts to be as open as she was, or the sense to try to stop her before it was too late. Each time she acted out one fantasy she went to a stronger one. More exciting, she said."

Atlene paused again, wetting her dry lips with her tongue and dropping her eyes from his before continuing.

"She came to work with a black eye once. She said the games had gotten out of hand. She was scared. She said she was going to stop."

He dropped his stare to the floor and Atlene, noticing, paused again. "You sure you want me to go on?"

He nodded without raising his face.

She took a deep breath and continued. "It wasn't a week later she showed up hurt again, had a busted lip. She moved around like she was hurting somewhere else, too. It scared the hell out of me. I begged her to stop. The psychiatrists at the hospital will counsel us free; it's part of the benefits. She wouldn't hear of that. She said it was all over; she was through with her games. She said she meant it this time."

Atlene took another deep breath, shaking her head. When she spoke again her voice had become higher pitched and was strained.

"Mr. Richards, it wasn't a week later—and this was not long ago—she got really hurt, didn't show up for work for two days. She called in sick, but I guessed what might have happened and went over to her cottage."

Atlene shifted nervously in her chair. "Whoever it was who did it didn't leave any marks you could see with her clothes on. He didn't bruise her face or arms. But she had been beat good. She said she had gotten hysterical, told the guy—this was the one in police work—that if he ever came back she was going to tell his wife, that she might anyway. That's when the guy told her he'd kill her if she did." She took a deep breath. "And a few days later, someone did."

Finished, she slumped back in her chair.

Several seconds of silence passed and then Richards raised his head.

"Atlene, we have to find out who he is." His brow wrinkled. "Hell, I don't even know if Winstead's married."

"Sheriff Tidmore is," she said.

He looked into Atlene's dark eyes. "I noticed you were uncomfortable around him this morning."

"He's in police work. He's married."

"That's all?"

She nodded.

He stood. "Thank you, Atlene."

She rose to her feet. "Mr. Richards, she wasn't a bad girl. She was really a good person."

"She was my daughter, Atlene. There wasn't a better person anywhere."

At the door, Atlene stared at him a moment, then reached out and hugged him.

"Thank you," he said, and she nodded and smiled softly as he walked outside. Then she closed the door behind him.

He was halfway across the lawn when her door suddenly flew open.

"Mr. Richards! Mr. Richards!" she called as she hurried from the house.

"Mr. Richards. I can't believe I haven't thought of this earlier. Minnefield. They have a man locked up in maximum-security named Minnefield. You need to talk to him. I don't know why I didn't think of it before."

"Think of what?"

"Judith told me once—she was being sarcastic, in one of her moods. She said he was the only man that'd ever been faithful to her, went to bed with her every night."

He angled his head slightly, a quizzical expression coming to his face.

Atlene's voice was excited, the words coming fast.

"She said that one night she noticed he was standing in his window staring at her as she was walking to her door. He got to where he did it every night. She started playing with him, waving at him before she would go inside her house. She said he could see in her bedroom window when the curtains were open."

She shook her head, her eyes narrowing. "I don't know, Mr. Richards, she never said it, but I think she got to teasing him. Maybe leaving the curtains open— another one of her games. I don't know what she was fantasizing, but she began paying as much attention to him as he was her. She said she'd sneak around to the corner of the house and look, and he was always standing there when her bedroom light was on. Then when she'd turn it off he'd leave. That was why she was saying he went to bed with her every night."

Atlene was staring directly into his eyes. "God, Mr. Richards. If she hadn't gone to bed yet, still had the lights on, he could have been watching. He might have seen the killer."

CHAPTER

15

It only took Richards twenty minutes to drive from Atlene's to the hospital's administration building, and it was a little after three when the secretary showed him into Dr. Thornburg's office—still plenty of time to meet with Minnefield and then return to the motel to wait for the sheriff and the ride to the dairy farm.

The doctor stood but didn't come around the desk to shake hands. "I'm sorry to have kept you waiting," he said.

Thornburg's voice was as gentle as his appearance. Considerably shorter than Richards's six foot, and of a slim, fragile build, the doctor sported an old-fashioned flat top of slightly grayed brown hair and wore simply framed, thick lensed glasses. His suit was neat but drab. He pointed to a seat in front of the desk, then seated himself.

"Your daughter was a fine person. I didn't know her personally, but her record was exemplary. Chief Nurse Johansen said she was one of her very favorite people."

"Thank you."

"Now how can I help you?" The administrator leaned forward, elbows on his desk, hands clasped, thumbs twiddling.

"I would like to speak with Marcus Minnefield again."

"I see."

Thornburg leaned back in his chair, his face taking on a reflective look. Then he leaned forward again.

"Alan told me you all's earlier visit didn't accomplish anything. Quite frankly, I don't think talking to the man will ever produce anything other than frustration, yet I can understand your wanting to keep trying. You're alone?"

"Yes, sir."

"Is the sheriff aware you're here?"

"No, sir, not specifically."

A small knowing smile appeared on Thornburg's face. "Think maybe you can persuade Minnefield to tell you something he wouldn't with the officers around? I doubt it, Mr. Richards, I seriously doubt it. I don't see any harm in your trying, though. Go ahead. I'll have my secretary call Alan and tell him you're coming."

When the guard led Richards into the maximum-security unit's outer office, the security captain was standing, waiting.

"Dr. Thornburg said you wanted to go up without a guard; that right?"

Richards nodded. "Yes, sir."

"You know to stay in the middle of the hall. You're not carrying any kind of weapon, are you?"

Richards shook his head.

"You sure you don't want an orderly to go with you?"

"I believe it would be better if I speak with him alone."

Alan nodded. "Okay. Listen up. Don't hand Minnefield anything. Don't take anything from him. I mean absolutely nothing goes back and forth. Understand?"

The captain paused, his tongue working under his lips at whatever he was thinking. "I tell you what," he finally said. "I'm going to have an orderly accompany you anyway. He can stop at the head of the stairs where he won't be any distraction to Minnefield, but still keep an eye on you. It's for your own good. It's just too dangerous to be in there not knowing anymore than you do."

As Richards came down the hall Minnefield rose from his bunk and moved to lean against the front of his cell. The flowered pajamas had been replaced by white cotton ones emblazoned with cartoon characters. He still wore the blue slippers.

"I thought it was you," he said. "You slide your feet along when you walk. So does Alan, though."

Richards stopped and forced a pleasant smile. "You know why I'm here, Mr. Minnefield. I just hope you'll decide to help me."

Minnefield smiled knowingly and nodded his head, then his expression changed to a serious one. "Revenge burns deep, doesn't it, Mr. Richards?"

"I don't know if you'd call it revenge. I . . . yes, revenge; you're correct."

Minnefield nodded. "It's nothing for you to be ashamed of, I have had the same feeling myself. It won't let you rest. Maybe I will decide to help you." A wry smile replaced the serious expression. "Then again why should I trouble myself?"

Richards didn't think he had shown his irritation, but Minnefield saw something.

"Do I detect a feeling of disgust, Mr. Richards?"

Richards was careful with his answer. "Disappointment."

"Disgust, disappointment, the feeling is much the same, only different in the degree of intensity. I have the feeling daily." Minnefield pushed himself away from the bars and spread his hands. "Observe how I live." He turned and strode to the back of his cell. There he turned back around and spread his hands again.

"Observe carefully," he said, his tone suddenly sharp. "My world. Ten by twelve. You talk of disappointment, disgust; I could not endure it except for my opening. Yet for the window I am forced to toil daily cleaning listless, filthy cretins." He paused, staring at Richards as if waiting for an answer.

Not knowing what else to do, Richards nodded.

Minnefield moved back to the front of his cell, grasping a steel bar with each hand. There were yellow smudges on his fingers—chalk dust. Richards saw the pieces of chalk lying on the bed; a notebook pad rested on the pillow. The sketch of a broad face was upside down, and he couldn't recognize the person, but he could see there were horns drawn protruding from the forehead.

"I have made a decision as to what I wish in exchange for the information you desire," Minnefield said. "I want this opening guaranteed to me forever. And I don't wish to continue to have to earn it by toiling like a dung bug. What I want you can provide. What I have to offer in exchange is the identity of your daughter's killer. Absolutely, in a way which will leave no doubt in your mind. I do know who the killer is, Mr. Richards, and I can prove it."

Richards managed to keep his face expressionless, but his heart was knocking. A tingling sensation swept his back.

Minnefield turned and walked to his cell's barred opening, staring out. He kept his back turned when he spoke.

"They have robbed me of much more than my freedom by putting me in here," he said, his voice now so low Richards had to strain to hear.

Minnefield raised his right forearm in front of his chest and, staring at it, flexed it. "I am measurably weaker. You have undoubtedly noticed my voice is raspy from disuse. Surprisingly, my vision has not suffered. It is in fact now more acute. Probably since it is now so much more important to me." He turned back toward the front of his cell.

"How is it I know who murdered your daughter? I observed the killer, of course. In fact, I witnessed the attack itself." A smile crossed Minnefield's lips, his eyes narrowing, obviously searching for a reaction. "You cannot comprehend that? You will when I explain it to you, which will be my proof; and which I will give when you have accomplished what I desire. Are you now excited, Mr. Richards?"

"Hopeful," Richards answered, his heart thumping so wildly it was a pounding noise in his ears.

Minnefield turned back to face the window. "From where you stand," he said, "you cannot see the oak to the other side of the perimeter fence, but it is there, a large oak, perhaps a hundred years old. It is home to a variety of birds depending on the season of the year.

Presently several sparrows are in residence there, but it also has year-round occupants. In particular, a pair of squirrels—just recently with family, by the way—one of whom has a minor disability. From accident or by birth I do not know, the disability was already apparent when the two moved to the tree.

"They're remarkably similar, in size as well as color. Sometimes I become confused as to which is the male and which the female. But when they move I know. The male carries the disability. He's a trifle slower up the tree when they are startled. His problem is even more noticeable when he is traversing a limb. His hind quarters are not so steady as his mate's."

Minnefield was silent a moment, then turned from the opening and leaned back against the far wall of his cell, crossing his arms.

"Mr. Richards, my opening gives me a clear view of your daughter's cottage. I am sure you can understand that if my vision is keen enough to discern a squirrel's disability, it certainly is capable of recognizing who entered your daughter's house."

Richards knew the long pause which followed was for dramatic effect, and it worked, his already rapid heartbeat increasing.

"You must forgive me," Minnefield finally said. "I have taken total command of our visit. I have not allowed you to speak. If you find what I am saying uninteresting, please interrupt me." A smile moved to his face as he pushed himself away from the wall and walked toward the front of his cell. There, he slouched against the bars once more, his hairy forearms resting on a cross piece, his smudged hands protruding limply into the hallway.

Richards's hands almost had a motion of their own, aching to clench into fists. Were he allowed to, he would have gladly climbed into the cell and attempted to beat Minnefield's thoughts from his head. But he kept his voice level.

"I can assure you I am listening to everything you say with great interest."

"I know that. I am only attempting to remain polite. It is seldom that I entertain guests and my social graces are rusty. Should I then tell you how to make us both happy?"

Richards nodded.

"Tell you who your daughter's killer was?"

Richards nodded again. He was afraid his voice would betray his rising anger if he spoke.

"The newspaper reported that a dozen maniacs roamed loose that night," Minnefield said. "That is correct if you are counting in bakery slang."

"A baker's dozen," Richards stammered. "Thirteen?"

Minnefield smiled. "Precisely. Thirteen roving lunatics under a storm-touched sky, among whom was the murderer of your daughter."

"Not among the dozen we know about? Another one was out?"

"I do not necessarily refer to a patient. Anyone who would kill can be characterized as insane, no matter the justification. Wouldn't you agree? If not, then why am I incarcerated here? I have never killed without justification." He smiled again as he paused for a moment. "The police are starting to suspect her husband now, aren't they?"

Richards's eyebrows squeezed closer together and he nodded again. "If none of the patients did it, Dr. Salter would be a logical suspect. What does that have to do—"

Minnefield raised his palm in a silencing gesture. "You are aware of the fact that Dr. Martin Salter is eminently proud of his prematurely gray hair, that when your daughter suggested he dye it he became highly insulted?"

Salter's hair had turned gray before he was twenty-five. That Judith had suggested he dye it was news to Richards, and he wondered how Minnefield had come by such information. Again, what did that have to do with the murder? Before Richards could ask, the man raised his palm again.

"My questions are mainly rhetorical. They do not require an answer. Though it might not have occurred to you, prematurely gray hair, especially the more silver variety such as Dr. Salter's, is easy to spot in the dark, given even a glimmer of reflective light from the moon."

"Was it Dr. Salter?"

Minnefield smiled. "You think I would confide in you before I obtain what I desire?"

"Was it John Winstead?"

Minnefield's face tightened, then as quickly relaxed. Richards could not read the reaction.

"Touché, Brandon, but what did my reaction mean, that I was shocked by your question, or that you are warm? Shall we continue the game: hot, cold, warmer?" The smirk he was affecting suddenly left his face, an expression of utmost seriousness once again returning.

"Are you listening carefully, Mr. Richards? Eddie Hopper had nothing to do with the death of your daughter, at least in the way you imagine. Listen carefully. Eddie Hopper arrived at your daughter's cottage after the killer had already arrived. Listen carefully. The attack took place a few minutes after the witching hour."

He turned and walked to his bed, casually lying down on it.

Was he finished? Was that all? Richards's mind was

racing. What was said about Hopper proved nothing. There was no way to corroborate the statement. Same with the time of death. Judith always worked the evening shift. Minnefield would have seen her arrive at her cottage enough times to safely assume she was home by eleven-thirty. He had not said anything which verified he was watching at the time. Nothing—and what had the change of expression at the mention of Winstead's name meant?

Lying back on his pillow, his arms folded behind his head, Minnefield began speaking again.

"The newspapers are quite detailed, their reporters quite explicit in their attempt to create sales. That they have not reported the time of the attack or when Eddie Hopper arrived at the cottage means such details are known only by the police—if indeed the police do know—by the killer, and by myself. Neither was it reported the killer entered and exited through the yard on the north side of the cottage."

"Mr. Minnefield—"

A silencing hand raised from the bed.

"You need to say nothing. I have told you what I have so that no doubt will remain in your mind that I know who the killer is."

All there was were doubts.

He continued. "As the sheriff requested, I have now done my part, though certainly there is more I have to tell. I will tell you the last of what played outside my opening when I have received from you your part. I want my window guaranteed to me, for all time, and without requiring further onerous labor on my part. I want these sickly, foul-odored patients moved from this floor, and a guarantee they shall never return. And I want a television placed in the cell next to mine, tuned to the channel I desire. And don't worry, Mr. Richards, I do not desire such programming as would horrify the psychiatrists, unless they are horrified by the world they live in. All I wish is a news channel so that I might learn and grow.

"My guarantees shall be in the form of a letter from the governor of this state. It will have to be in such form as will cause my attorney to verify it as a legal, binding guarantee. Nothing less will do.

"Finally, I wish to see you back here four days from today, at precisely one P.M. I can see the parking lot quite clearly from here. It is of the essence that you arrive at exactly one P.M. You must come alone.

"Oh, yes, one important requirement. If any details of our discussion are made public prior to our next meeting, the agreement will be forthwith canceled. After our next meeting, and assuming the guarantee you bring me is acceptable, I will let those who wish take credit for the solving of this crime. You might tell the governor that. Elections are only a few months hence. Now run along. You have a lot to attend to."

Richards forced himself to turn and start down the hall without asking any further questions—better to leave Minnefield feeling in total control for now.

"Oh, Mr. Richards! One last thing. Neither was it reported that the killer stripped naked before he murdered your daughter."

Richards had to force himself to continue his slow walk. He had the urge to run—to Judith's. Minnefield had boasted too much, had strayed from his teasing, tantalizing remarks to substance, to something which could be verified.

A few minutes later Richards stood in the front yard of Judith's cottage, his nerves beginning to tingle. Glancing toward the third story of the maximum-security lockup he stared at Minnefield's opening.

While at night the hall light would outline a figure standing at the opening—as he had pointed out to

Tidmore that predawn morning at Judith's—in the late-afternoon sun the gossamer fabric covering the opening served as a sparkling reflector. He couldn't discern whether Minnefield was now there watching or not . . . but he knew he was.

The only way Minnefield could have known the killer was naked was if he could see clearly into the bedroom through its window. If there was not such a view then he had invented the fact, and everything else he said was most likely also a lie.

Taking a deep breath, he smoothed his hair back from his forehead and then moved toward the cottage's front door.

Entering his daughter's bedroom he paused for a moment. The smell was still there. It was an odor he had begun to sense nightly while he slept. He wondered if he would ever again be rid of it.

The single window in the bedroom was directly behind the bed, the short headboard blocking much of the view. Half curtains hung to the top of the headboard. They were parted with a gap of maybe eighteen inches between them.

He walked around to the left of the bed, moving himself back and forth, bending a little at the knees, arranging himself where he could line his view up with the maximum-security building. Then he could see it. The barred opening.

When he moved only a step to the left he lost the view. Back to the right it was gone again. Any movement in the narrow field, from back to the bathroom door to forward where the pillows would have rested against the headboard would be in Minnefield's view, even to his being able to see someone on the bed if that person raised or sat above the headboard. Richards's heart raced happily. Minnefield *did* know.

CHAPTER

16

The sheriff's dairy farm was located in an area of gently rolling pine hills, a few miles south of the hospital and a half-hour from the motel. Richards was silent most of the drive, only politely answering when spoken to.

He had been wildly excited as he had driven to the motel to meet Tidmore, anxious to tell him all he had learned. But then he had found himself strangely hesitant to say anything.

He glanced at the sheriff once again. He knew he was going to have to trust someone. But Atlene's all-encompassing warning kept running through his mind —someone in police work.

After Tidmore guided his Lincoln through the entrance gates emblazoned with the initials *RPT,* he began pointing out items of interest and Richards tried to appear interested.

There was the sixty-acre lake stocked with bass, bream, and catfish, and monitored monthly for the proper Ph; the small wooded plots which dotted the pastures were left intentionally uncleared as wildlife habitats—the hunting was excellent. The eighty-acre pasture the road cut through was of a new experimental fescue variety.

The sheriff's home was a large modern colonial, a two-story structure of white brick with a drive-through columned portico fronting its entire length, one-story wings to each side of the main structure. The sheriff explained that the entire area had once been a hardwood forest; the oaks surrounding the mansion were more than a hundred years old.

Turning into the circular driveway they stopped under the portico.

A woman emerged from the house. She was a big woman, not fat, but strongly built. She walked with a gait more suited to crossing furrowed fields than city sidewalks and she wore flats, probably to minimize her over six foot height. Thick brown hair, neat but not fashioned, surrounded a pleasant round face. She had a very pretty smile, big white teeth gleaming, lips pulled back wide in sincerity. She held out her hand.

"I'm so happy you could make it," she said in a soft, genuine voice. Her grasp was friendly, ladylike, but the strength of her hand was evident.

She bussed her husband as he came around the Lincoln. He slid his arm around her waist.

"This is Leeanne," Tidmore said. "Twenty-five years she has put up with me."

Entering through the home's stained-glass front door, they crossed a white marble foyer into a large professionally decorated room. The huge fireplace at the back of the living room was covered in marble identical to the foyer floor.

"Go on and change," Leeanne said to her husband. "I'll show Mr. Richards to the family room."

"It'll just take a minute," the sheriff said, turning toward the master bedroom door at the far side of the living room.

Richards followed Tidmore's wife through French doors on the left side of the fireplace, emerging into another equally large room.

"Raymond decorated the family room in a man's taste," she said apologetically.

Mounted above a black marble fireplace was a deer head, the coarse hair of the neck out of sync with the smooth marble. A pair of boar heads flanked the deer, the taxidermist having mounted the hogs in a gaped-mouth, tusk-brandishing snarl.

The room's more normal furnishings included a long leather couch in front of the fireplace, and a pair of leather-covered reclining chairs, one to each side of the couch. One end of the room housed a large octagonal slate table complete with eight chairs. A poker-chip container and two decks of cards lay on the black top.

To the other side of the room was a leather-covered, marble-topped bar, the glass cabinets behind it filled with a variety of liquor bottles. The floor was covered from wall to wall by a thick, white carpet.

A disjointed collection of furnishings chosen without the overall effect in mind, Richards thought, but everything expensive.

Through a glass door at the back of the family room, he could see a covered porch, a large hot tub at its center, with exercise equipment surrounding it.

Leeanne offered him a drink which he politely declined, then the two engaged in small talk until her husband reappeared.

"Not many people get the grand tour," the sheriff exclaimed as he entered the room. He was dressed in a blue jumpsuit, yellow cowboy boots, and a beige Stetson. He had a smile on his face.

"Don't believe that, Mr. Richards. Raymond shows everybody around that he can."

She moved to her husband and hugged him from the side. The two were virtually the same height, the heels of the cowboy boots the only difference.

"He's just like a little boy," she said, "that's why I love him. How do you like his new outfit?"

"Leeanne," the sheriff said self-consciously.

"Ever since I met him," she said, "he's had to have his costumes. His working-on-the-farm costume is different from his showing-you-around-the-farm costume. When we went to Grand Cayman last year he spent more money on shorts and outfits than we did on the vacation. When we were married he had a specially made tux. You should have seen the first outfit he had made when he was elected sheriff. I didn't dare let him wear it."

The sheriff, a smile on his face, kissed his wife on the forehead. "Come on, Brandon, before she starts getting personal." He laughed.

"Now don't be walking around on that leg of yours too much," Leeanne called after them. "Ruby doesn't want to have to be massaging it all night again."

Climbing inside the sheriff's pickup, Richards made his decision. "I went by to see Minnefield. He said he saw the killer."

The sheriff's eyebrows bunched as he glanced toward Richards. "Well?"

"He said he would tell me later, when I had done some things he wanted."

The sheriff smiled and shook his head.

"I believe he really knows. He's aware the killer came in through the north side of the yard. He couldn't know that unless he saw him. He said he was naked."

The sheriff's smile grew bigger.

"No, Raymond, he could know," Richards insisted. "He has a view through his opening directly into Judith's bedroom."

Tidmore's brow furrowed in thought as he guided the pickup onto the dirt road leading deeper into the farm. After a moment, he glanced toward Richards. "We want to remember to think everything out carefully. If we assume one thing's correct when it isn't, then everything we build onto it could come out wrong."

Richards's expression was quizzical.

"Things have a way of getting out," the sheriff explained. "One of my deputies, one of the other officers could have said something about the killer's entry being on the north side of the house. It could have got back to Minnefield through the hospital security people who came by the cottage. It could also be a logical assumption on his part. There's only the front door and the side door. He could have assumed a killer wouldn't walk in the front door, visible to anyone on the street. Anyone could say the killer was naked, or wearing a clown's suit with green ears. Who's going to dispute it? That doesn't mean anything."

"But he can see in her window, I verified that myself."

"From a couple hundred feet? What kind of angle did he have? There were curtains on the window."

"The curtains were open . . . about eighteen inches."

"Eighteen inches at two hundred feet," the sheriff said, shaking his head as he glanced toward Richards.

"He also said Hopper arrived after Judith had already been murdered."

"That's all he said, no explanations?"

Richards shook his head. "I believe he's going to say Martin did it. Talked about his gray hair, how it would stick out in the moonlight. He meant to leave the impression he's going to say it's Martin anyway." He was sure of that.

"Hopper coming up after the killing . . ." the sheriff mused out loud, his eyes narrowing with his thought. "If he did . . . remember J.J.'s theory? Hopper stumbled in on Salter. Salter shot him with Judith's gun, and then left him there for a cover-up. If Minnefield's right about Hopper then maybe J.J.'s right, too."

The sheriff remembered something else. "By the way," he said, "Salter was in the city the night of the murder. His second alibi is that he was at the male prostitute's apartment. His lawyer told me that this afternoon. Our good doctor would have been better off without that alibi. His lawyer's going to bring him in to talk to me in a couple days." The sheriff pointed toward the right. "Here's the first thing I want to show you."

He had stopped his pickup in front of a white block building.

Inside, the milking was in progress, a pair of men in overalls monitoring the extracting equipment.

Sixteen Holsteins stood encased in the metal milking stalls which sat on elevated concrete ramps to each side of the building. Stainless steel milking retractors enclosed the teats hanging from each cow's swollen bag. Richards watched the white liquid rhythmically squirting into the clear plastic containers mounted to the side of each stall.

"We run four hundred fifty through here each milking," the sheriff said. "Probably got a hundred to a hundred-twenty in the maternity lot. We're milking three times a day now. Four in the morning, twelve-thirty, and at this time. In the winter we cut back to two milkings. We're running about eight percent more milk from our number ones than the area average."

One of the attendants moved along the line of cows, pulling a lever at each stall. As he did, the retractors fell from the teats to hang suspended from the ball-shaped collecting containers.

After a second attendant medicated the Holstein's teats, another lever was thrown and the Surge Stall's steel gates opened, the Holsteins shuffling forward and down the ramp to the feeding lot outside. As their replacements followed up the entrance ramp, the lever was pulled again, the gates angling back to form narrow stalls filled one by one by the cows.

Richards was impressed with the assembly line-like efficiency. "You have a big-time operation here, Raymond."

The sheriff shook his head. "Big enough for a workday, but not big enough for a payday. We've been losing money for three years, a lot this year. If something doesn't change we're going to have to shut down. City folks don't think about the farmers anymore. They will when all us independents go out of business and the big companies triple the price. But I'm afraid that's going to be too late to do me any good." With a gesture of his head he led Richards on through the milking house and out the back entrance.

As they walked toward a smaller white block building a hundred yards ahead, Tidmore said, "Let's assume Minnefield saw the killer—while I don't put any stock in him being able to see through the gap in those curtains, I do believe he might have seen someone approaching the cottage—what does he want for his telling you who it was?"

"A guarantee that he never loses his view. And he wants the patients who can't take care of themselves moved from the third floor."

"That's all?"

Richards nodded.

"Alan won't be happy," the sheriff said, "but if it turns out Minnefield can finger the killer, he'll go along with it."

"He's not taking anybody's word but the governor's. He wants a legal document his attorney will okay."

Tidmore shook his head slowly. "That's something else. Governor's already catching hell about the escape. He's not going to be in any mood to be doing anybody out there a favor."

Richards disagreed. "He's not really asking for anything new. He already has the view. You told me the only reason those patients are on the floor is because of an arrangement Minnefield himself instigated. Nothing that I can see would make it appear the governor was doing any favors. On the other hand, if we could work it where the governor gets the credit for solving the murder . . . I can't see a politician turning such an opportunity down. Raymond, we have to try. I'm telling you he knows."

Tidmore nodded. "Might fly. I don't care who gets the credit, just as long as we get it solved. The governor doesn't owe me any favors, but he'll talk to me. I've got a lot of friends in this county and he knows it. Let me see what I can do."

"Raymond, part of the deal is that the agreement has to be signed, sealed, and ready to be delivered four days from now. He said the agreement's off if we miss the timetable. He also said it's off if he hears any publicity on this before he gets a chance to look it over. I don't know what his reasoning is, but those are his terms."

"Not any reason," Tidmore said. "He just wants to call the shots. That's all. And by the same token, if we don't do exactly what he says, it might just make him mad enough to not help. If I can get the governor to go along with it, time shouldn't be any problem. One way or the other I think I can get a quick answer. Now, the bulls we house in this building live better than you and I do."

Inside, the eight stalls were empty.

"This is the part of my operation that makes money." A smile came to the sheriff's face. "It's been my salvation."

The enclosure was immaculate, the concrete floor and walls still damp from a recent cleaning. Tidmore continued through the building to the doors at the back, pushing them open to reveal a small feed lot.

Several large bulls looked toward the opening of the doors, and then turned their attention back to their troughs. A man in blue overalls was walking toward the building, a pair of empty feed sacks draped over his shoulder.

Tidmore had a proud smile on his face. "Big money right there," he said. "You're looking at the sires of the best milkers in the state . . . several states. Your typical dairy farmer can't afford to own bulls of this quality. We supply them with the semen and they inseminate their stock."

The man in overalls stopped before them. "Sheriff," he said, "searched high and low, but can't find a nary nuther one."

Tidmore nodded. "Okay, thank you, A.C."

The man walked on into the building.

"Some calves missing," the sheriff said. "We found one outside the fence on the road, but a couple are still missing. Second time in a month. Beginning to think rustlers; coyotes would have left something. I've borrowed some night-vision equipment the city cops have. Gonna put a stop to whoever's crawling in here at night. Well, let's go eat." He turned back toward the building's open doors. "All Minnefield mentioned about Salter was his hair?"

"Uh-huh. Specifically his prematurely gray hair, and about Judith wanting to dye it. Dye it. That's news to me. She always told me it made him look distinguished."

"And Hopper didn't show up until after your daughter was attacked?"

Richards nodded. "That's what Minnefield said."

"He knew the killer came in on the north side of the yard?"

Richards nodded again.

"Nothing else?"

"Well, he went to great lengths to impress me with how keen his vision was—which he did—giving me a lot of detail about birds and squirrels which lived in the trees along the perimeter fence. Nothing that would have anything to do with the murder."

CHAPTER

17

Ruby Tonkon, a full-blooded Choctaw Indian, was the Tidmore's live-in maid and cook. She had prepared a meal consisting of a roast, chunked potatoes and whole carrots, plus scratch biscuits laden with gravy and a side dish of English peas. It was excellent, made more so by Richards being ravenously hungry for the first time since he had left his Lake Ponchartrain home.

"Delicious," he pronounced, placing his fork on his plate and leaning back in his chair. He had to resist the urge to pat his too-full stomach.

"More coffee?" Ruby asked.

He smiled politely and shook his head. "No, thank you. It really was delicious."

She lowered her eyes from his, blushing faintly at his praise.

"Ruby has fresh banana pudding for dessert," Leeanne said. "It's one of her specialties."

"Oh, my goodness," he said. "I can't, but I must."

Ruby beamed.

The sheriff laughed. "I'm going to get a cigar. Care for one?"

"No, thank you."

Ruby glanced back at Richards as she walked from the dining room. She was very pretty, big black eyes staring from a light brown face, a brilliant white smile. Though her white uniform was loose and casual it was obvious the figure under it would be difficult to improve upon.

"She's been with us eight, no, nearly nine years now," Leeanne said.

Richards self-consciously broke off his stare, turning back to the sheriff's wife. "She's an excellent cook," he said.

"Oh, much more than that. We couldn't do without her. I'm going to go help her with the dessert. It's past the time she's supposed to be off."

Left alone, Richards studied the chandelier hanging above the dining table. He had seen a nearly identical one at a shop on Canal Street in New Orleans, the one in the shop not as exquisite as the one he now viewed. The price tag on the chandelier in New Orleans had been eighteen thousand dollars.

And the table he sat at, hand-carved mahogany, an antique. Five thousand, ten thousand, twenty-five thousand? He didn't know the first thing about art, but the frames hanging on the wall obviously contained real oil paintings.

A happy home, plenty of love visible, and the two very well off. He realized the only thing he hadn't seen were any signs of children, though hanging in the foyer was a picture of a young boy.

"Here you go," Leeanne said, setting a large bowl of banana pudding topped with whipped cream in front of him. She refilled his coffee cup and moved the pitcher of cream next to the cup.

He ate it all, then shut his eyes a moment at the pain his full belly was causing him. Then he turned toward where Leeanne had seated herself.

"I saw a picture of a boy in the foyer," he said. "Your son?"

"We lost our child, too, Mr. Richards."

Richards was awkward for a moment, the sheriff speaking before he did.

"We lost Jack seven years ago. He was just a kid, seventeen years old, but he had become heavily dependent on drugs. One night someone gave him some crap that was pure poison."

"I'm sorry." How many times had he heard those well-intentioned but hollow words the last few days. There was nothing else to say.

The sheriff nodded, but did not comment.

Leeanne said, "That's one of the reasons we so hope your daughter's killer is brought to justice. We never really knew who was responsible for our son's death. You see, there were others there that night. A neighbor saw two people leaving and they had left Jack's door open. Jack was on the floor, already dead. We were never able to find out who the two were."

"If we did, I'd have killed the sons of bitches," the sheriff said loudly. His face carried the first angry expression Richards had seen on it.

"Raymond," Leeanne cautioned. "We've talked about that. God knows who was responsible." She turned her face toward Richards. "Please don't take Raymond's comment literally, he wouldn't hurt a fly unless he was forced to. He doesn't even carry a gun. There's been a couple of times I've wished he did." She looked back toward her husband. "When Dr. Salter came out here, I was scared for you then."

The sheriff shook his head. "I can handle Salter without a gun."

"He came out here?" Richards asked.

"When J.J. was after information to help your daughter out, Salter got upset. J.J. carries a badge as a part-time deputy in our department, does just enough work that I can afford to supplement his income a little."

"Used to," Leeanne corrected.

Tidmore nodded his agreement. "After Salter sued him I took the badge back. I was afraid he was going to get the department in trouble. Actually it was Leeanne here and Jerry who were worried. Jerry's my younger brother. You haven't met him, yet. He's my chief deputy. A little nepotism at work. Besides it's usually a chief deputy that ends up running against a sheriff in an election. I can control my brother; whip his little butt if I have to." He smiled.

Leeanne was serious. "Raymond and I haven't disagreed on a dozen things in twenty-five years of marriage, I mean really seriously disagreed. But John Winstead isn't the kind of man my husband needs working as a deputy."

"Leeanne!"

"I'm sure Mr. Richards understands. He knows John. He just doesn't show good sense in the way he operates. When he gets to thinking someone's guilty he'll prove it if he has to—"

"Leeanne!"

She glanced at her husband, frowned, and then looked back at Richards. "I don't want you to think I don't like John. To the contrary. Kathy, his wife, is my best friend . . ."

Winstead was married, a married man in police work who had killed someone. Richards continued to listen intently.

". . . A month doesn't go by that they don't spend a weekend with us. Raymond and John fish and Kathy and I shop. As a private person John is great, but when he assumes his role as a detective he has a weakness in seeing good and evil as one hundred percent one way or the other." She paused a moment, glancing toward her husband. "And when he knows someone's done something wrong he doesn't care what he has to do to see they're punished . . ." She looked again at her husband, and he didn't stop her this time. ". . . even if what they're finally punished for is something they really didn't do."

"That's not all that bad," her husband said.

"Oh, flitter," she said. "You know better than that."

"I think Mr. Richards would prefer a different line of conversation," Tidmore said, his words spoken deliberately and in a slightly raised voice.

Leeanne glanced at her husband and then lowered her gaze to her plate.

The sheriff finally broke the silence. "Would you like some more coffee, Brandon?"

"No, thank you. Raymond, you said Martin was upset when he came by here?"

Leeanne answered. "He was upset over the questions John was asking in his hometown. I guess it was embarrassing, though I can't imagine a man who does some of the things Dr. Salter does as being embarrassed very easily."

Tidmore laughed. "Here she goes again."

She smiled and the tension was now completely gone.

"Well, never mind about the things he does," she said. "He came out and wanted to see Raymond. Raymond was in his shop, down where he keeps his antique cars. Did he show you?"

"Saving the best for last," Tidmore said, "going to go show him now."

"So I told Dr. Salter where Raymond was and he went out to see him. Next thing I knew Raymond came in the house with his cheeks flushed, and said that Dr. Salter had threatened him. I told you before, Raymond's not the type to hurt anybody, and he's not a man easy to anger." She looked at her husband. "I don't think you ever did tell me all he said. Probably didn't want to scare me. I believe Dr. Salter's a dangerous man."

"I told her what he said," the sheriff explained, "all of it. It wasn't any big deal. He claimed J.J. was some kind of red-necked bozo and that I was the real brains behind the investigation. Said if I didn't get J.J. off his back he was going to take care of me."

"You said he was going to make you sorry," his wife said, a concerned expression coming to her face.

Richards glanced back to the sheriff.

Tidmore shrugged. "Take care of me, make me sorry—what difference does it make. I've been threatened before. There isn't anybody in police work that hasn't been. That's why cops carry guns."

"And you should," she said. She stood and walked to the buffet, opening a drawer. "You can ask Raymond," she said. "I've never, not one time, said anything about any of the crimes he's investigated. It's easy to throw stones. I've had my suspicions a couple of times, I'll grant you that, but I've never said anything. Yet I told him when I first heard about your daughter that it was probably her husband who committed the murder. He's mean enough, and he had the motive. I'm scared of him."

The sheriff laughed. "For somebody who just got through talking about J.J., you sound remarkably like him."

Richards smiled.

"Here," she said, "here's what I was looking for." When she turned around she held a cassette in her hand. She looked at her husband.

Tidmore rolled his eyes and nodded wearily. "Okay. There's a recorder in the bottom of the cabinet. You can play it on that."

It was a taped telephone conversation between Martin Salter and Tidmore. Other than it was obvious Salter was angry with Judith's trying to force him to return the twins, the conversation told Richards nothing he didn't already know, until the last exchange.

"Dr. Salter, if you would just go ahead and return the children nothing more would come of this."

"The children are none of your damn business. And I'm warning you, you better not send Winstead down here again. One more time and you'll be sorry. Stay out of my county and leave me alone. I mean it."

"Dr. Salter, I don't like being threatened. I—"

"I don't give a damn what you like."

The slamming of a receiver ended the taped conversation.

It was not so much the words but the viciousness of tone which was new to Richards.

CHAPTER

18

Following an after-dinner drink Richards went with the sheriff to view the antique cars. One was a 1939 Ford, chocolate brown with a beige interior, and the other a 1949 MG, yellow with its two doors opening from the front into a brown leather interior. The MG was ten years older than the one Richards had bought for his daughter. Judith had made daily use of hers while Tidmore's was in pristine condition, not a speck of dust to be seen.

Seeming to read Richards's thoughts, Tidmore said, "Occasionally I take them to a car show. I've driven the MG to the city and back a couple of times, but they're mostly just to look at. Beautiful, aren't they?"

Richards nodded and having noticed the empty spot

in the three-car garage asked, "Do you have another one?"

"Just my Lincoln. Some of the hands are washing it right now. Leeanne keeps her car in the house garage and I keep mine out here with the antiques. She's got a 1972 Cadillac convertible that's really a nice car itself. She drives it a lot though, doesn't keep it in real good shape. But then she bought it to drive. She doesn't see much sense in having a car just to look at. Come on back into my office."

Through a door at the back of the garage was a plain concrete-floored, block-walled office. The luxurious touches Richards had seen in the house were not totally absent, though.

The large expensive leather couch sat against one wall and Richards eyed a roll-top desk and chair which were antiques. A more modest six-drawer office desk and an overstuffed executive chair were placed at the far end of the long narrow office.

"This is where I was when Salter came by. He burst through that door down there." The sheriff pointed to the door leading out at the end of the office. "Burst in, talking sort of normal at first, then started to raise his voice. I told him to get the hell out."

Richards smiled. "When he told you you'd be sorry?"

"When I told him to get the hell out it was because he'd just threatened to kill me if J.J. didn't stay out of his area. Naw, didn't say it exactly like that. First he said something about if J.J. keeps sticking his nose in other people's business he might find himself floating in the Tombigbee River someday. A little further in the conversation he said something about what he said about J.J. went for me, too.

"Don't tell Leeanne that. She only found out about the tape she has now because she walked in when I was sitting here playing it a couple nights ago. It was the day after your daughter was murdered. I was playing it back to see if there was anything Salter said that I might have forgotten. You know, something that might tie back to your daughter. You heard it. There wasn't anything."

"I never heard Martin sound like he did on the tape, the viciousness in his voice."

Tidmore pointed Richards to the end of the couch, then perched himself on the edge of his desk. "How much did your daughter tell you about what J.J. turned up on her husband?"

"Really nothing. Just that they had enough stuff to get the kids back. I told her they weren't going to need anything to do that. She was the mother. They were living with her and Martin took them away forcibly, and after him having run out on her. The only specific thing I know I heard from Winstead yesterday, when he told me he had discovered Martin was seeing the male prostitute. Evidently Judith used that information in the court proceedings."

"Your daughter must not have wanted to worry you. There's a lot more to it. Salter's father is a big shot in the Dixie Mafia—was, guess you'd call him retired now. No one was able to convict him, but everybody in law enforcement knows that's what he was."

Richards knew his surprise was showing in the crinkling of his face.

"You can trace it all the way back to the grandfather. Bootlegging, then untaxed whiskey, prostitution, bookmaking, and we're pretty sure the father graduated into dope about the time Salter was starting college. I don't know if it was the father's idea or Salter's, but the kid decided to be a straight arrow—good grades, fair athlete, medical school—hell, he's vice-president of the state psychiatric association. He'll be inducted as its president at their convention here in the city in a couple days. Anyway, coming up he pretty well kept his nose clean, except for one time. Don't know if the old man cut off the money or if it was just in Salter's blood, maybe something for kicks, but he had a conviction his senior year in college for running a numbers racket.

"He's not clean anymore, though. Since he went back to his hometown he's started running with a lot of his dad's old pals. Nashville's got an informant that swears he fenced a truckload of stolen Levis. It doesn't sound big time until you stop and think how many pairs would be in an eighteen wheeler. Big bucks.

"The part of the state where he lives has always been a rough spot, lot of the power down there is held by thugs. Goes way back. Ever seen a movie called the *Phoenix City Story*? Years ago thugs had pretty well taken over Phoenix City, Alabama. Finally got so big they killed an attorney general.

"The Alabama governor called out the national guard. Law enforcement didn't have the same kind of civil liberties to contend with we've got now. They ran the thugs out of town on rails, killing the ones that didn't want to leave. Splinter groups out of there settled all over the place, one bunch down by the coast in Salter's area. They've never taken control, least ways not like they did in Phoenix City, but they've got a lot of power. Not uncommon to have an unsolved murder down there."

"And Judith knew all this?"

"J.J. said she knew—most of it anyway. You've seen the way J.J. already feels. I didn't want to egg him on, but when I first got the word about your daughter's death, her husband's the first one I thought of, too. Right now he's the odds on favorite, even though I don't want to close my mind to any other possibilities. Can't ever do that in a murder, not until you know for sure." He glanced at his watch and slid from the edge of the desk to his feet. "It's already after nine," he said, bending over idly to massage his left thigh where the edge of the desktop had been pressing against it. "Want to get one more for the road or would you rather have a cup of coffee?"

"Coffee would be great."

"Take you this way," Tidmore said, starting for the door at the end of the office. "Show you Leeanne's favorite toy. Her dad built us a pool. She wouldn't like it if she heard me call it a toy. He passed away right after he built it. She was an only child and he spoiled her rotten." He smiled wistfully. "Makes it a little rough on me, too, not being able to give her all the things her dad got her used to."

"From what I've seen, I don't think you have deprived her of much."

Tidmore smiled proudly.

The pool was built in the shape of a heart, the neatly trimmed hedges around it trimmed likewise—a little overdone. The shrubs were probably Leeanne's idea. He could understand. It had been her father's last gift to her. He thought of his last present to Judith —the MG would never be sold.

"It's hard to match gifts like this," the sheriff said reflectively as he stood staring into the pool's blue water. "The dairy's not doing well, and me a man making his living in police work."

At the sheriff's words, Richards looked up. He had to trust somebody. He had to, even though a nervous sensation passed through his stomach at the thought.

"Raymond. You really don't carry a weapon?"

"I have a shotgun in my car, keep a couple pistols in

my offices, but I don't pack one on me. That way I don't get too brave." Tidmore chuckled.

Richards looked directly into the sheriff's eyes. "Then you've never had to shoot anybody?"

Tidmore laughed and shook his head. "God, no. Probably still be shaking if I had."

"Raymond, I need to speak to you confidentially. A couple of things are bothering me."

"Sure." The sheriff turned from where he had been staring into the pool and faced Richards.

"A nurse out at the hospital called me. She said Judith was dating a married man who was a policeman, or at least in some kind of police work. Judith told this nurse that she had told the man to stay away from her, threatened to tell his wife, and that the man had threatened her. In fact, said two men had threatened her. Whoever they are, they have to be suspects."

Tidmore was staring into Richards's eyes now. "When did you learn all this?"

"Yesterday."

The sheriff stared a brief moment longer, his eyes slightly narrowed in puzzlement, but he didn't make a point of asking why he had not been told earlier, and Richards appreciated that.

"Just threatened her," Tidmore asked, "nothing in particular?"

"That's all she said."

The sheriff shook his head. "Something like that's fairly typical. She threatens to tell a man's wife, he threatens she better not. A guy running around and his wife finds out, he might have to sleep on the couch awhile. That's all. You don't kill someone to stay off the couch. I wouldn't put much stock in that."

"There's more. Today I went out and asked around at the cottages, trying to find out if anybody knew who

Judith might have been dating. A neighbor said she was dating J.J."

Tidmore's eyes narrowed more dramatically this time. His tone was sharper, too. "What exactly did he say?"

"He told me that about a month ago J.J. had been coming by Judith's."

The sheriff's features relaxed, a wry smile coming to his face. "That was when he was working for her, Brandon."

"That's what I told him. But he didn't change his mind. He claims J.J. stayed there all night. Something else—the guy's wife was on him hot and heavy. There is no doubt she thinks he was trying to make time with Judith. I guess he'd have to be a suspect himself. J.J.'s the one who worries me though. If he was dating Judith, with what the nurse told me about a threat coming from someone in police work, a married man, that bothers me. His feet are the correct size, too."

"Good God, Brandon, so are mine." The sheriff's tone was sharp again. He nodded at Richards's feet. "Yours look like they might be. Don't start jumping to conclusions. If it turns out J.J. was dating your daughter I'll have to talk to him, but I don't believe for a moment he had anything to do with her death."

Richards knew he was speaking about a man Tidmore had trusted for years, a fellow law enforcement officer, and from what had been remarked on around the dining room table, one of the sheriff's closest friends. Still, there was no reason to back off now.

"I feel the same way, Raymond, yet I can't keep him out of my mind. If he has dated Judith then I want him to prove where he was that night; pass a lie detector test, something."

There was silence for a moment, then the sheriff

nodded. "Fair enough." The sharpness was gone now, his tone was resigned.

"And, Raymond, I'd like to be there when you first ask him. I'd like to see his initial reaction, judge it for myself."

The sheriff nodded again. "When do you want to do it?"

"The sooner the better."

"I'll set it up for first thing in the morning. Wait at your room for my call."

CHAPTER

19

The drive from the sheriff's dairy farm back into Jackson was a peaceful one, the traffic sparse. After taking a long shower and slipping on a pair of pajama bottoms, Richards felt more relaxed than he had at anytime since receiving the original call about Judith from the Davis County Sheriff's Department. But he ordered two Scotch and waters from room service, anyway. If two didn't work he was going to order two more. He was determined to enjoy a good night's sleep.

After finishing the first drink he decided to do one last thing before retiring.

Removing some stationery and a pencil from the dresser drawer he seated himself at the table by the window. There he started listing everything he knew about the attack and the possible suspects, trying to make some sense out of the whole affair.

It was nearly eleven when the telephone rang.

"Hello."

"Brandon, baby, how are you making it?"

It was Flora. He had left her standing at the door of his Lake Ponchartrain home. She had wanted to come along, but he had told her no coldly. Even worse, he told her there was no need for her to come to the funeral—not to where Stella lay.

Stella had always teased him about who he would marry if something ever happened to her. He had promised nobody—and he hadn't. Flora was only a friend of two years standing. But still, to bring Flora there, to where Stella was, he couldn't do it. He was a bastard, no two ways about it.

"Thank you for the flowers," he said. "They were nice."

She should have told him to go to hell, not sent anything, not been there when he came back. But Flora wasn't that kind of person.

"When are you coming home?" she asked.

He moved the telephone with him as he slipped onto the bed. "Soon."

"The New Orleans paper said Judith was killed by one of the patients, but that the police aren't sure who. Do they have any leads?"

"Too many leads. Too many suspects. I'm not even sure it was the patients who murdered her. It's driving me crazy."

"Baby, you sure you don't want me to come and stay with you? Your voice sounds so down."

"There's not much else I can do here," he admitted resignedly. "I have to be back for a meeting in four days, but maybe after I attend to a couple of things in the morning I'll come home for a day or two. I need some clean clothes anyway."

"I'll take off work."

"Good, I've missed you. Listen to me a minute. I wrote some things down. I need somebody to talk to. Okay?"

"Okay."

He hurried to the table and retrieved the piece of paper he had been working on, then returned to sit on the edge of the bed.

"Okay, first, the same blood type that Martin has was found in Judith's bedroom. It's rare, only three percent of the population have it. Of course three percent is still a lot. You know he had threatened her. Since I've been here I've found out he not only has a violent personality, but the law enforcement people here say his father's in the mob. I'm not sure now, but the patients escaping might just be a coincidence. There's a good chance he's the murderer."

"Oh, God!"

"Judith's best friend told me Judith had been threatened by some married man she was dating who was involved in police work. She said the man bragged he had killed somebody. John Winstead . . . he's the detective Judith employed when she was trying to get the twins back from Martin . . . well, a neighbor of Judith's says Winstead was staying all night at Judith's. Flora?"

"Yes, I'm listening."

"Flora, Winstead's in police work, and now he's told me he killed someone—"

"What?"

"In the line of duty, in police work, like the man told Judith. He could be the killer. Oh, yeah, the next-door neighbor's a real lout, big man, probably has close to the same shoe size. Don't know what his blood type is . . . and Martin's alibi, it really places him in the area. So you have Martin, maybe Winstead. If not Winstead then there's possibly some other policeman or someone in police work, the next-door neighbor, and of course it could still be one of the escaped patients. In fact, it could be a patient we don't even know was out that night. A patient I talked to yesterday said there were thirteen who escaped rather than the dozen we know about, though he might not have been referring to a patient per se. He says he saw the killer. I was convinced he had when I was listening to him. Now, after speaking with the sheriff, I just don't know. What do you think?"

There was silence on the other end of the line.

"Flora?"

"Baby, you need to come on back to New Orleans. Let the police handle this. What you were saying wasn't even making sense to me. Staying up there's doing nothing but keeping it on your mind every second. Please come on back, now."

"I said I was . . . tomorrow. I have to meet with Winstead first, though. The sheriff said I can be there when he questions him about dating Judith."

"Good, I'll be waiting."

"Flora, everything's becoming so mixed up. Salter's a doctor, a psychiatrist, a healer, yet if he didn't kill Judith he already destroyed her in a way. And his mind . . . he has to be as screwed up as any patient he's ever treated. Winstead, a peace keeper—maybe he's the killer. Minnefield's a crazed, brutal mass murderer. He could end up being the one who names the killer. Everything is twisted. . . . It's crazy."

"Baby, please, you're just torturing yourself."

"Flora?"

"What?"

"I should have talked with Judith more."

"What do you mean?"

He shook his head. "I just should have discussed more things with her. You know I never even told her about the birds and bees. How do you tell a little blond-haired girl playing in the backyard with her puppy about sex? When she was a teenager . . ." He shook his head. "She still seemed so young. Finally, I looked around one day and she was grown up. I assumed everything had worked out for the best; she had found out what she needed to know on her own. Was I really embarrassed to talk to her or just didn't take the time? You know, I only visited her at college one time, the day she graduated."

"Oh, baby, don't start something like that. A girl's never had a dad who loved her anymore than you did."

"Love's easy, responsibility isn't, and I'm all she had after Stella died."

"Baby . . ."

"When she first started having trouble with Martin, I should have gone up there immediately. If I had maybe she wouldn't have become involved with a married man. Instead, I was wheeling and dealing, flying all over the country closing syndications, being a big shot, thinking about myself."

"No, you were doing like everybody else does, like you were supposed to do. You were making a living . . . and not just for yourself. Where did she get her MG?"

He took a deep breath. "I was all she had, Flora. I needed to be more interested in what she was doing. The money wasn't enough. It didn't mean anything."

"Yes, it did. The money, and the love, and the sacrifice. You couldn't have done anymore. I don't know how you managed what you did. Stop and think. You worked your way through law school, supported a wife and then a little girl, you paid off your school loans by working seven-day weeks . . . and then after Stella was gone, you took time off from your work every day to pick Judith up at school, doing your work at night after she was asleep, and then getting up again in the morning to feed her and take her to school. I've heard the stories. My God, what else could you have done? I've always been envious of how anybody could be loved as much as Judith was.

"You have your shortcomings. You're domineering, too sure of yourself, keep a sloppy house, and you're too stupid to marry me, but not having done enough for Judith is not one of your weaknesses.

"Now I don't want to hear anymore about it, and if you don't come back home tomorrow afternoon, I'm coming up there after you."

CHAPTER

20

Richards woke early, then ate breakfast in his room so as not to miss the sheriff's call. It was nearly ten, however, before the telephone rang.

"Haven't been able to catch up with J.J. yet," Tidmore reported. "I've been calling his home since eight without an answer. I got us an appointment with the governor, though. I'll pick you up in a half-hour."

The Governor's Offices took up the entire top floor of the State Office Building. Richards stood in the visitor's lounge off the main hallway. He was looking through the large plate-glass window in the room, staring down on the city.

The sidewalks were full of people scurrying about

their work. He could imagine them exchanging pleasant greetings. He looked up. The storm front had finally passed. The thick clouds present ever since Judith's death were now replaced by a brilliant sun and a clear blue sky. He heard laughter as a pair of the governor's staffers passed in the hall. All he felt was sadness. He wondered when his normal emotions would return, and how much of them never would.

He turned toward where the sheriff sat on the couch in the middle of the room.

"Raymond, what do you think our chances are?"

"That the governor agreed to meet with us means it's at least fifty-fifty. Elections are in November. That's in our favor. Politicians are always looking for some way to do a good deed right before the elections, especially him. He's a liberal in a conservative state. Each time he's run he's used a coalition of blacks and liberal whites to get to the point where it's a tossup. Depends on publicity in the state newspaper to put him over the top. Getting credit for helping solve a murder would look good. Other side of the coin is he doesn't want to have something backfire, give an opponent any ammunition."

"Sheriff Tidmore." It was the governor's aide. "We are ready now."

The governor was pressed for time. After a quick exchange of pleasantries the meeting came directly to the point. Richards explained everything, including the timetable and the need to keep the matter confidential until Minnefield had seen the agreement.

"Anything I can do to further justice," the governor said perfunctorily. "But I don't have the power to arbitrarily sign such a guarantee. The attorney general does. But even then there are certain procedures he would have to follow, certain officials he would want to contact: the district attorney, the circuit judge who committed the patient."

"Sir," Richards began, "Minnefield will only accept your signature."

"I understand that, and I am going to try to help you. I want you to understand, though, that I am not agreeing to sign anything at the moment. . . ."

The governor paused, apparently waiting for a response, and so Richards nodded. "Yes, sir, I understand."

"What I am thinking of doing," the governor continued, "is asking the attorney general to work out the details with the appropriate parties. Then I will sign that my office has no legal objection to the arrangement."

Richards relaxed. The governor was putting himself in a no-loss situation. If Minnefield's information led to the crime being quickly solved, the governor would take credit for instigating the agreement. If Minnefield's revelations led to any sort of controversy, the governor would say he was not involved one way or the other, that he had in fact only informed the contractual parties his office had no legal objection to the agreement.

Descending in the building's elevator, Richards voiced his only worry. "Will the attorney general take on the responsibility?"

"AG's a former law partner of the governor, the same philosophy—sort of the governor's disciple. And he's sharp, too. He'll go along and make sure the fine print will pull him out of any problems that might come up."

Richards noticed Tidmore's stare and self-consciously smiled. "What?"

"You still look like you could use some sleep. I've got some other duties I'm going to have to attend to today. Why don't you go on back to the room and take a nap. I'll call you if I hear anything about the case."

"I thought I might check and see if J.J.'s back yet."

The sheriff nodded. "Okay. It's you that looks like you're going to pass out, not me. If you do find him, call my office. I'll do the same. After thinking about it I'm pretty interested in talking to him myself, now."

"Thank you, Raymond."

"That doesn't mean I have the slightest worry about him being involved in your daughter's death. But if he was dating her he should have been up-front with me about it. He owed me that."

After the sheriff drove him back to the motel, Richards went to his room and checked his answering machine, then he removed the phone book from the drawer of the bedside table.

Winstead's number was busy, and remained so. The operator said the telephone was out of order.

Winstead's address was listed as a rural route, and Richards had to stop twice along the way to ask directions.

The big detective's home was a double-wide trailer. It sat a hundred yards back off a blacktop road in a thinly populated area five miles south of the city. His automobile sat in front of the trailer.

At the entrance to the property, embedded in the center of the dirt road leading to the trailer, was a square, four-inch post. Nailed to it was a sign: KEEP OUT.

Guiding his Cadillac around the sign he followed the road to the trailer.

Winstead's wife answered his knock with a smile on her face.

A short attractive blond, she was more wholesome than pretty. Her makeup, though subdued in color, was applied perfectly with sharp lines; her hair was coiffed on top of her head without a single strand out of place. A plain white cotton dress covered her trim, toned figure. She was a study of perfect order, if somewhat plain, and not what he had expected in the wife of the rough-hewn Winstead.

"Mrs. Winstead, I'm Brandon Richards. I was wondering if I might speak with your husband."

"I'm sorry, John's not in right now." She glanced at the automobile in front of the trailer. "You saw his car. Its engine is messing up. He took mine."

"You don't know when he might return, do you?"

She shook her head. "He's working on your daughter's case and you never can tell about John when he's on a case. He always becomes so involved. I tell you, Mr. Richards, you have a good man working for you in my husband."

Richards smiled politely and nodded.

"He goes days at a time sometimes, like a hound trailing a coon. He strikes a scent and he doesn't stop until he's treed it. Days, nights—don't mean anything. He's tireless. Like when he was working for your daughter, he'd spend the day over in the city gathering information for the case, then more than once sat up all night watching over her."

Richards worked to keep his expression the same and his voice casual. "Stayed with Judith?"

"Oh, yes. I know of two times, right after her husband called and threatened her, that he stayed over at her cottage the whole weekend. Then there were a couple of other times, just because John knew the doctor was in the city, that he stayed over there all night. With what Judith was able to afford to pay him, I doubt if he made minimum wage considering the hours he was on the case. But I'm not complaining. I mean, that's his life, I mean, he—"

"Mrs. Winstead, your husband wouldn't happen to keep any kind of time sheet, something that would show when those nights were?"

"When he stayed at your daughter's?"

He nodded. "Yes, ma'am."

"Why, yes. He keeps a log on every case he's on. When he has to testify he has to have exact times and dates. Why?"

"I can afford to make up the difference if she wasn't able to pay him what she owed."

"Oh, no." She shook her head. "That's behind us. John agreed to do what he did for a certain price and she paid it. I was just meaning that when you pay him for a day's work, you've really got a day's work."

"Do you know where the log he kept on Judith's case is?"

"Sure. In fact, it's lying on his desk right now. With that lawsuit Dr. Salter's thrown against him John's been reviewing what he did."

"I'd like to see it."

"Oh, no. John would be mad if he even knew I said anything about his not being paid enough. He wouldn't like that one little bit."

"I won't tell him you showed me. But I'd like to make it up to him somehow. Maybe I could do it in the form of a bonus for what he's doing for me now."

"I don't know, Mr. Richards."

"It'd make me feel better, Mrs. Winstead. Something I can do for Judith, now."

He didn't like saying that, acting. He felt guilty at doing so, but he had to know.

She stared at him for a moment, her features softening, a compassionate expression coming to her face. "Well, okay. Come on in the living room and I'll get it for you."

The perfect order expressed in her appearance was

duplicated in her housekeeping. The inside of the trailer was spotless, everything in its place. Like her appearance, though, everything was also drab, to Richards's taste. Subdued colors blended into monotony, except for the vase of freshly cut flowers sitting on the dining-room table.

There was nothing more than the needed furniture in the small living room, certainly nothing whimsical: a beige-colored couch; a pair of chairs divided by a table and lamp; and a television sitting on a second table. He seated himself on the couch as she disappeared down the trailer's hallway.

When she returned, she carried a letter-size looseleaf notebook. "Here it is. I doubt if you can read his handwriting."

He found the information he wanted, the dates Winstead had spent at the cottage, and wrote them on the back of a card from his billfold.

Replacing the billfold in his back pocket, he stood. "Mrs. Winstead, I really appreciate this. You've helped me understand your husband a lot better. Thank you."

She smiled. "Don't you be telling John I showed you this."

"I promise you I won't."

It only took thirty minutes to drive to the sheriff's office, but Richards had to wait another hour until Tidmore returned from a meeting in the city.

"Brandon," the sheriff said as he walked through the door into his office.

Richards rose from the couch. "I went out to see if J.J. was home yet. He wasn't, but his wife gave me these dates out of his log book." He handed the card to the sheriff. "They're nights he spent at Judith's."

The sheriff's eyes narrowed as he studied the dates.

"Raymond, these were nights he was sitting up at Judith's because Martin had threatened her, and a couple of times just because Martin was in the city. If there was some way to match these dates with the nights Judith's neighbor said J.J. spent there, then we'd know he wasn't dating her."

"I've already had some deputies out to talk to them, the husband and the wife. God, she's a bitch. If I was him I'd be looking for strange stuff, too. . . ."

At the sheriff's embarrassed pause Richards said, "That's okay. Go on."

"I wasn't thinking."

"Go on."

Tidmore took in a deep breath, releasing it audibly. "Anyway, my deputies didn't get any specific dates, just that J.J. had spent the night there several times. Looks like you might have something though. The neighbors said he always parked his car in the drive, and that's not something I would figure a man slipping around on his wife would do. Too much of a chance that somebody might recognize the car and the word get out. I'll send some deputies back down there now, see if the couple can recall any actual dates."

Richards nodded. "I already feel better."

"Brandon, after you brought up what the nurse said, I'll admit I wasn't dead certain that J.J. didn't have something going with your daughter. She was a beautiful girl. But I never harbored the slightest thought that he was involved in her death. If you knew his background like I did you wouldn't either. Now plant some cocaine on a drug dealer he couldn't catch with his own stuff on him, he'd do that. Beat a confession out of somebody? He's done that. If you've got a second, sit down."

As Richards moved to the couch, the sheriff walked

around behind his desk and seated himself, opening a drawer and taking out a cigar.

"J.J. was born to his mother's second marriage. Her first husband had been a thug—terrible man. He had ended up being sent to the pen and she'd divorced him. When she remarried, he threatened to kill both her and her new husband."

The sheriff paused a moment as he lit his cigar. "Fifteen years later this thug got paroled. That's when J.J. had just turned twelve. A week later, while J.J. was over visiting at his grandmother's, somebody broke into his home and killed both of his parents. Wasn't much question about who did it, but there was no evidence. Everybody's hands were tied. J.J. couldn't understand that. He still doesn't. The good news is that a couple of years later this guy turned out to have a conscience, or he went bananas, who knows. He was shooting himself full of drugs every night, might have just went off the deep end. Anyway, he left a note confessing to killing J.J.'s parents and blew his brains out."

His eyes narrowed. "Wasn't a month later some bartender was quoted in the newspaper as saying the guy had told him he'd killed a couple—meaning J.J.'s parents. Bartender said he thought the guy was just blowing hot air. A couple of months later the girl who had been shacking up with this guy sold her story to a detective magazine. Says he'd told her, too. Of course she thought it was hot air. At least that's what she said to keep her little buns out of trouble.

"Anyway, J.J.'s still bitter about it, says the cops didn't do enough, that all they had to do was dig deep enough and they could have gotten something out of this bartender and the girl themselves. He believes if the guy hadn't up and killed himself he'd still be running around loose." He paused a moment, a reflective expression coming to his face. Then he nodded. "Probably right."

He looked back at Richards. "Anyway, as soon as J.J. was old enough he started working in law enforcement. And if you define a good cop as one that gets convictions, J.J.'s been a great cop. If you define a bad cop as one who doesn't care how he goes about it, lives by the premise that the end justifies the means, then he's a bad cop, a terrible one. In any case, that's J.J."

He leaned forward, his elbows resting on the desk, and looked straight into Richards's eyes. "Now you tell me J.J.'s broken the law to put a bad guy away, I wouldn't doubt you for a moment. But you tell me J.J.'s broken the law for personal gain, I'd swear to my dying day you're crazy. He can't. His whole career he's justified the things he's done by getting rid of the bad guys. I don't believe he could live with himself if he did anything that made him one of the bad guys, at least in the way he defines the term."

Tidmore leaned back in his chair again and then laughed. "You know, come to think about it, despite what I said a while ago, I really doubt J.J.'s the type to be steppin' out. That little five-two wife of his you met today, he's scared to death of her, and she's so straight-laced and prudish she'd make an angel uncomfortable. They haven't got any kids, you know. Some say it's because he's never been able to find her in the dark and she won't strip with the lights on." He laughed again. "She found out he'd been running around she'd probably have a heart attack, literally."

CHAPTER

21

Returning to the motel a little after six, Richards ate a hurried meal from the evening buffet, then checked at the front desk for messages. There were none. There were none on his answering machine either.

Calling room service he ordered a Bloody Mary, then hurriedly undressed and took a quick shower, moving back into the room to slip on his pajama bottoms and turn on the television.

"Good gosh!" Flora was going to kill him. Lifting the telephone receiver he punched in her number, but there was no answer. He punched in his Lake Ponchartrain home number.

"Hello."

"Flora?"

"Brandon, where are you? I've been waiting."

"I'm sorry, I haven't been able to leave yet. It's getting pretty late now. . . ."

"Ohhh, baby, you promised. I went to the seafood market. I have grouper, oysters—everything you like. I was going to prepare—"

"I'm sorry, I really am. Some things just came up." He looked at his watch. Might as well, he thought, he needed clean clothes. He smiled. "What I was getting ready to say is that I was afraid if I didn't call and tell you how late I was going to be that you might think I'm not coming and leave." He shook his head. "I'll be there in four hours if you can wait up. But I'm going to have to come back tomorrow."

"That's okay. I'll at least be able to see you."

"You have everything ready to pop in the oven. I haven't eaten yet." He rolled his eyes. "I've been waiting until I could eat with you. I'll be famished."

"Don't forget to bring everything with you."

"I won't."

"I've heard that before. I don't know how you can have a reputation as such a detailed lawyer when you go off and leave your toothbrush and razor so often. You left a hair dryer once."

"See you in four hours."

Smiling, he replaced the receiver and moved toward the bathroom. He would pack his toiletries first.

The telephone rang.

He lifted the receiver at the second ring. "Hello."

"Brandon, this is J.J. The hooker that Salter's using for an alibi, they just found the son of a bitch dead in his apartment. Man I had watching the place just called me. He thinks the hooker might have been dead since your daughter was killed. Stink got so bad it was getting out in the hall and the landlord called the cops. When I get back in town I'm gonna talk to the medical examiner. Call you tomorrow."

"Wait a minute, J.J. Where are you?"

"Down in Salter's area. Doing some checking around. Gotta go. I'm late."

"J.J., wait a minute. J.J.? Crap!"

He stared at the dead receiver for a moment, then reached and depressed the cradle button. He punched in the sheriff's home number.

"Tidmore here."

"Raymond—"

"Brandon, I was getting ready to call you. Jack Graff's the one that killed the guard. Hospital security just called the office and they transferred the call out here. He's the only one that refused to take a polygraph and they been on him hot and heavy ever since. He up and admitted it tonight. That's why he was hiding in the attic, I guess. Like I told you, don't ever try to figure those people's way of thinking."

Richards felt an exciting surge race through his body. "He could be the killer, then."

"No, him killing the guard doesn't change anything. He might have followed Hopper out of the dorm—they lived on the same floor. But even if he did, he didn't stay out long. I think he climbed in the attic pretty fast. That's security's feelings, too."

"How do they know he didn't go to Judith's and then come back?"

"Hell, I guess you can always say anything's a possibility. But security thinks they got it out of him straight. And remember, none of the other patients ever saw him leave or come back. Plus, it was raining. His clothes would've dried during the length of time he was in the attic, but he'd have had mud on his shoes. All the ones that got outside did. He didn't have a speck on him. Most important, he didn't have a drop of blood on him, either. There's no way he could have done the beating and not gotten blood on him."

"The bath, remember. The killer took a bath."

"No. When they found him in the attic they went over him with a fine-tooth comb. There would have at least been a trace of blood under his fingernails . . . somewhere."

Richards shook his head, his excitement ebbing. "Do you have any ideas about the male prostitute?"

"Like what?"

"J.J. said he might have been dead since the night Judith was killed."

"I don't know what you're talking about, Brandon."

"The hooker. J.J. just called and told me. I thought you knew. That's why I was calling. He said the city cops found him dead in his room after the apartment manager started complaining about the smell."

"Damn. No, I didn't know, and that's gonna be somebody's ass. I'll head over there right now. I'll call you after I know something. Is J.J. at home?"

"No, he's still down in Salter's area. Can I meet you at the apartments?"

The sheriff paused a moment. "Yeah, if you want. Boys over there won't know who you are. If they give you any trouble tell them I told you to meet me there. You know where it is?"

"No."

"Walter's Apartments. Take Normandy off the Interstate north, go west to Lee, turn right a block from there. See you in about forty-five minutes."

After replacing the telephone receiver Richards slipped his pajama bottoms off and dressed in the same coat, trousers, and shirt he had been wearing when he arrived at his daughter's the first morning. His only other suit he had worn for two days straight. The socks he had washed in the sink the night before were still slightly damp, but he slipped them on rather than the pair he had worn that day.

Dressed, he looked in the bathroom mirror and frowned. Despite his recent shower he felt unclean in the rumpled clothes, and that made him mad. Every little irritation was now making him mad: slow traffic; the cashier at the restaurant taking so long to fill out his credit card; everything. His nerves were a wreck. Shaking his head, he started toward the door, and as he did the shrill ring of the telephone once again filled the room.

"Hello."

"It's Atlene, Mr. Richards. Have you heard about Jack Graff?"

"Yeah, the sheriff just called."

"The guards just returned and were talking about it. I believe he saw something, don't you? I don't believe he imagined it all."

"I'm not following you."

"About the monster," Atlene said. "I mean, I know he's really screwed up mentally and he has it all mixed up in his mind, but he had to have seen something. What do you think?"

"Atlene, all the sheriff told me was that Graff killed the guard."

"The guards say he's contending a monster tore Hopper's head off. He says he saw it. That's pretty specific, isn't it? I don't think he went to Judith's, but I don't believe he hid in the attic immediately, either. Maybe he went to the fence with Hopper, but was scared to leave the grounds. He could see Judith's yard from there. I think he might have seen something, twisted it around into being a monster. I don't know. I was calling you to see what you thought."

"Can you talk to him?"

"I can't go inside maximum-security. I don't want

to, either. I'm going to have to run. I'm on evening medication delivery and I still have half a dozen dorms to cover. If I hear anything else, I'll call you."

Room service had yet to deliver the Bloody Mary as he stepped from his room and hurried to his Cadillac.

CHAPTER

22

Richards had to wait outside the entrance to Walter's Apartments and Boarding House until the sheriff arrived. The city police wouldn't allow anyone to enter who didn't live there.

"Brandon," Tidmore said as he walked up, beckoning with a gesture of his head for Richards to follow him inside the building.

The policeman at the entrance obviously knew the sheriff, stepping aside and holding the door open for them.

The officer on duty at the bottom of the stairs also recognized Tidmore.

They hurried up the rickety wooden stairway, Richards staying near the wall, away from the loose and tilted banister.

No policeman stood outside the prostitute's open door and they walked into the apartment.

A short, stocky man dressed in a rumpled brown rack suit was standing in the middle of the small living room.

"Hey, Sheriff. This going to tie back to your case in Davis County?"

"Might," the sheriff said. "This is Mr. Richards. He's the Salter girl's father. Brandon, this is Detective Carlisle. He's with city homicide."

The man nodded and Richards did, too.

"What do you have so far?" Tidmore asked.

"Not much. Somebody caved his head in with part of an old steel bedrail. It's down at the station. No fingerprints. His watch was broken, stopped at seven-thirty. Seven-thirty A.M. or P.M.—your guess is good as mine. Bruise on his wrist looks like he held his arm up to protect himself and the watch was smashed when he was hit. Drawers were all opened and ransacked; his pant's pockets were inside out. Whoever did it was looking for money. If there was any here they got it; not a penny lying around anywhere."

"Medical examiner set the time of death?"

"Preliminarily, three days plus."

"Stretch that out a little bit, be close to when Salter was with him. Was he dressed or undressed?"

"Fancied out. Florsheim shoes, tight pants, silk shirt. Scarf to match. His coat was lying on the floor by the door. He was either on his way out or letting in someone he was to leave with. Can't think of any other reason for him to be slicked up and toting his coat."

Richards looked to the sheriff for his opinion.

Tidmore nodded. "As good a guess as any. If he got surprised when he opened the door then it wasn't Salter."

"Why?" Richards asked.

"Salter's a pretty big guy, wouldn't have had any trouble handling the hooker. But if it was him I doubt he would have popped through the door starting a ruckus. Be more likely that he would have talked awhile, catch him unaware, keep it quiet."

Richards's eyes narrowed. "Why do you keep mentioning Martin, Raymond?"

"Just thinking out loud. Trying to see if I can ignite a spark."

"I still don't understand. He was Martin's alibi. Martin already admitted he was in the city and now he doesn't have anyone to say where he was. The last thing he'd want is the prostitute dead, right?"

"That's not necessarily the case. The alibi wasn't going to help him much, anyway. After leaving he still had plenty of time to go by your daughter's and get back home when he said he did. No, he doesn't lose much with the guy dead. But he could have kept the hooker from ever being able to testify about anything else, like maybe some private conversation where Salter had talked about how pissed off he was at your daughter. Could be anything."

The sheriff turned back to Detective Carlisle. "If you find out anything, let me know."

"Sure, Sheriff." The detective looked at Richards. "Sorry about your daughter."

"Thank you."

Moving back down the creaking steps, Tidmore was still thinking out loud.

"Martin's fingerprints gonna be in there, but that isn't going to prove shit. He was a long-standing customer. Only place any fingerprints in that room would make any difference is if they were on the piece of bedrail. If the medical examiner could narrow down the time of death a little bit, we might be able to learn something there. At least make Salter have to account for where he was then."

The sheriff continued to mumble, Richards catching only bits and pieces of it as they walked across the lobby through the door and out to the curb.

"Well," the sheriff said, pulling a cigar from his breast pocket as he looked reflectively into the clear summer sky. "Another piece to add to the puzzle." He lit the cigar and took a puff off it, then turned to face Richards. "Everything's gonna fit together one of these days," he said reassuringly.

Richards nodded.

"Brandon, didn't you say J.J. had a man watching the apartment?"

"Yeah, since the day of the funeral. No one's been in or out of the apartment since then."

"I'd like to talk to him anyway."

"Raymond . . ."

"Uh-huh?"

"The nurse I told you about, Atlene. She called to tell me about Graff just after you did."

"Uh-huh."

"She said Graff told security a monster killed Hopper. You didn't mention that." He wondered why.

The sheriff didn't speak for a moment, staring off across the street, then a gentle expression crossed his face, and he turned and looked into Richards's eyes.

"You've got enough bullshit to worry about without me adding to it by telling you about every cock-and-bull story I hear. It was just a nut's mind working. Hiding in the attic like he was there's no way he could know anything about Hopper being killed. But don't worry. Starting in the morning he'll be questioned a half-dozen times. I'll personally talk to him at least once. If there's anything else to be found out I'll find it."

He laid a hand on Richards's shoulder. "Brandon, you're too caught up in this. You can't tell it, but I can see it. It's getting to you. I'm beginning to think I'm not being a very good friend by letting you hang around seeing things like this, filling your mind full of crap all the time. A murder investigation's even rough on seasoned officers. Being personally connected, her father, I don't believe you can keep taking it. Maybe after you take the guarantee to Minnefield you need to head on back to New Orleans for good. I'll keep you informed about the investigation, daily if you want."

"I won't need to be here if Minnefield tells us who the killer is. It'll all be over then."

The sheriff shook his head. "There's no way in hell we'll be able to use whatever Minnefield says to get an indictment. God, we try that and the judge would commit us. All we can hope for is that he'll give us enough information for us to know he's right. If he does, we'll single out whoever he names and start trying to uncover something. But that's a long way from a conviction. This day and age it doesn't matter whether you know who did something or not, you've got to prove it, and you've got to play the game by rules that are one-sided in the thug's favor. It's not easy to get an indictment, much less a conviction."

"If Minnefield proves it to me, that's all I care about. That's all I need."

The sheriff's forehead wrinkled. He removed the cigar from his mouth and stared directly into Richards's eyes. "Brandon, I know how you feel. But whatever we find out you need to let it move through the proper channels. Maybe I shouldn't have said what I did about the rules being one-sided. They're there for a reason. It's just easy to be lazy and complain about them. Minnefield tells us who it was, we'll get him. It'll take a while, but it'll get done. Whoever killed your daughter, they're not worth you ruining your own life by doing something stupid."

CHAPTER

23

There was a message on Richards's answering machine when he arrived back at the Holiday Inn.

"Mr. Richards. This is Robert Furby, an attorney in Memphis . . ." The man's number followed, and that he had information regarding Judith's murder.

Richards quickly punched in the digits, an answering service operator coming on the line to take a message, but refusing to give out the attorney's home number.

He called Memphis's residential information and was in luck. Robert Furby was listed.

A sleepy voice answered on the third ring.

"Mr. Furby, this is Brandon Richards. You left me a message regarding my daughter's murder."

"Oh, yeah, yes."

Richards could hear a rustling of sound in the background and then the dropping of the receiver.

"Sorry," the voice said a moment later. "Let me turn on a light here. . . . Okay. Mr. Richards, I represent a client who says he has information which can help convict your daughter's killer. My knowledge of this information is very limited, but I can tell you that what little I do know lends some credibility to his claim. Other than telling you that, I am bound by his instructions to reveal nothing until he has met with you. As you might expect he wants something for his information."

"That's fine with me. Who is he?"

"He doesn't want me releasing his name at the moment—Hell, its Ernie Henchcliff. He's a con; both con man and convict. He's currently in the state pen. I was appointed to represent him. What he wants is for you to come to the pen and meet with him. If you're agreeable to paying him what he wants, he says he'll give you the information. If you wish to proceed I'll prepare an agreement on his behalf and meet you there."

"When?"

"As soon as you can. I've already worked it out with the prison authorities."

"How far is the prison from here, the city?"

"Better make it three hours to get inside the gate and to the meeting."

"What's the earliest you can arrange it?"

"My schedule is open after lunch tomorrow," Furby said. "How about three o'clock?"

"Fine."

"I'll meet you at the front gate of the main entrance. Now remember, Mr. Richards, I don't know if this man's information will end up being valuable or not. But I felt bound to forward his request."

"I understand. I'll meet you at the main gate at three o'clock. Thank you."

As soon as Richards was disconnected he called the sheriff's number.

"Sheriff Tidmore here."

"Raymond, this is Brandon. There was a message from a lawyer on my answering machine. He represents a prisoner at Parchman who claims he has information that will help convict Judith's killer."

"What could he possibly know?"

"Hell if I know. If I had to bet I'd say nothing. I have to meet with him, though. I can't afford not to. The only thing, I have to go to the state pen and the appointment is not until three o'clock. I'll lose the whole day. What if the governor or attorney general needs to talk to me about the guarantee?"

"I apologize, Brandon. I should have thought to tell you when we were at the apartment building. Guess my mind is getting overloaded, too. The attorney general called earlier today. It's all set. He read a draft over the phone. Minnefield will go for it. AG says they'll have it ready tomorrow afternoon or the next morning at the latest." The sheriff paused a moment. "I think you're right. You better run on up to the prison. Never can tell, could be something. I'll pick up the guarantee and have it here at the office when you get back."

"Appreciate it."

"You listen to the news in the last few minutes?"

"No, why?"

"Salter didn't have anything to do with the hooker's murder. Kid looking for crack money did it. Guy who lives in the same building saw the kid coming out of the hooker's room a few nights ago, same night Salter

was there. Looks like it must have happened right after he left. City picked the kid up a little while ago and
he broke down right off the bat. It can happen just
that quick, Brandon. Work your butt off, seem to
never get anywhere, then, bam, it's solved just like
that. Can't tell, maybe it'll happen when you find out
what this attorney's got set up for you."

After replacing the receiver Richards sat a moment
staring at his suitcase. Then he lifted the receiver
again and called Flora.

CHAPTER

24

Robert Furby was a short, stocky man with a thick neck. In his late forties and overweight, he still gave the impression of an athlete through the way he carried himself. A baseball catcher and a football guard, Richards guessed. Decked out in a blue three-piece suit and a red bow tie, the attorney wore white shoes.

The two rode in Furby's Buick from the entrance gate of the prison farm to the main facility and were checked in without any delay. They walked to a conference room off the main cell block on the first floor of the prison.

A guard brought Ernie Henchcliff inside the room, unlocked his handcuffs, and left, moving to stand outside the plate-glass viewing window built into the wall.

The convict seated himself across the metal table from them.

"Ernie," the attorney said, "I've explained to Mr. Richards what you want. He's agreeable if your information is helpful."

Richards decided that if there were ever a man whose features doomed him to a life of crime it was Henchcliff. The man's face would be ideal for a low-budget gangster movie. He had big ears and a long hooked nose which seemed bigger than it really was due to the narrowness of the gaunt face on which it sat. His eyes continually moved up, down, and sideways, not holding eye contact for more than a moment at a time.

The convict stared back across the table at Richards, and then he leaned forward. "Five thousand dollars, mister. I get five thousand dollars for my appeal. You sign that there paper and leave the five thousand with my attorney and we've got a deal."

The attorney had laid the document on the table and Richards reached out, sliding it in front of him.

Henchcliff cocked his head to the side as if he were trying to read the paper from where he sat. "It's supposed to say if you use anything I tell you I get five big ones."

"It does," Furby said. "Specifically, it says if the prosecution enters into evidence any information gleaned from what you tell Mr. Richards, you'll be entitled to five thousand dollars. The document is quite explicit and leaves no room for misinterpretation."

"I agree to the terms," Richards said, pulling a pen from his pocket and scribbling his name on the document. He pushed the piece of paper back to the attorney. "Now what is the information?"

"Mr. Richards," the attorney said. "You didn't

spend much time reading the agreement. I want to stress the fact that the five thousand dollar fee will be earned by Mr. Henchcliff even without a resulting conviction. Simply entering the information into evidence completes his end of the arrangement."

"I understand."

The convict bobbed his head forward several times, a satisfied smile coming to his face.

The attorney turned his face to the man. "You may proceed, Mr. Henchcliff."

The convict nodded. "Yeah, thank you, man. Okay, I know where there's a tape recording of Doc Salter saying he wants his wife dead. He was trying to set up a hit and it's on tape. How's them apples?" He smiled broadly.

Richards continued to stare into the man's face.

"Wants to know how much it would cost and how it's to be done," Henchcliff continued. "Have I got some good information or have I got some good information?"

Richards leaned back in the metal folding chair. "And how was this conversation taped? By whom?"

"You don't believe me," the man said, "do you? You think I'd waste my time calling you up here if I didn't have anything? I got better things to do."

Richards smiled.

The convict leaned forward over the table again. "See, there's this man in Memphis who's got a reputation. A big businessman gets in financial trouble and he hears 'bout this man. The businessman looks this man up and says I've got a lot of insurance on a building that's not worth piddlin'. You torch it for me and I'll give ya a couple thousand bucks. So this man goes and torches the building. The businessman pulls in big insurance bucks and hands the man his couple big ones. As the man sticks the money in his pocket he says, now each month you send me another thousand. Businessman looks funny and says, what you talking 'bout? The man says, oh, I forgot to tell you, I recorded our little conversation when you were asking for the building to be torched. You don't bring me a thousand dollars first of ever' month I'm gonna turn it over to the cops.

"The businessman laughs and says, and go to jail yourself? This guy that does the recording he looks surprised and says, for what? I get word some guy's got me confused with somebody else and wants to talk to me 'bout torching a building. I tape record the conversation for my own protection. I don't know where the man got my name. I damn sure don't do things like torch buildings. Then a couple days later I notice in the newspaper the building is burnt. I say, gosh almighty, I need to do my civic duty and let the cops know 'bout this. So I give 'em the taped conversation. I'm a hero.

"The businessman's hooked and he knows it. He turns pale and stands up and walks around, but he sends a thousand dollars first of ever' month. I saw that happen."

Henchcliff smiled at the cleverness of the scheme, first looking at Furby and then back to Richards. When neither's expression changed, the smile left his face and he started speaking again.

"Now Doc Salter he hears tell 'bout this man, too; hears he can arrange a hit. Salter waltzes in and offers him twenty-five thousand dollars. Now your daughter's dead, Mr. Richards. Guess who's gonna be paying a thousand dollars a month for the rest of their natural-born life?"

Richards glanced at the attorney. Furby shrugged. Richards turned his face back to the convict. "How do I obtain this tape?"

"Not by asking for it," Henchcliff said. "Worth a lot more to my man holding it over Doc Salter's head than it is selling it. Besides, knowing 'bout someone's trying to get a body killed and not telling the cops, that could be serious. My man would think twice before he really went to the police with that conversation—even though Salter's not gonna take that chance. I know where the man keeps his tapes. That's what I'm gonna tell you. You got any money on you now?"

"A little."

"I could use 'bout fifty in advance, to get me some cigarettes and stuff I been needin'."

Furby shook his head. "We have an agreement here, Ernie."

Henchcliff threw the attorney a dirty look, then smiled as he saw Richards reach into his pocket.

"Mr. Richards," the attorney said, "you don't need to—"

"It's okay."

"Don't hand it to him now." The attorney nodded toward the plate-glass window. The guard was staring intensely at Richards's movements.

"If it's okay," Richards said, "not breaking any rules, I'll give it to the guard when he comes back in."

Henchcliff smiled then looked back over his shoulder at the guard, winking and giving an okay sign with his fingers. The guard's eyes narrowed, a disgusted expression coming to his face.

Richards turned his gaze away from the convict toward the attorney. "I'm not familiar with rules of evidence. How do we go about obtaining the tape?"

"Where is it, Ernie?" the attorney asked.

"In a house about five miles from where the doc lives."

"I thought it was in Memphis," Richards said.

"Naw, said the man works out of Memphis. Got a

brother down near the coast in Salter's hometown that stores his valuable information. Keepin' the goodies in the far end of another state, that way he doesn't worry 'bout one of his customers pitchin' in the towel and bringin' the cops by."

Furby scooted his chair back and stood. "Search warrant would be best," he said. "But in that county you're taking a chance. The man doing the storing might receive a phone call if the wrong cop hears about it. When the police arrive, there might not be anything lying around. You'd never know if this character's telling the truth or not."

"I resent that," Henchcliff said.

Furby rolled his eyes. "I'm going to step outside for a few minutes, Mr. Richards. I've brought you together with this . . . gentleman. I'm sure you'll bear in mind I have also advised you that a search warrant is the only legal maneuver open to you. I'll be waiting outside. Anything you say to Mr. Henchcliff will remain between you two. The prison is not allowed to eavesdrop on any conversations in this room; attorney-client privilege."

After Furby exited, Richards turned back to the convict. "Do you know the home's address?"

"Going south on the highway that runs through the center of town, it's the last house on the right before you cross into the city limits. It's in the main bedroom's closet. Look up to the right on the top shelf and you'll see some books. They're hollowed out. The tape's in an old history book. I saw it put there with my own two eyes."

Richards stood.

"Leave the fifty bucks with the guard."

CHAPTER

25

At a quarter to eight Richards saw the orange Gulf County school bus stop in front of the ranch-style home. After it left, he guided his Cadillac from the side road where he had parked and drove toward the house.

He had driven to the police station the night before, had even stopped and parked on the street outside the old building, but had been unable to make himself stop and go inside. If the wrong cop hears about it, Furby had said, when the police arrive there might not be anything lying around. And it wouldn't just be the police who would hear about it; a judge would have to issue the search warrant, a secretary type it. The town was small, it wouldn't take long for even an innocent mention of why he was there to spread.

He shook his head, tapped his fingers nervously at the top of the steering wheel, and glanced at the home as he drove past.

He knew the likelihood of there actually being a tape was tenuous—at best. He had met many a con man in his security's law practice and had developed a sixth sense when it came to recognizing them. Henchcliff's story, despite its seeming plausibility, had not rung true.

On the other hand, why would the convict have lied? For him to have concocted such an elaborate deception made no sense. He didn't stand to gain anything if there was no tape. Richards shook his head. If there was a tape, could he himself risk losing it through informing others he was aware of where it was hidden—lose maybe the only evidence there would ever be connecting Martin back to the crime? He couldn't do that to Judith. Flora was right, Judith was a grown woman, would have resented him checking on her, questioning her, trying to direct her relationships. If she had wanted his advice she would have asked. There was really nothing he could have done for her before—but this was different. He had sworn an oath to her at the funeral home and at the grave, and nightly as he lay in bed. He had no choice.

On his third pass by the home the wife left in her white Ford. He didn't see the husband leave, the man's pickup truck disappearing from the yard between Richards's fourth and fifth pass.

Two hundred yards past the home the highway intersected a gravel road. A wooden sign tacked to a four-by-four post identified the road as Town Limits Street. Turning right, he followed the road, passing a pair of trailer homes and a boarded-up shack and coming to the street's intersection with a second gravel road.

Turning right again, he drove about two hundred yards farther and stopped his Cadillac. He was directly behind the home, separated from it by a pecan grove.

Guiding his Cadillac to the shoulder, he parked it. Reaching into the glove compartment he took out the .38, hefting it in his hand a moment before replacing it and then stepping out onto the road.

Hurrying to the barbed-wire fence at the edge of the grove, he climbed it and dashed into the trees.

A third of the way through the grove he heard the noise of a vehicle coming down the road where he had parked. Stepping behind a large pecan trunk, he shielded himself from view. It was a pickup, several pigs squeezed into its caged bed. It passed in a cloud of dust and bouncing gravel.

He hurried on toward the home.

A split-rail fence separated the house from the grove. He crawled through the lengths of post and moved to the back of the home. His breathing was slightly labored and perspiration had formed on his back. Nerves. He took several deep breaths to settle himself.

Edging to one of the home's windows he peered inside. The front of the house faced the east and the rays of the morning sun coming through the front windows gave him a clear view inside.

Twenty feet past the window was a back door. It was unlocked. Opening it, he stepped into a small kitchen.

A black miniature poodle charged from the living room, its barking rapid and shrill. He tried to grab it but it dodged away and circled him, yelping as if he had kicked it.

A plate of half-eaten eggs and ham sat on the counter top. He grabbed it and dumped its contents on the kitchen floor.

The dog first jumped away, then quieted and moved

back to the food. With a tilted head it looked one last time at Richards, then began hungrily gobbling the bits of leftover breakfast.

Richards pounced, grabbing the animal by a single leg and pulling it yelping to him, muffling its mouth.

Walking to a broom closet he deposited it inside and shut the door. Then he passed through the opening to his right, crossing the living room into the hallway and on to the bedrooms. The dog quit barking.

The bedroom to the right and the one to the left were both small, and he went on past them to the larger bedroom on the far side of the home.

Inside it he first went to the windows facing the road and looked out. A pickup truck pulling an empty cotton trailer was moving down the highway past the front of the house. Nothing else was in sight.

He moved quickly around the bed and opened the sliding closet doors. There were no books on the shelves.

The shelves in the small closet in the second bedroom were also devoid of books.

In the final bedroom, the bed had no coverings, the mattress bare. The closet was also empty, neither clothes nor books.

He heard the poodle start barking again, its quick high pitched tones grating on Richards's nerves.

Back in the master bedroom he looked a last time in the closet, then dropped to his knees and peered under the bed.

Standing, his eyes swept the room. No books of any kind. The dog's barking had risen to a fevered pitch, nearly constant, its high tone almost a howl. Then, abruptly, the barking ceased again.

Were there bookshelves in the living room? he wondered. He hadn't noticed. He hurried through the door and out into the hall, his heart jumping when he saw the police officer walking toward him.

The officer dropped into a crouch, the revolver he held at arm's length swinging up to point at Richards's chest.

Richards froze.

A second taller officer stepped from the kitchen into the hallway, walking up behind the first. He wore sergeant's stripes. His revolver was also unholstered and pointed at Richards.

Not knowing what else to do, Richards raised his hands. "I don't have a gun."

The sergeant glanced at the shorter officer and nodded.

The officer cocked his revolver, the metallic click clearly audible in the quiet hall.

Richards felt his stomach tighten. He had to fight the urge to run.

"Turn and put your hands against the wall," the officer said, "slowly."

Richards kept his gaze riveted on the two revolvers as he did as he was told.

The officer came down the hall, Richards's eyes following him until the flat of the man's palm thrust Richards's face toward the wall.

A hand swept his body, moving around his chest and under his arms, down both the outside and inside of his legs. His left arm and then his right were jerked from the wall and twisted behind him; the cold steel of handcuffs snapped closed around his wrists. Gripped by the shoulder he was swung around and slammed backward into the wall.

A revolver barrel jammed into the skin under his chin, forced his face upward, and he could smell warm, stinking breath. He felt the side of his mouth tic; his legs suddenly became so weak he feared he would collapse.

A hand jammed into his hip pocket and jerked his billfold out.

The back of his head pressed against the wall, his face lifted toward the ceiling, he glanced from the bottom of his eyes to see the officer flip the billfold down the hall to the sergeant. The man rifled through it, then raised his head. "Where's your buddy?" he asked. "Winstead."

The barrel jabbed deeper at Richards's silence, his mouth gaping open in pain.

"Easy, David," the sergeant said. "Let's take him in."

A sudden yank at Richards's arm and he was propelled around and down the hallway toward the sergeant. After only two steps a leg intertwined with his and he went sprawling onto the hallway floor, his face bouncing against the dirty carpet. The toe of a boot jabbed into his left side, and he rolled to his back and looked up at the smiling face.

"That's enough, David!" The sergeant's tone was sharp.

The officer continued to smile. A little man, five seven or so, and skinny, but now wearing a badge and with a pistol. Richards glared into the man's slitted eyes as the officer reached down to pull him to his feet and push him back against the wall once again.

"Try to run again and I'll blow your brains out!"

"David! I said that's enough."

Richards was shoved roughly down the hall.

Pushed through the front door out onto the small porch, he stumbled down the stairs and went sprawling onto the front lawn, bumping his face once again.

Looking back at the leveled guns, he pulled his knees under him and rose.

Barely back to his feet, he heard a vehicle swerve off the highway and turned to see a police van brake to a sliding halt in the gravel driveway. The van's front doors opened, a blue-uniformed police officer emerging from the right seat. From the driver's side, a big man in a brown three-piece business suit stepped out. In his fifties, he was at least six five, easily over two hundred-fifty pounds. He sported a gray crew cut and carried his Stetson in his hand as he walked toward Richards.

"Hey, Chief. Caught a Brandon Richards breaking and entering into Doc Salter's house."

Richards's blood chilled. He glanced at the officer who had spoken, then back to the house.

The chief nodded, his thick neck creasing and a double chin bulging at the movement. "Your information's old hat, Mr. Richards. Dr. Salter moved from here a week ago. He's renting the place now. Weren't planning on leaving something inside, were you?"

Richards stood in stunned silence, his mouth wide open, his head moving slowly side to side. The flat of a palm jabbed hard into his back. "Did you hear the chief ask you a question?" came the voice from behind him.

The chief's face crinkled in irritation. "I can handle it, David."

"Yes, sir."

"Did you all read him his rights yet?"

"Yes, sir," David said, "first thing."

Richards glanced at the officer and David smiled back. The sergeant looked away.

The chief gestured with his head and rough hands sent Richards stumbling toward the van. Pushed hurriedly into the back seat, his head cracked solidly against the edge of the door frame. "You son of a bitch," he said, and heard David laugh.

CHAPTER

26

A single three-story building housed the small town's police station, jail, welfare office, and volunteer fire department. Richards was hustled from the police van and down three concrete steps through a double door opening into the building's partially buried first level.

Prodded down a hall smelling of mildew, he was guided to a pair of elevators. Above one a laminated sign said: POLICE DEPT. AND JAIL; above the other was a sign proclaiming OTHER CITY DEPARTMENTS. At the bottom of the second sign, scribbled in a felt-tip pen's blue ink was, "City Janitor," and a scratchy arrow pointing down the hall.

When the elevator stopped on the second level, a

man in a business suit wearing a badge pinned to his breast pocket stepped forward. "The reporters are here," he said.

The chief nodded, adjusted his tie, then clasped Richards by the arm and led him out into the hallway.

The television lights bracketed Richards and the smiling chief. A reporter stepped forward and thrust a mike towards Richards's lips.

"Do you have anything to say, sir?"

One of the reporters said, "Is it true you were caught planting evidence in what you thought was Dr. Salter's home?"

Richards's eyes only jumped from one reporter to another as they hurled questions.

"Mr. Richards, was it your intention to murder Dr. Salter? Do you hold Dr. Salter responsible for your daughter's death?"

"Did you intend to plead insanity because of your daughter's murder?"

"Why did you want to make it appear that Dr. Salter murdered your daughter?"

And in the background Richards could hear a lower voice: "In an extraordinary change of events, the father of the murdered Judith Salter, an object of state-wide sympathy after his daughter's death, has now been caught breaking into the former home of her estranged husband, Dr. Martin Salter. No official police statement has yet been given, but WDON has obtained word from a source high in this police department that it is thought that Mr. Richards broke into what he thought was Dr. Salter's home to plant evidence which would implicate the doctor in Judith Salter's murder. The question now is why? What vendetta does Mr. Richards carry against Martin Salter. What caused . . ."

A shout drowned out the WDON reporter. "Chief

Crowley. My station just received word that Mr. Richards's revolver was found in the master bedroom of the home. Would this indicate to you that Mr. Richards in fact intended to murder Dr. Salter, rather than plant evidence?"

Richards stared at the reporter, then the chief.

The chief shook his head, using a sweeping motion of his thick arm to clear a path through the crowd of reporters, pulling Richards along behind him. "I'm not aware of Mr. Richards having been armed. Other than that, I will have no comment."

"My station picked it up over the police band when one of your officers called it in. They say that evidently Mr. Richards disposed of the pistol when he realized the police were there."

"No comment."

Chief Crowley led Richards into the booking room and the officer stationed there closed the door behind them, cutting off the reporter's questions.

The chief unlocked Richards's handcuffs, then pointed to the booking desk and the smiling jailer.

"My pistol is in my car's glove compartment."

The chief pointed again.

Richards walked forward, laying his hand on the desk top at the jailer's instructions. He was quickly fingerprinted and handed a paper towel to clean off the heavy blue stain. The jailer nodded toward the wall at the far side of the room, and gestured for him to move there.

An officer stood Richards next to the feet and inch markers on the wall, then walked back to his camera.

"Good . . . turn to the left . . . head up . . . back to the right . . . head up . . . good!"

Chief Crowley had stepped out of the room without Richards noticing and now walked back inside. In his hand he held a clear plastic bag containing Richards's revolver. He held it up in the air.

"I didn't take the gun in the house and you know it."

"How come Pimbly here found it there then?"

The lanky Pimbly had a smile on his narrow face. His tongue came out and washed his lips as if he were looking at something he couldn't wait to devour. "Yeah," he said.

"You're crazy," Richards said. "You got that out of my glove compartment."

"They tell me you're an attorney," the chief said. "You should have known better."

"I went in the house because I was told there was information hidden there which would prove Martin tried to hire someone to murder my daughter. It was a setup. I didn't know Martin had lived there. I have witnesses who—"

Witnessess who had set him up in the first place? Other than visiting the penitentiary and meeting with a convict and a lawyer, he didn't have anything. What a stupid bastard I am, he thought, and dropped his head.

"Mr. Richards," Chief Crowley said.

Richards raised his head.

"You broke and entered. That alone is enough to send you to the penitentiary. Doesn't matter why you did it, and doesn't really matter about the gun."

Richards didn't have to be a criminal attorney to know the chief was right. "Can I make a phone call?"

The chief nodded. "In here."

Richards followed Crowley through the door into a small office.

The chief pointed to the telephone sitting on the desk. "My dime," he said and moved to sit in the chair behind his desk.

"Am I going to receive bail?"

"District attorney will file breaking and entering charges. My judgement is he won't go for anything stronger until after an investigation. He doesn't like to lose cases. Breaking and entering the home of a man as respected as Dr. Salter is in this community, even if he's just renting it now—I called Judge Gresham—it's going to be about a ten thousand-dollar bail. That is unless you get Judge Coleman, a friend of Martin's, probably double then, maybe triple—all according to which one hears the case."

Richards lifted the receiver from its cradle and began dialing.

Chief Crowley leaned forward, using a thick finger to cut off the dial tone, then stared a moment into Richards's eyes. Finally he said, "I have mixed emotions about Martin's family. The main thing in their favor is that they've never given me any trouble and they control a lot of votes they've always sent my way. You understand the position I'm in?"

"You apologizing for setting me up?"

The chief's expression didn't change, but his voice was colder. "There's some people going to believe anything you say Mr. Richards, cause they don't like the Salters. There's some going to say you're lying no matter what you say. That's the bunch the Salters control. That leaves about sixty or seventy percent in this town going to listen honestly and render a fair judgement. You're going to be standing trial here. Judges in this county aren't going to give you a change of venue. You better keep in mind those who don't have their mind already made up. What I'm saying is those sixty or seventy percent have known me all my life. They know I don't set nobody up. If you don't want 'em to start thinking you're a chronic liar, you better watch what you say about me."

Richards laid the receiver back in its cradle, then explained to the chief about the meeting with the attorney and the convict.

Chief Crowley sat silent for a long moment after Richards finished, then leaned forward, his elbows on his desk, his hands clasped in front of him. "Who knew you were going to break into the house?"

"Nobody. I wasn't sure myself until this morning; wasn't absolutely positive until I started through the pecan grove."

The chief sat silent for another long moment, nodded his head at his thoughts, then leaned back in his chair.

"Okay, from the beginning: the convict and the attorney set you up, then somebody followed you after you left the pen. They would have figured you only had two choices. One, go through my office and hope I wasn't Salter's friend or, two, slip in and get the tape yourself. You're already desperate enough to hurry down and talk to a convict, and believe him. You're in an emotional state right after your daughter's death, grabbing at straws. They figured the odds pretty good. All they had to do was have someone follow you until you made your move, then call us." He shook his head. "For what it's worth—given you're telling the truth—I'd have done the same thing for my daughter. Course all that means is we're both crazy."

Richards took a deep breath and let it out. "I guess I'd better make my phone call."

"Tell 'em ten thousand. I can make sure which judge you go before. I'll do that much for you just in case you're telling the truth. Won't either one of 'em see you before tomorrow, though."

Tomorrow was the fourth day. "Chief, please, I have to be back at the state hospital by one tomorrow. I have to."

"Sorry."

"Is there any way at all one of them could see me today, even the other judge? I'd rather have the higher bail than have to stay."

The chief shook his head in exasperation. "Hell, man, you're acting stupid again. You're an attorney. You should know it's not just the bail. Whichever one you get now will be who sits on the case. You don't want Coleman, believe me. In any case you'll be spending the night with us. You're just going to have to forget about that appointment."

CHAPTER

27

After dialing his law firm's number Richards leaned back against the wall of the office. Chief Crowley was rummaging through his desk's drawers searching for something.

"Wilkinson, Heath, Richards, and Ward."

"Sylvia, this is Brandon. Grab a pencil."

"Mr. Richards, Fire Safety, Inc., has been ringing your phone off the hook. They say they're offering—"

"Later, Sylvia, I have a problem. Find a pencil and write this down."

"Yes, sir. Just a minute . . . I have one."

"Call Charlie Bordeaux. Tell him he needs to wire ten thousand dollars to . . ." Richards glanced at the chief, received a weak nod and a shrug. "Make that thirty thousand, just in case. I want it wired to me in care of the Chief of Police, Gulf City. I need it done immediately. Then call Sheriff Tidmore in Davis County. Tell him I've been arrested—"

"Ohh!"

"Listen! Tell him I've been arrested in Martin's hometown. They've charged me with breaking and entering. Tell him I'm having the bond money wired, but the police chief here says I'm not going to be released until tomorrow, too late to keep the appointment with Minnefield. Tidmore will know what you mean. Tell him he has to do something to get me out before then."

The chief rolled his eyes, shaking his head, but didn't look up. He had found the pair of nail clippers he had been searching for and was working at the ends of his fingers.

"Sylvia, also tell them that if there's anything they can think of, to do it. Maybe one of them knows the judges down here. I can't miss the appointment. I have to get out of here by tonight at the latest."

The chief shook his head again, then held his hand up, palms down, studying his nails.

When Richards finished with the call and replaced the receiver, Crowley leaned forward and pushed a button on his desk.

The door opened, Pimbly and the officer named David came in to escort Richards out and down the hall toward the cell block.

The renewed questions and glare of television lights ended as the cell block door clanged shut behind him.

The afternoon and night passed maddeningly slow. It was nearly daylight when Richards heard the footsteps coming down the cell block. Hopeful, he moved to the front of his cell and stared down the dimly lit hallway.

It was Pimbly, the officer called David, and Martin Salter.

Stomach tightening, he backed to the rear of his cell.

Pimbly unlocked the barred door and the three stepped inside.

"Brandon," Salter said.

Richards stood quiet.

Salter had a quizzical expression on his face. "I want to know why, Brandon."

Richards saw movement out of the corner of his eye and saw that the man in the adjoining cell had moved to stand at the barred partition between the two cells. Across the hallway another prisoner had moved to the front of his cell, also listening to the conversation.

He felt emboldened.

"Come off the crap, Martin. You and I both know why I was in your house. Did Henchcliff do you a little favor so he'd have a pension waiting when he gets out, or did he already owe you? Furby—all I had to do was ask some other attorneys and I'd have discovered he works for your family, right? What's the plan? I can't figure out your plan. You know this isn't going to stop me."

Salter's brow furrowed. "Robert Furby?"

"Don't know what I'm talking about? You're full of shit, Martin."

"Where did you meet him?"

Richards shook his head, smirking. "Ah, that's good, real good." He glanced at the prisoner standing at the side of the cell and the other one across the hall, and then at the two police officers standing behind Martin. "This part of the game? They going to testify how you claimed you couldn't possibly have known anything? What are they going to testify I said?"

"Furby works for my poppa," Salter said. "What has he to do with you?"

Richards laughed. "I'm tired of this crap. Why don't you get the hell out of here?" He moved to his bunk and sat, swinging his legs up on the bare mattress and laying back.

Stepping quickly forward, Martin grabbed him by the shoulder. "I said, what have you to do with Furby?"

Richards slammed his forearm back against Martin, knocking his grip loose. Then all reason dissolved in anger. Richards lunged from the mattress, throwing his shoulder into the doctor's chest and driving him back against the cell wall.

Arms grabbed Richards from the side as the two officers wrenched him backwards and wrestled him to the floor, pinning his back against the cold concrete.

"YOU SON OF A BITCH," he shouted. "GET THE HELL OUT OF HERE!"

The prisoner across the hall was smiling, the one in the next cell had an excited expression on his face, his cheeks flushed.

"Let him up."

At Martin's order, the two officers released Richards and stepped back, but remained between he and the doctor.

Richards looked up from where he lay, staring at the confused expression on Martin's face.

"In God's name, Brandon, what's wrong with you? You really think I killed Judith? I had nothing to do with her death, Brandon. I swear to God. I couldn't have. She's the twins' mother."

Richards pulled his legs under him and stood. "Take a lie detector test then. Prove it!"

Across the hall, the smile on the face of the prisoner widened. He was nodding his head.

Salter shook his head. "Winstead has friends all over the state. Test results are not always black or white, it's according to who does the interpreting. I can't take the chance it'd be some pal of his. I know him. You ask around. He has it in for me. He doesn't care who murdered Judith. He just wants to pin it on me."

"Bullshit. It can't be used in court against you, but it could show you didn't do it. Have the FBI administer it."

Salter shook his head again. "No, I'm not going to. Brandon, I told you Furby works for my poppa. Will you tell me, please, what has he to do with you?"

Richards stared a long moment. Furby worked for Martin's dad. A father protecting his son. Maybe. He nodded his head. "Okay. Furby and a con told me you had tried to hire a man to kill Judith. This man supposedly taped the conversation to blackmail you later. It was supposed to be stored in his buddy's house. That's why I was there. The buddy's house turned out to be yours. Ask that character behind you." He looked at the officer called David. "He just happened to come by and catch me there."

Salter glanced over his shoulder.

"I got a call on my car radio," David said hurriedly. "Somebody saw him slipping in the back. That's all. Honest. Dr. Salter, this isn't getting anywhere. It's gonna be my ass anyway when the chief finds out I let you in. We'd better go."

Richards, his brow crinkling, looked from David back to Salter. "The chief doesn't know you're here?"

Salter addressed his remark to David. "I told you I could take care of it. I'll smooth it over. Don't worry."

"Martin," Richards said. "You don't know, do you?

Your dad . . . your dad did set it up. He meant to get me off your back. Well, you can tell your old man that if you didn't kill Judith all he did was screw up. All he did was prevent me from finding out who did."

"What do you mean?"

"There's a patient back at the hospital who says he knows who the killer is." He looked for a reaction from Salter, saw only curiosity. "I believe him. I worked out an agreement where the governor was going to give him some privileges in exchange for him telling us who the killer is."

"How would a patient know?"

"It's a man named Minnefield. He—"

"Marcus Minnefield?"

Richards nodded. "He said he was looking out his window and saw the killer enter the house. He knows enough detail about what went on to where I believe he's telling the truth. What does that do for you?"

"I hope he does know, Brandon, believe it or not."

"Then help me keep the appointment. If you don't want him to tell me, then keep me here." Richards stared intently into Martin's eyes, trying to read the reaction.

Salter smiled a little. "Your own little lie detector test, huh?"

Richards nodded. "If you didn't do it, help me make the appointment so I can find out who did."

Salter stared at Richards a long moment, then turned and strode from the cell. "David, bring him down here."

"Dr. Salter, I—"

"Now!"

By the time Richards was escorted into the chief's office, Salter was already on the telephone.

"Poppa. I'm down at the jail. . . . No, it's all right. . . . Listen. I know about Furby. . . . No, don't give me any of that. I appreciate what you're trying to do, but that's not how I want it. I want Mr. Richards turned loose now. . . . No, immediately! There's a patient at the hospital who says he knows who the killer is. Mr. Richards has to keep an appointment with him. . . . No, Poppa, I told you I appreciate it, but that's what I want. Trust me. I want him released. Please, Poppa?"

CHAPTER

28

Martin Salter, his eyes bleary, obviously tired, was sitting in a straight-back chair just inside the door of the chief's office. Richards sat in the soft leather chair behind the desk. His thoughts centered on his attack on Martin in the cell.

Richards knew the attack only reinforced what he had already come to realize. His obsession with finding Judith's killer was taking its affect on his ability to act rationally, was taking control of his life. What surprised him most about the realization was that he didn't care.

He heard the groaning of the elevator and raised his face to the office's open doorway. He heard the voices of the officers in the hall as they greeted Martin's father.

Martin said, "You better be careful with what you say," then stood.

A wheelchair entered, the old man sitting in it smaller than Richards remembered, much smaller than Martin, though his face was broader and his neck much thicker than his son's. White haired, his thick bushy eyebrows and large drooping mustache were black. A heavy tan camouflaged but didn't hide the liver spots on his forehead and left cheek. Pointed patent-leather shoes stuck out from under the brocade quilt which covered his lap and legs.

"Poppa."

The man didn't acknowledge his son's greeting, or even look at him, instead staring directly into Richards's eyes.

Richards rose. It was the second time he had met Martin's father, the only other time just after their two children had returned from eloping. The man hadn't needed a wheelchair then.

The old man finally broke off his stare and looked up at his son. "You really want to turn this bastard loose?"

Martin nodded. "He's not like Winstead."

The man looked back into Richards's eyes. "I'm going to listen to you," he said, "but, first, who do you think done it?"

Richards stood silent a moment, then moistened his lips with his tongue. "I don't know. That's what I'm trying to find out."

"You think Martin here done it?"

Richards caught Martin's taut expression, the slow shake of his head.

"No, sir, I told you I don't know who killed Judith."

"Then why are you harassing him?"

"I wasn't harassing him. I was set up. I—"

The old man raised his hand in a silencing motion,

shaking his head. "I know about all that. It doesn't make any difference. If you wanted to know something you should have come to me."

Richards couldn't help but smile a little.

The old man's face instantly turned red. His eyes slitting, he dropped his hands to the rims on the side of his wheelchair and jerked it forward a few inches before stopping. "You're a cocky bastard, aren't you!" The eyes remained slitted.

Unnerved at the sudden anger, Richards felt his pulse increase.

Martin was shaking his head again.

The old man continued to stare for a long moment. Then he leaned back in his wheelchair, the muscles in his face softening, but his eyes remaining the same. "Answer what I asked you. Who do you think done it?"

Richards glanced at Martin, then back to his father. "There's a neighbor of hers, he's a possibility." He spoke slowly, carefully choosing his words. "I have reason to believe the killer could even be a police officer."

The old man's eyes widened.

"Also, one of the patients can't be ruled out." Pausing a moment he studied the old man's expression. "Then, there's your son."

It was as if Martin's father hadn't even heard the last phrase, the man's face retained the same quizzical expression it had at the mention of the police officer. He met Richards's gaze again. "This nut at the state hospital; why would you believe anything he said?"

Martin answered. "Poppa, I've treated the man. He's intelligent. The only question is, if he does know will he tell the truth?"

"And you're willing to gamble on that?" the old

man asked, glancing up at his son. Then he returned his cold stare to Richards.

"What if the nut says Martin's the killer?"

"It doesn't matter who he says, Mr. Salter. He's going to have to prove it to where I know he's telling the truth."

"And what makes you think you're going to know if he's telling the truth?"

"If I don't know for sure, then I'm not going to do anything."

The man's eyes squinted. "And what would you do?"

Richards took a deep breath, touched his tongue to his dry lips, then, seeing Martin staring at him with widened eyes, decided to remain quiet.

The old man sat silent for a long period. Finally he looked up at his son again. "You all go on out of here," he said.

"I don't know if that's a good idea, Mr. Salter," David said, staring with wrinkled forehead at Richards.

The old man laughed. "And you think I need your protection?"

David's eyes dropped to the floor, his cheeks reddening.

The old man stared at the officer for a moment. "That embarrassment or anger?" he asked.

David shook his head. "Sir?"

The old man laughed again and then gestured toward the door with his head. "Go on. All of you, go on and get out of here."

Martin nodded at the two officers. "It's okay," he said, then followed them through the open door, shutting it behind him.

Martin's father said, "Raising children is hard, isn't

it?" The man's voice was suddenly so low Richards had to strain to hear it.

The old man shook his head and rolled his eyes. "Don't guess there's anything I could tell you about your daughter," he said, "that you don't already know. And I dare say there's nothing you can tell me about Martin I haven't already heard. Made no difference Martin grew up sitting on a stack of untaxed whiskey in the back of a pickup, your Judith, she grew up playing with Barbie dolls. Not much difference in 'em in the end, huh? You're an educated man, what caused 'em to turn out like they did?"

The old man's face had carried a blank, introspective expression as he spoke, not looking at Richards so much as in his direction. But now the expression was serious and the gaze focused.

"Well, I'm truly sorry about your daughter, Mr. Richards, and I understand your grief. But that's no damned reason to be getting after Martin. Man's got a right to leave a woman he don't think's right for him, and that's all he done. Martin didn't kill nobody, you understand that, NOBODY!"

Richards remained silent.

The old man shook his head. "You're not taking my words to heart, are you?"

Richards kept his voice low, his tone level. "Would you, if it were your daughter?"

"NO!" The answer was quick and sharp. Abruptly he said, "Enough of this bullshit. Let's get down to brass tacks." He settled back in his chair. "Martin's going to come to no good. With his preferences nothing else can happen." He pointed with an index finger to his own chest, then thumped it. "But while I'm alive, whatever time I've got left, I'm going to do what I can to protect the boy. You understand that? I'd do it even iffen he did the killin', but he didn't. I know that. I'll be damned if I'll stand by and see anyone stick that on him. I'd do some of my own killin' before I'd let that happen, you understand?"

Richards didn't move, staring directly into the old man's eyes.

"Okay, Mr. Brandon Richards, here it is plain. I don't want Winstead up here anymore, and I don't want you sending nobody else neither. You agree to that and I'll let you go. When this is all over, I'll see to it the charges against you are dropped. You put in a lot of sweat to earn your big-shot lawyer degree. You know what a felony's gonna do to it."

Richards continued to stare.

A smile formed on the man's face. "You think by not talking I can't tell whether you're lying or not? I can see it in your look. You're not going to call him off, are you?"

There was silence for several seconds then finally the man spoke again, nodding his head when he did so.

"Martin said you were a man of your word. Don't usually pay much attention to his judgment of people, but I think he's right this time. If I let you go will you call me with any questions you got before you sneak somebody up here? That's not much. Give me your word on that and I'll let you go."

Richards knew his expression must have changed, because the old man laughed.

"Don't ever set in on a game of poker, son. You'd give away anything more important than a ten. You'd like to lie, tell me whatever I want to hear, but you don't know how to do it without giving away it's a lie. You don't even know it yourself, yet, but you're not coming after Martin unless you're sure he did it. I can see that, and he didn't. I'm going to let you go and hope that nut holds up to what you and Martin think about him."

The man looked back over his shoulder.

"Hey, boys!"

David immediately stepped through the door.

The old man laughed.

Martin stepped around David into the room. "Poppa?"

"You're going to have to give me a little time to soothe things over with Chief Crowley," the old man said, looking up at his son. "But he's free. I believe you judged him right, Martin. Doesn't happen very often you read people right, but I'm betting you did this time." He looked back at Richards. "Other than letting you keep your appointment, doesn't make much difference to me, anyway. Judge would turn you loose by lunch. Only difference is you miss breakfast on the county."

"How long until I can leave?"

A smile came to the man's face. "Well, you haven't totally lost the use of your tongue. Persistent cuss, too, gotta give you that. I'll go by the chief's home now. I'll call the judge from there." He looked at his watch. "You won't have time for any sightseeing, but you'll make it."

"I need to use the phone a minute."

The old man nodded and pointed to the one on Chief Crowley's desk.

After the Davis County Sheriff's Department answered and Richards asked for the sheriff, there was the normal wait. He drummed his fingers nervously against the wall and held the receiver loosely to his ear. He glanced at his watch.

"Sheriff Tidmore here."

"Raymond. They're going to let me out. I'm going to make it to the hospital in time to meet with Minnefield, but it's going to be close. Can you meet me at the main entrance with the guarantee?"

The sheriff didn't answer immediately.

"Raymond . . . ?"

"I don't have it, Brandon."

He felt his stomach jump; his hand tightened on the receiver.

The sheriff continued.

"The governor won't sign and he won't meet with you again. You getting arrested scared him to death."

"No! He has to." *He has to.*

At Richards's tone Martin quirked an eyebrow.

"Give it a couple of days," the sheriff said. "I'll talk to him. I'll tell him you're out of it, it's for me. He'll still be able to get credit if Minnefield breaks the case. I believe he'll go along. And Minnefield's not going to cut off his nose to spite his face. He'll be sullen for a couple days. If he sees he's gonna get what he wants, though, he'll come through."

Richards shook his head. "No. I'm going to keep the appointment. You said it yourself. He has a need to dominate. If I don't meet with him, I've slapped him in the face, acted like I don't care. At least if I keep the appointment maybe he'll give me a chance to explain."

Martin nodded his head.

The sheriff was silent for a moment, then said, "It can't hurt anything. Go ahead."

"How is Dr. Thornburg going to react? Will he let me in?"

"He's out of town. It's unlikely he's even heard about you being arrested. Even if he has, he's not going to call back here and cancel a meeting he thinks the governor's okayed. You haven't got anything to lose, anyway. Give it a shot. I'll be waiting outside, want to hear how it went as soon as you're through."

"He said alone, Raymond. I'd hate for him to see you, give him something else to be upset about."

"I won't come inside the grounds. Call the office the minute you're finished. They'll patch you through to my car. I'll be close by. We'll meet outside somewhere."

CHAPTER

29

Marcus Minnefield watched from his third-floor cell as Alan Molpus left on his lunch break, the captain passing through the dual security fences on his way to his brown Ford. Alan's leaving meant it was twelve-thirty. He took his lunch break at the same time every day. He would be back at precisely one-thirty.

"Until then," Minnefield whispered, and raised his hand in an unseen wave.

Walking to the front of his cell, his smile changed to a frown as he stared down the hall to the head of the still-empty staircase. The rest of the staff was not as punctual as the guard captain. The orderly who was to let him out to clean the third-floor cells was late again.

This recurring tardiness was a source of considerable annoyance to Minnefield. Ever since he had changed his time to be let out to coincide with Alan's lunchbreak, it had been a constant struggle to keep the orderlies punctual, especially Jonah. Once, when Jonah had been over five minutes late, Minnefield had chastised him by refusing to clean the cells at all that day.

A form appeared at the top of the stairs and then emerged into the hallway. The short black orderly took his time as he moved down the cell block. The long billy club hanging from his belt swayed lazily in time with his steps.

Minnefield moved his eyes from the billy club to the way Jonah walked. The two had strikingly similar builds. Wearing Jonah's uniform and imitating his slow elongated stride, Minnefield knew it would be possible to walk down the dimly lit hallways of the building and be mistaken for the orderly, except that Minnefield was not black—an easily remedied situation.

"You're late," he said as Jonah walked up to the front of the cell. "You should be aware by now that I abhor a lack of punctuality, Jonah."

"Now, now, Marcus, where ya fixin' to be off to?" Jonah's smile faded as his eyes made contact with Marcus's cold stare. Turning away, he slipped his key ring from the metal clip on his belt and unlocked the manual door bolt on the cell adjacent to Minnefield's. A backup electrical lock was still in place. The door would not open until Jonah pushed the proper button on the big electrical panel mounted at the head of the staircase.

Moving to unlock the manual bolts on each of the other four occupied cells on the floor, he returned to stand in front of Minnefield's cell.

"Stand back away from the door, Marcus."

Minnefield's eyes saw nothing he had not already committed to memory. The orderly's uniform consisted of blue denim trousers and a white, long-sleeved shirt, its cuffs unbuttoned and folded back a single time. Jonah always wore his cuffs that way. He preferred wearing his big leather weapon belt like a gunfighter's rig, low on his hips and slanted toward the weight of the billy club. While standing still, he tended to shift most of his weight to one leg.

"You gettin' hard of hearin', Marcus?" Jonah emphasized the sudden sternness in his voice by moving a hand to rest on the metal mace canister at his belt.

Minnefield smiled and backed to the center of the cell.

Jonah inserted the large metal key into the manual lock, but before turning the key he bent and peered through the narrow crack between the door's lock plate and the solid steel of the frame.

The light which could be seen through the narrow threadlike opening was interrupted twice by steel bolts; both the manual lock and the electronic one were properly seated. Jonah straightened and turned the key to the left, then hung the keyring back on his belt.

"What'cha gonna be needin' today?" he asked.

"Clorox, towels, and I will be requiring some Drano, also. Mr. Vanderford's toilet is slow in flushing."

Jonah glanced at the listless form lying on the bunk in the adjacent cell, then shook his head. "He remind you of your father or something?"

"I do not have a father."

Jonah laughed silently. "I can believe that. Probably never had no mother, neither."

"I had a mother, Jonah, once."

The side of the orderly's mouth lifted into a one-sided smile and he shook his head. He then sniffed the air. "Lord," he exclaimed, "this joint gets to smelling worse every day. What is it about you nuts that stinks so bad?" He turned and started back toward the staircase.

"I would be able to accomplish a more proper cleansing if permitted the use of a scouring pad," Minnefield called after the orderly.

Jonah didn't look back. "And the answer is no, again. Towels only, no steel pads. Captain's orders."

Unlocking and opening the closet door next to the staircase, Jonah removed a plastic container of Clorox, setting it outside on the floor. From a commercial-size metal Drano canister he scooped a double handful of granules into a small yellow plastic bucket, and placed the bucket next to the Clorox. Finally, he lifted a towel from the stack in the closet. After wiping his hands with it, he pitched it into the bucket.

Shutting and locking the closet, he walked to the head of the staircase and swung shut behind him the heavy barred door that sealed the third floor from the rest of the building. Looking back into the hallway through the heavy metal bars of the door he said, "Which'un you wanna clean up first, Marcus?"

"I will attend to Mr. Vanderford first."

"I hadda ask?"

Jonah reached for the panel and pushed button number six, Minnefield's cell, then button number five. Separate metallic clangs indicated the electronic locks to the two cells were now released.

"Get a movin', Marcus. I'm takin' off early today. Got me a high-butted, wild woman for tonight. Got to get to the house and rest up first. You miss that stuff, Marcus?" The orderly chuckled to himself, then leaned back against the dirty gray wall of the staircase, fumbling in his breast pocket for a pack of cigarettes. He struck the wooden match on the metal NO SMOKING sign hanging on the wall beside him.

Minnefield pushed open his cell door and walked to the end of the hall, bending to pick up the containers and towel. He nodded deferentially when Jonah glanced through the barred door toward him.

Inside Vanderford's cell Minnefield stopped next to the old man's bunk, staring down at the gaunt face.

The man's eyes were slits, parts of the pupils and the white to each side of them visible, but he was asleep. Mouth gaped open, jaw hanging down, his snore was rattling and broken. The institution-issue pajamas he wore were soiled and the bare mattress showed a wet circle under his buttocks. The bed-clothes were lying on the floor beside the bed. Minnefield picked them up and laid them across the old man, making sure the faded cover hung down far enough to conceal the ancient bed's corroded iron legs. He then knelt beside the bed and laid his hand against a pale, stubble-covered cheek. The old man did not notice.

Jonah shook his head and leaned back against the wall again.

Continuing to stroke the listless figure's face, with his other hand Minnefield reached under the bunk and found the recess in the iron plate. It was where the countersunk bolt connected a leg to the frame. Wedging the side of his knee under the edge of the frame, he began to apply and release pressure rythmically with an up-and-down movement of his leg.

The frame slipped and sagged only an inch—like it had two weeks before when he had first noticed it, and then discovered that one of the leg's connecting bolts was broken. He had immediately known what he would use the bolt for. He had worked it back in place then, and since had checked every day to make sure the old man's restless movements had not caused the frame to sag again. He would need both hands now. He glanced toward the staircase.

The orderly was leaned back against the wall, his lips moving with a silent song, his right foot tapping time.

Minnefield used his knee to lift the bed slightly off the floor, the emaciated body on it adding little weight to the task.

Holding the leg at its very bottom, prying it outward, Minnefield pulled its top far enough from the frame to slip his fingers into the gap. A painful push with an index finger and the bolt moved. It now protruded out of its recess under the bed and he was able to work it loose and into his hand.

Easing the leg back as near as possible to its original position, he rose. Picking up the Drano container, he left the bottle of Clorox behind as he moved to the toilet in the corner of the cell. Jonah was still leaned back against the wall, his face angled toward the ceiling, blowing smoke rings.

Minnefield dropped a handful of Drano granules into the bowl and pushed the handle. Jonah glanced down the hall at the sound, then turned away again.

When he did, Minnefield grasped another handful of granules and moved quickly back to the bed. Kneeling, he removed the top from the Clorox bottle.

The old man opened his eyes, blinked, and recognizing his friend, smiled a faint, toothless grin. He made a slight hissing sound, the only sound he knew how to make. He had been a deaf-mute since birth.

Minnefield smiled back and moved his empty hand to the thin face, cupping the protruding chin, then jabbed his thumb and index finger hard into the hollow cheeks. The old man's eyes widened in pain as his mouth was forced into a fishlike pucker. Minnefield dumped the Drano granules inside. The narrow tongue jumped, tested the granules, then thrashed wildly. Minnefield lifted the Clorox bottle and sloshed some of the liquid into the opening. For a brief moment he observed the turquoise crystals starting to boil, then released the pressure of his fingers and used the heel of his hand to clamp the mouth shut.

The old man gurgled. Ropey neck muscles strained as he tried to turn his head. His bony hands came up to clutch at Minnefield's wrist.

Minnefield glanced toward the still silently singing orderly, then back to the wide eyes and pale face. When he saw the Adam's apple work twice in a swallowing motion he smiled. Smoke seeped from the man's tightly pressed lips and Minnefield's smile grew broader.

Suddenly he jumped to his feet and hurried into the hallway. "Jonah!"

"What?"

"Something is wrong with Mr. Vanderford. I think he might be sick."

"He's okay."

"No, he is definitely not okay. Will you come see about him . . . please?"

"Lordy, Marcus, I told you I was needin' to be takin' off early today. All right, get on back in your own place."

"Thank you."

Minnefield moved to his cell door, palming the piece of broken bolt into the electric lock's female slot as he moved inside.

The bolt protruded a fraction beyond the face of the slot and he had to apply extra pressure to close the door. The orderly was too far away to hear the scraping of metal on metal.

Jonah pushed the locking button to cell six. The electrically activated bolt shot forward, clanging as it was stopped short by the piece of broken bolt—the same sound it would normally make when firmly seated in the female coupling. He waited for the signal the electric circuit was complete, the security bolt's sensing end locked in contact against the steel at the back of the female slot. The light glowed green. Unlocking the door at the head of the staircase, he hurried, can of mace in hand, down the hall to stop at the front of Vanderford's cell.

The old man was thrashing wildly on the bed, his hands clutching his throat, guttural choking sounds emanating from his gaping mouth.

Pushing the cell door open, Jonah cautiously stepped inside.

He saw the tears streaming from the wide eyes, and then heard the gurgling gaseous sound in the man's stomach. He bent closer when he noticed the light green foam boiling from the corner of the mouth. Then a whisp of smoke came out.

"Jesus!"

Hooking the mace back onto his belt clip, he hurried outside the cell and pulled the door shut, using his key to relock it.

Turning to leave, he heard behind him the scraping sound of metal on metal, and then the sudden step. His eyes widened, his body paralyzed for a split second with sudden terror, then he grabbed for the can of mace at his belt.

Minnefield's hands clasped the orderly's neck, slamming the man face first into the bars of Vanderford's cell. The mace clanged to the floor and rolled down the hall. A hard blow to the back of the neck jammed Jonah's jaw between the vertical bars, his chin pressed down against a crosspiece. Another blow followed;

now the front of the cheeks were between the bars. The third blow to the neck was accompanied by the audible snap of a cervical vertebra.

Jonah went limp, the hands which had been wildly grabbing back over his shoulders falling to dangle at his sides.

Minnefield stepped back to study the limp form hanging against the front of the cell. Jonah's chin and lower face were wedged between the bars, his knees bent, toes pointed inward. A jaw muscle quivered, and there was the curious twitch of the left ear. The heart would beat for several more seconds.

The old man rolled off the bed to fall hard to the floor where he convulsed once before lying still. A thin whispy column of smoke rose from his open mouth.

Minnefield's face was flushed with excitement. His eyes darted back and forth between the two men, not wanting to miss anything.

CHAPTER

30

Jonah hung from the front of Vanderford's cell as if from a hangman's noose. The old man lay silent on the floor, smoke no longer coming from his mouth. No smoke had ever come from his ears. Anatomically speaking, Minnefield knew it couldn't, even though characters in the newspaper comic strips he studied each day were often shown with smoke boiling from their ears as well as their mouth. But knowing better didn't keep him from sneaking a glance from time to time as he hurriedly smeared his face and hands with the crushed black chalk. He would like to have seen smoke coming from the ears.

He already wore the orderly's uniform, the corpse's dignity now preserved by only an undershirt and jockey shorts, plus the socks Minnefield decided against wearing. Athlete's foot fungus was highly contagious.

With no mirror to guide him, Minnefield had left a round white spot about the size of a dime on his upper right cheek despite patiently rubbing the chalk a full two times over each part of his face. Though it was overly snug, he buttoned the collar of the uniform shirt, a dress code Alan strictly enforced. The sleeves were turned back—one precise roll.

The can of mace retrieved and properly snapped to his belt, Minnefield carried the orderly's billy club in his hand as he moved from his cell. He particularly liked the weapon. It had been bored longitudinally with lead poured inside. He slapped his palm heavily with it as he moved down the staircase toward the second floor.

The fat white orderly was seated at his desk on the second floor, only a few feet from the stairwell. Leaned back in his seat, his feet propped up on a desk strewn with sandwich wrappers and empty cigarette packs, he was reading a newspaper. The old floor-lamp, its light across his right shoulder, made him nearly blind to anyone approaching from the stairwell. Minnefield started toward him.

"That didn't take long," the orderly said. "What did you do to jack him up?" Then, noticing the white spot on his friend's cheek, he squinted his eyes against the light.

"Jonah, you've got something on your . . . MY GOD!"

He tried to jerk his feet off the desk and stand, the newspaper spilling across his lap, his hand grabbing at the mace on his belt, but the whole effort tilted his chair backward. Swung in a flat arch the billy club slammed into his chest, turning him upside down on the concrete floor.

Five minutes later the trembling orderly stood at the door leading from the first-floor cell block into the front office. An even six foot, and heavy enough to have been told at his last physical to lose twenty pounds, his body nearly completely hid the shorter man standing behind him and slightly off to his side. All the guard who peered through the peephole from the office could see was the orderly named Gene, and part of the cheek and ear of Jonah standing behind him. He didn't notice the white spot on Jonah's cheek, and it probably wouldn't have alerted him if he had. He turned away from the peephole and nodded to the black security officer sitting at the desk. At the nod, the officer raised from his chair and reached back up over his shoulder to push the button releasing the door's electronic lock.

At the buzz and metal clank of the sliding bolt, Minnefield swung the billy club hard into the back of Gene's neck, nudging the orderly off to the side as he fell. Minnefield's narrowed eyes were then at the small square window.

The black officer at the desk turned back around to resume thumbing through his copy of *Playboy*. The lanky white guard who had looked through the peephole stopped with his back to the door, lighting a cigarette.

Minnefield pushed open the door and strode inside, slamming the billy club into the back of the man nearest the door. At the *thump,* the black officer looked over the top of the magazine, then lurched wide-eyed to his feet as Minnefield moved past the crumpling body of the first guard toward him.

A shot of mace into the black's face and the man was blinded, his thumb fumbling as it tried to release the safety loop of his holstered revolver. The billy club then caught him in the throat, knocking him backwards and sideways into the wall. A second swing caught him on the side of the face and his knees buckled, his body sliding slowly down the wall.

The white guard was on his hands and knees in the middle of the room. Shaking his head, he raised his face to stare up into Minnefield's eyes, then glanced toward the gunbelt and revolver lying on the top of the desk next to the television monitors.

Minnefield clasped the billy club in both hands, raising it high over his head. With three rapid blows he quickly beat the guard to death.

Minnefield returned his attention to the black officer.

The man was on his knees moaning, reaching out blindly, then finding the desk, he started to lift himself up.

Bored, Minnefield swung the billy club hard into the man's forehead, the force of the blow driving his head back into the wall again. Once more the officer slid down the wall, this time his eyes rolled back in his head.

Minnefield was breathing heavily, in much worse physical condition than he would have imagined. Without turning his head, he rotated his eyes to the left, then to the right, locking on the door back into the cell block. He walked that way and disappeared inside, closing the door behind him. The sound of Gene moaning something could be heard through the door, then a thump of billy club into flesh, then several more thumps.

There was a long silence, followed by the sound of the billy club clattering to the floor and rolling across the hall.

Minnefield, face flushed and still panting, opened the door and walked back into the office.

Stepping over the body of the guard lying in the center of the room with a "Pardon me," he moved to the bathroom door in the corner of the office. Inside it he rested his hands on the edge of the wash basin for a moment, then turned on the faucet and began washing his face, cooling his feverishness at the same time as he removed the black stain.

When he emerged from the bathroom he was a new man, refreshed and with a pleasant smile on his face.

"Pardon me," he repeated as he knelt and started unbuttoning the shirt of the guard lying in the middle of the office.

In a few minutes he was completely dressed in the guard's uniform, and stood admiring his new look in the bathroom mirror. The uniform fit relatively well, except that his massive hairy forearms prevented him from buttoning the cuffs. He decided to wear them as had been Jonah's fashion and turned them back one precise roll.

Not looking at the bodies crumpled on the floor, he moved out of the bathroom to take a seat behind the desk next to the bank of television monitors.

CHAPTER

31

Richards arrived at the hospital's main entrance gate at twelve fifty-four. The lone security guard was retrieving a visitor's pass from an outgoing vehicle. He looked across his shoulder and, recognizing Richards, smiled and waved him on into the complex. At the brief squeal of rubber, the guard glanced back again.

Just past the administration building Richards had to slow his Cadillac, edging it past a group of men shooting craps against the street's curb. It was the after-lunch recreation hour for the general-population patients. He tapped his fingers nervously at the top of the steering wheel as he had to slow again, steering around a resident standing in the middle of the street.

Off to the side, over on the buckling and cracked

sidewalk, an old woman no taller than five feet and nearly as wide held her arms lifted toward the sky, crying uncontrollably.

At the maximum-security unit, the electrically controlled gates to the dual fences opened as he approached them. He gave a last glance to the barred window on the third floor and started forward.

The main door to the building opened as he approached it, and he moved inside without having to announce himself. The flood lamp above the remote television camera in the short hall was blinding, and he lowered his eyes until he heard the bolt release on the outer office door. He stepped forward into the office.

My God!

Minnefield sat leaned back in the chair at the far desk, pistol holster and ammunition belt draped across his lap. He was smiling. The Smith & Wesson revolver he held in his hand was loosely pointed at Richards.

"You're punctual," Minnefield said softly. "That is in your favor." He gestured with the revolver for Richards to move on into the room.

Then Richards saw the two bodies. Sitting propped against the wall between the desks, they stared blankly across the room. Horror mixed with his fear, then anger.

One of the guard's faces was so mutilated as to be featureless. The forehead of the other was split across the hairline, two other blood-matted wounds on top of his head.

Minnefield gestured again with the revolver. "Please, Brandon. You should not test my patience."

Richards pushed the door shut and stepped to the middle of the room.

"As I'm sure you have gathered," Minnefield said,

"I have made a decision to depart this institution. That is the purpose for requesting your presence at one o'clock. I thought your Cadillac would be properly comfortable for the initial stage of my journey, and I needed a driver the guards at the main entrance were accustomed to seeing come and go, particularly a driver with intelligence." He looked down at the bodies. "I shudder to think what the results of an IQ test would reveal about those two." He raised his face again. "One of them might very well have been so bereft of reasoning ability as to try and foil my attempt at leaving, had I honored him as my driver.

"You on the other hand are obviously quite intelligent. I am sure you have already assessed the situation, realized that it would be fatal not to do as I say— and that I am likely to make it through the gate in any case.

"Finally, I realized it would be especially desirable to have a driver with his own personal reason for hoping that I made it safely through the gate. You, of course, have such a motive. If I am successful in exiting this place without a disturbance, then I will reveal to you who your daughter's killer is. You do still wish to know, don't you?"

Richards raised his gaze from the bodies to Minnefield's eyes, but said nothing.

Minnefield smiled. Reaching into his lap he unsnapped a leather pouch on the ammunition belt, removed a pair of handcuffs, and held them up. "Here," he said, and pitched them toward Richards, who didn't extend his hands quick enough. The cuffs clanged to the concrete floor.

Richards looked down at the cuffs, bent slowly, and retrieved them.

"Try again," Minnefield said, pitching a key. Richards managed to catch it, then raised his face back to Minnefield's.

"Attach the cuffs to one of your wrists, then string the links through the handle of that top drawer and attach your other wrist." He pointed to a heavy legal-size filing cabinet sitting on the side of the room opposite the desks.

As Richards did as he was told, Minnefield rose, walking around the desk to hold out his hand. "Please."

Richards handed him the key.

"Thank you. Now all that is left is to wait for my host to return. I wouldn't want to depart without bidding him good-bye. Then we'll be on our way." He glanced at the guard's watch he now wore on his wrist. Wetting a thumb, he rubbed the red stain from the crystal and looked again. "About nineteen minutes. Alan is always punctual."

Richards glanced into the hate-filled eyes, a swirling mixture of impending horror, anger, and helpless frustration twisting his stomach.

Long minutes passed, the only sound the ticking of the round clock hanging on the wall above the silent, staring bodies. At one twenty-eight, Minnefield moved to the bank of television monitors. A minute later a broad smile spread across his face.

Richards was unable to see the monitor screens from where he stood, but he knew what they displayed.

Minnefield reached to the control panel in the wall and pushed a button. Glancing back at the monitors, he pushed another button, waited a minute, and pushed a third. Then he hurried to the door leading to the short entrance hallway and disappeared through it.

Richards pushed the drawer-release button.

Locked! He quickly glanced around the room. The black officer still wore his gun belt, the butt of a revolver protruding from its holster. Richards yanked at the handcuffs.

The drawer handle was steel, attached solidly, two bolts to each of its sides. He yanked again, trying to twist the handle with his hands. He stepped back and attempted to drag the cabinet with him. Its weight was enormous. He strained, desperately pulling. It wouldn't budge.

Taking a deep breath, he lunged backward as hard as he could. The cabinet tilted slightly, then steadied again. He looked at his bleeding wrists.

Taking another deep breath, he lunged again. It tilted, stopped—he pulled frantically. It toppled over, yanking him downward as it crashed to the concrete floor.

Pain shot through his wrists. His hands, unseen under the bulky cabinet, felt like they were caught in a vise. A drop of perspiration rolled off his nose.

Leaning backward, he shut his eyes, and ignoring the excruciating pain, pulled hard. The cabinet slid forward. He pulled again. It slid another six inches. His eyes were stinging from the salty sweat running down his brow; his shirt was wet now. Trying to dig his heels into the concrete floor, he lunged backward again.

Minnefield walked through the door, pushing the grim-faced Alan ahead of him.

"Brandon. Brandon," Minnefield said, shaking his head. "What am I going to do with you?"

Richards slumped back on the floor, shutting his eyes.

"Help him up, Alan. . . . Now!"

After Richards was on his feet, Minnefield removed the cuffs, having Richards in turn lock one of them on

Alan's wrist, the empty cuff left dangling. Then he ordered them into the cell block.

Once inside, he locked Alan to the front of an empty cell by snapping the free cuff to the cell's bars.

"Have you met Ronnie?" Minnefield then asked, smiling at Richards. He gestured with the revolver and walked two cells down from Alan. Richards followed. Two enormous meaty hands came from the dark to clasp the bars, and even Minnefield stood back.

"He doesn't like anybody intruding on his territory," Minnefield observed. "Ronnie, a rather innocuous name for this. You talk about insane—that's one thing—but what you're witnessing here is crazy, pure crazy. Absolutely no sense, a base animal according to the psychiatrists, but that's not description enough. An animal only kills for a purpose, is responsive to pain, can be trained, can at least learn rudimentary skills. Ronnie has none of those attributes. He has been here since he was fourteen years old. I have been told he was just your run-of-the-mill, totally deranged, vicious child. Then something snapped.

"He not only dispatched his parents, he included the dog, cat, a particularly handsome and rare parrot, crushing it with the bars of its own cage—he didn't understand how to open the cage—then went into a neighbor's pasture and killed thirteen cattle before the police arrived."

The hands never moved, no sound came from the shadowy figure. "He is my going-away present to Alan," Minnefield continued, "for all he has done for me since I have been his guest here." He reached to his belt for the key ring.

A wave of revulsion swept Richards. His throbbing hands tightened into fists at his sides. He shook his head back and forth, imperceptibly at first, then strongly.

"NO!"

A long silence passed, Richards bereft of the courage needed to raise his eyes and see what expression his exclamation had brought.

"That is your decision," Minnefield finally said, his voice soft, his tone conciliatory. "I will accept that by your presence here you have done your part and I am in your debt. But only once must I repay you. The name of your daughter's killer or Ronnie not released from his cell—it's your choice, but only one or the other."

Richards raised his face to stare into the cold, mocking eyes staring back into his.

After a long moment, Minnefield's eyes slitted and he spoke again. "You wish then for me to make the decision? I understand, Brandon. You have to know who your daughter's killer is. It's more important than anything else, any moral values you thought you held. I'll make the decision for you and then you'll bear no guilt. As you wish."

"No!"

Minnefield smiled. "No, because you don't wish to have Alan meet an early end in exchange for a simple name? Or no, because you're afraid if I make the decision I will choose to leave Ronnie caged and then you will never know who your daughter's killer is? Which is it?"

Richards slowly shook his head. Minnefield was serious. He really thought he had offered a choice. He was beyond insanity. "If you don't hurt Alan, I'll do anything you say."

"Admirable in a broad moral sense, but such a decision doesn't speak well of your family ties. Were it my child who had been murdered I would not hesitate in opting for the killer's name."

"Leave him alone. That's what I want."

"If that is your wish, I have no real objection. I am an easy man to get along with." He gestured with the revolver toward the office door.

At the outer door to the maximum-security building, Minnefield paused a moment and stared into Richards's eyes. "You are not intelligent enough to dupe me. Think of your own life, and also what will happen if I am forced back in here with Alan again. Perform especially well in carrying me safely through the entrance gate and I might, in my gratitude, decide once again to reveal the name of your daughter's killer."

Passing through the inner-security fence, Minnefield told Richards to close the gate. Richards stared back.

A little smile came to Minnefield's face. "I turned the electricity off." He laughed. "Have faith in me, Brandon."

After they passed through the outer gate, Minnefield shut it himself, then followed Richards to where the Cadillac was parked. There he opened the door on the driver's side and stepped into the automobile first, motioning with the Smith & Wesson for Richards to follow. Richards slid behind the steering wheel.

As he was about to turn the car on, he spied movement out of the corner of his left eye. The sheriff's Lincoln was pulling into the parking space next to the Cadillac. Tidmore lowered the Lincoln's passenger window, then leaned across the seat to speak. "I couldn't wait any longer. I was wondering how it . . ." His eyes focused past Richards to the figure sitting on the far side of the Cadillac.

"Leave, now!" Minnefield said to Richards.

Tidmore ducked low back to the driver's side of the Lincoln, yanked the twelve-gauge from its rack between the seats and scrambled out the door, moving to crouch behind the hood.

"COME OUT OF THERE!" he yelled.

"Leave, now!" Minnefield repeated, and Richards felt the cold barrel of the Smith & Wesson press against his temple. He reached forward and turned the ignition key. Minnefield chuckled.

At the sound of the Cadillac's motor, Tidmore snaked the barrel of the shotgun across the hood. Richards stared into the black hole of the muzzle.

"COME OUT OF THERE NOW, MARCUS, OR I'LL SHOOT!"

The revolver pressed harder. For a brief moment, Richards thought of making an attempt to grab the barrel. Then he reached for the gearshift and pulled it into reverse, pressing his foot against the accelerator.

The shotgun bucked in Tidmore's hands, the muzzle flash first clear then blurred as the Cadillac's windshield dissolved in a shower of fragmented glass, and the Smith & Wesson fired. Richards, pressed over against the door, deafened from the revolver blast, slapped a hand to the great pain in the side of his head. No blood, but a ruptured eardrum—the revolver had fired wildly. His eyes darted to the passenger seat. Minnefield, his face a mass of bright red blood and shredded flesh, lay slumped back against the seat. Clasped in a limp hand, the revolver lay in his lap, a wisp of smoke trailing up from its barrel. The hand tightened, starting to lift. Richards's eyes jumped to the gore that had been a face, saw an eye pop open, dart, and begin to rotate toward the driver's side. Richards yanked at the door handle, threw himself sideways out of the still-backing Cadillac. Slamming to the pavement, the side of his head hit the blacktop hard. He saw a flash of light, then tiny dots of light, darting fireflies, the dots fading, then black. . . .

CHAPTER

32

Wheeled on a stretcher from the emergency room into the flashing bulbs of the photographers, Richards self-consciously moved his fingers to touch the stitches on his forehead and across his cheek.

He felt stupid.

He had tried to talk the doctor into at least allowing him to sit in a wheelchair. He wasn't injured that badly.

He saw Flora's face among the smiles grinning down from each side of the hall. Her widened eyes made him wonder if he looked even worse than he thought. He smiled back at her and she dropped the hand that had been nervously covering her mouth.

Then he heard the familiar voice: "In another bizarre turn of events, Brandon Richards, father of the slain Judith Salter, and a man who only yesterday was arrested . . ."

A police officer was standing at the hospital-room door and when Richards was wheeled inside everyone was left behind, except Flora.

She bent to help the two orderlies and nurse slide him off the stretcher onto the fresh-smelling sheets of the bed. Then the orderlies left, the nurse tarrying only long enough to check his blood pressure and take his pulse. After the nurse's departure, Flora bent and kissed him on the forehead.

"I'm ready to go back home now," he said.

Flora smiled and nodded, and her gaze kept darting all over his face.

"You're going to make me nervous if you keep staring like that."

She moved her eyes away, awkwardly, glancing back one more time after she did.

He smiled and patted the bed and she sat beside him, reaching out to take hold of his scraped hands with her manicured ones. She held gently.

He glanced toward the door. "Wonder what they'd do if I left now?"

"Oh, you can't," she said. "They have to keep you under observation."

"The doctor probably wants me here for the publicity. He let the damn reporters in the emergency room, spent more time talking to them than stitching." He started to shake his head, but stopped at the swirling dizziness, and then raised a hand to the throbbing.

"Baby, you have a concussion."

"Anybody who's been knocked out has a concussion, honey. In a little while I'm going home." He saw her lips draw tight and the determined shaking of her head, but he didn't feel like teasing anymore—the faces of the two guards in the outer office of the maxi-mum-security building had flashed through his mind. He then remembered the other one lying in the hall-way inside the building. A wave of nausea swept his body. He didn't know if it came from the throbbing in his head or from his revulsion at recalling the scene. He tried to relax. The bed was comfortable, the pillow cool and soft around the back of his head. He shut his eyes.

Almost immediately he was dreaming. He knew he was, but couldn't wake up, though he wanted to—the dream quickly becoming a nightmare. He squirmed, tried to force his eyes open.

"Aiieeee!" he screamed, and sat upright in the bed. "Brandon!"

His head jerked toward Flora's frightened shout, dizziness sweeping over him at the movement.

"What is it?" she asked, her voice only slightly lower.

"Jesus!" he exclaimed in relief, his muscles relaxing as he became fully awake and realized where he was.

"Baby, what is it?" Her face was flushed with her increased heartbeat.

"It's okay, honey." He held his hand out to hers as he lay back. Taking a deep breath, he let it out slowly. "A nightmare, honey, that's all. I had a nightmare."

The police officer standing in the doorway shook his head and shut the door.

Flora glanced toward the closing of the door and then back to him. "You scared me," she said. She touched the side of his neck with the back of her hand. "You're all covered in sweat."

He was. He wiped at the wetness on his forehead with the back of a bandaged wrist.

He looked up at her. "I was following Judith's killer through a jungle. I didn't know who he was, but I knew it was the killer. I had a rifle and was going to kill him. But everytime I started to, he went around a corner behind some bushes and I'd have to run after him. God, that went on forever. Then suddenly there was no jungle, he was standing there facing me. It was Martin. When I started to pull the trigger he became Judith's neighbor, and then he was Eddie Hopper. I knew I had to shoot him before the jungle came back and he could hide again. Then I heard this horrible shrill laughter behind me. Something grabbed me around the waist and yanked me up in the air. There was this terrible pain. That was the most realistic part of the dream." He glanced down toward his stomach, ran a hand across it. The headache was growing worse.

Flora patted at his forehead with a folded washcloth from the bedside table.

"Some kind of giant claw was digging into my stomach. And then I saw Judith in her bed screaming, something huge and fuzzy on top of her, digging at her with the same kind of three-toed claw, like a giant bird's talon. It kept digging into her and she kept screaming for me to help her."

He felt his hands tremble, and gripped them into fists. His head swirled again and he moved his hand to his forehead. The dampness was increasing. He was growing nauseated.

"You're turning pale, baby. Just rest, please."

He shut his eyes, careful not to let himself fall asleep again. He then heard the door opening.

It was Winstead. He was dressed in the same too-tight polyester suit in which Richards had first seen him. The smile on his face was tilted toward the bulge of tobacco in his cheek.

"Hey, Brandon. How do you feel?"

Richard didn't risk trying to sit. "Headache and

some scratches . . . No, I feel like crap. Pavement knocked the hell out of me, didn't it?"

"Raymond said you were out until the ambulance got there, and went out again when they were loading you. Almost to the hospital before you come to for good."

"I still can't believe he shot."

"Best chance you had. Let Minnefield carry you off and you got no chance. Besides, he knew what he was doing, knew from that distance the pattern wouldn't spread enough to get you."

Richards shook his head and looked at Flora.

"Honest," Winstead said. "Raymond's an expert when it comes to firearms; you've seen the hunting trophies at his house. He's won every police shoot-off ever been held in this state. Only thing, he didn't figure the glass cutting you up—couldn't be helped though. What'd you go jump out of the car for, anyway? That's what like to killed you."

Richards smiled a little. "If you had a bloody head turn to look at you and it still had a gun in its hand, what would you do?"

"That was just some kind of reflex."

Richards started to shake his head again, then stopped. The dizziness was increasing.

Winstead's face took on a serious look. "Raymond's worried you might do something foolish if we break the case and you find out who the killer is. Asked me to come by and talk to you, make sure you were going to act right."

Richards smiled and would have laughed if he hadn't feared the consequences. "Break the case? I don't know which is the funniest, you talking about breaking the case with Minnefield dead, or Raymond sending John Winstead to tell me to act right."

The detective didn't smile. "I know what I'm doing,

you don't. I'm not gonna leave myself open. Well, I did what Raymond asked me to do. I talked to you!"

"I'll tell him you were convincing."

The big detective was silent a moment, looking past Richards and staring into the wall, then he moved his eyes back to the bed.

"Why didn't you ask me if I'd been dating your daughter? That's all you had to do, just ask."

Richards ran his tongue over his lips and shook his head slightly. "Sorry. I wasn't sure what to do."

"Raymond said to tell you those dates you got from my wife matched with the times your witnesses said I was at your daughter's."

"Good. I'm glad."

Flora dabbed the washcloth one last time at his forehead and then edged off the bed, moving from between the two men, glancing back at Winstead as she walked to the side of the room.

"Letting Minnefield use me to set up his escape screwed everything up royally, didn't it?"

Winstead picked the plug from inside his cheek and deposited it in the waste can sitting next to the bedside table. "Way I got it figured, Brandon, he hadn't really seen nothing. The break in that bolt was an old one. My bet is he would'a been takin' off soon anyway. Your daughter being murdered and you and Raymond coming by just gave him the idea about using you for a ride outta the place. Made up what he saw. You hadn't come by he would'a split anyway."

"He saw something, J.J. Had to. He knew too much."

The detective shrugged. "Makes no difference no how now." His brow furrowed. "They told you anything about maybe his son being in the area?"

"Huh?"

"Highway patrolman stopped a guy speedin' about

ten miles from the hospital. Happened about an hour before Minnefield tried to break out. Patrolman came by the hospital after the shooting, saw a picture of Minnefield one of the reporters had. Swore the guy he stopped was a spittin' image, only younger. Minnefield has a son. Was involved in that cult shit down in Mexico. Nobody's seen him since. Maybe nothin', but that's why you got a cop on duty outside the door. If it was him, he's probably out of the area by now, but Raymond didn't want to take any chances."

"Brandon," Flora said, "I brought my semiautomatic. It's in your glove compartment—I didn't know whether the hospital would have a metal detector or not. Want me to go after it?"

Winstead smiled at Flora. "Nobody's gonna bother your boyfriend here." He looked back to Richards. "But I'd keep the gun close the first few weeks you're back in New Orleans, just in case. You are headin' back now, aren't you?"

Richards nodded slowly. "Yeah, nothing left here for me to do. I'll go back and hope you or Raymond come up with something. J.J., there's a nurse out at the hospital named Atlene Johnson. Go by and see her. Tell her I said you're okay. She thinks a cop, or at least someone in police work, might have killed Judith. Maybe you'll think of something to ask her I didn't. She also believes Graff might have been outside of R-14 for a while. He's the guy they found hiding in the attic. He believes he saw Hopper killed." He smiled wryly. "Said a monster tore Hopper's head off."

"I'll talk to her. Anything else you been holding back?"

"I'm sorry. I promised Atlene. I had to be sure about you, J.J., especially when I thought you'd been dating Judith."

The big detective's features relaxed. "Don't worry 'bout it. What I'd done myself in the same situation. Well, guess I'll be runnin'. Kathy and I are gonna spend the night at Raymond's. Little fishing tomorrow will help take the edge off, always does. You head on back to New Orleans and relax yourself. Come Monday Raymond and I will be back on the case hot and heavy."

He fumbled in the pockets of his coat, producing a cash gas ticket and a pen, turning the ticket over and writing on the back of it.

"My other home number," he said. "It's unlisted. We leave the one in the phone book off the hook when we don't feel like being bothered. Call me anytime you got something on your mind."

CHAPTER

33

A glorious dawn painted the eastern horizon in bright colors. Leeanne Tidmore smiled as she glimpsed the scene from her kitchen window. Lifting the coffeepot from the stove, she carried it to the breakfast table and refilled Winstead's coffee cup. Her husband laid his hand over the top of his cup and shook his head.

"Anything else, John?" she asked.

"I might take just a bite more of those eggs," Winstead said, picking up his plate and holding it out to her.

Kathy Winstead, standing by the sink, shook her head and closed her eyes for a moment.

"Have you heard any more from the hospital?" Leeanne asked her husband.

The sheriff nodded. "While ago. He's okay, no problem. I talked to Flora. She said the doctor only knocked him out as a precaution. Knowing Brandon that's the only way they could get him to rest. Anyway, she said the CAT scans were okay and they told her they were going to take him off the sedative tonight. He'll probably be on his way back to New Orleans by tomorrow night, next day at the latest."

Winstead forked a lump of scrambled eggs into his mouth and spoke out of its side.

"He looked fine to me yesterday, maybe a little pale."

Leeanne nodded. "I hope so. It worried me when his headaches kept increasing."

Raymond pushed away from the table and stood. "Ready?"

Winstead forked the last three bites of eggs from his plate, then stood. "Mmmm . . ." He swallowed. "Just one more little sip of coffee."

Leeanne half-filled the cup, Winstead nodding his thanks as he reached back to the table for a biscuit. She smiled.

Kathy frowned.

"I guess you'll be out all day," Leeanne said, turning to kiss her husband on the cheek.

"Until they stop biting."

"We ought to be back from shopping around noon," she said.

Kathy looked at the two one hundred dollar bills her husband handed her and smiled. "Whose birthday is it?"

"Just wanted you to have a good time," Winstead said. "Brandon gave me a little bonus." He leaned forward and pressed his cheek to hers. "See ya."

"If you all are still fishing when we come back,"

Leeanne said, "Kathy and I'll throw together some sandwiches and we'll have a picnic on the bank."

"Sounds good," Raymond said. "J.J., you coming or not?"

With the closing of the backdoor behind the two men, Leeanne turned to Kathy. "Like a couple of kids. You ready?"

Kathy nodded.

After raising the garage door, Leeanne slid in behind her convertible's steering wheel and turned the ignition key.

Nothing happened.

Kathy glanced at the key. "Battery down?"

"I don't know." Leeanne tried the key again. "Usually hear something clicking when it's the battery."

"What do we do?"

"We'll take Raymond's car," Leeanne said, opening her door.

At the antique garage, Leeanne backed the Lincoln from its parking place, then waited while Winstead's wife lowered the garage door.

As Kathy slid into the front seat and shut the door, Leeanne said, "Sorry. Moisture control." She laughed. "Raymond has a fit if anybody leaves the door up. He even has a dehumidifier for when he thinks the humidity's too high." She glanced through the tinted windshield up into the sky. "Which is most of the time, lately. Looks like a new front is moving in." She shook her head and pulled the gearshift into forward.

Tidmore braced himself from where he sat at the bow of the aluminum fishing boat. Winstead gave a final shove, then hopped into the back of the boat as it glided out into the still water of the lake. Lowering the trolling motor he flicked its switch on. The silent swirling propellers strained to break the boat's inertia for a moment, and then propelled the craft toward the clump of willow trees on the far bank.

Whooom!

Winstead's head turned toward the sound.

Tidmore's forehead wrinkled as he also looked that way.

Several seconds of silence passed, and then they saw the column of oily black smoke rising above the pine trees.

CHAPTER

34

Richards stirred and opened his eyes.

"Baby," Flora asked, "how do you feel?"

"Fine." He looked over her shoulder to the dark outside the window. "What time is it?"

"Almost ten."

"I slept all afternoon?"

"Remember the headaches you were having?"

He did. He nodded.

"The doctors were worried about swelling. They put you on a drip to control it. Put a sedative in it to make you rest. That was yesterday afternoon, right after John left."

He moved his head, slowly at first, and then more rapidly. Feeling no pain or dizziness, he sat upright in the bed. "Been nice if they'd asked my permission."

"They did."

He moved his head from side to side again. "It worked. I'm hungry."

"They said you could have anything you wanted."

"How do you summon room service?"

"What about me going down to the cafeteria and selecting some of the things I know you like?"

"Great. Has Raymond or J.J. called?"

He noticed her expression. He had already noticed the subdued tone in which she had been speaking. "What is it?"

She shook her head, her lip trembling. She suddenly looked like she was going to cry. A chill swept over him.

"What, Flora?"

"It's terrible. There was an explosion out at the sheriff's . . . both their wives were killed."

"What?!"

He threw back his covers, swung his legs from under the bedsheet and came to his feet on the floor. A dizziness passed through him and he reached back to the mattress.

Flora stepped to him, reaching out to steady him as she looked into his eyes. "Baby, you have to stay in bed. The doctor said you needed twenty-four more hours, at least."

"Kathy and Leeanne. My, God! What . . . ? How did it happen?"

"There was a bomb in the Lincoln."

"A bomb? What in hell do you mean? What . . . who?"

She dropped her hands away from him to her side, shaking her head. "Martin planted a bomb in the sheriff's car. The women were going shopping. Their car wouldn't start and they were going to use the sheriff's."

"Martin? Why are you saying Martin?"

She shook her head, her eyes misting. "It was on the news. They found his fingerprints on something he touched when he put the bomb in the car. I think it said they were found in the garage."

He pushed himself away from the bed. "Where are Raymond and J.J.? I have to go there."

He moved toward the closet, shoving past Flora when she reached out to steady him.

At the door he paused a moment, shut his eyes, waiting until the dizziness subsided. Then he reached inside the closet, speaking back over his shoulder as he did.

"Call Raymond's office and find out where they are."

Everything hanging in the closet was clean, the clothes Flora had brought him. He grabbed a pair of slacks and a shirt. Removing the hospital gown, he hastily began dressing.

"Okay, just a minute," Flora said, moving her hand to cover the receiver's mouthpiece. "They said the sheriff went to the crime lab. They don't know where Winstead is."

"Find out the address."

He glanced briefly in the mirror hanging above the bedside table, brushing his hair back with his hands. The dizziness was almost completely gone now.

Driving through the city toward the lab, Richards glanced at Flora. "When did it . . . ?"

Her head was drooping.

She sat upright. "What . . . I'm sorry?"

"You want me to take you by the motel?"

"No," she said, shaking her head. "I'll be okay."

She was red-eyed and had circles under her eyes. He hadn't noticed until then. She had probably stayed awake all of the time he had been out. "I'm going to. I want you to rest. After I see Raymond and J.J., I'll come back to the room. I'm not going back to the hospital."

She nodded without saying anything more.

When Richards walked into the outer office of the crime lab a man in a Davis County deputy's uniform looked up, then walked toward him.

"Mr. Richards, I'm Jerry Tidmore, Raymond's brother."

"I just heard."

"Bastard was after Raymond."

"Is he inside?"

The man shook his head. "He left a half-hour ago, going back by the funeral home and then on to the farm."

"The doctors had me knocked out," Richards explained. "All I know is that they're saying Martin did it. They found his fingerprints."

"Two fingers and a partial palm. He's already dead, they just haven't thrown the switch yet."

Richards eyes narrowed. "What is J.J. doing?"

Jerry shook his head again. "Knowing him I'd thought he'd already have gone after Salter. But he went to pieces, much worse than Raymond. There's a couple of deputies with him—Raymond's idea. He thought like me, figured J.J. would go after Salter. But all he's done is sit and stare. Can't hardly get around by himself, his legs all rubbery and everything. It's killing him."

"And Raymond . . . ?"

"He's not in good shape, but he's taking it better than I would have figured."

"Where did they find the fingerprints? Flora said something about in the garage."

"He slipped in the garage and wired Raymond's Lincoln up. There was a small wrench lying just inside the garage. He must have dropped it down in the engine when he was working, couldn't find it or couldn't get to it. Probably didn't worry about it, knowing the amount of dynamite he packed in that car. It must have slipped out as Leeanne backed out."

"Are you positive about the fingerprints?"

"No doubt, both fingers and the palm had ten points."

"What does that mean?"

"Ten points makes it where even the FBI's satisfied, that's points of comparison. Each of the prints on the wrench had at least ten different places that compared exactly with Salter's. There're copies in the back. You want to see?"

Richards nodded.

"Come on."

Inside the laboratory a technician in a white lab coat was sitting at a desk, his feet propped up and eating a sandwich.

"Prints still on the counter?" Jerry asked.

The man nodded and Richards followed the sheriff's brother to the side of the room.

"See," Jerry said, picking a pencil from off the counter and pointing to the prints on the copies of the evidence cards. "This is the partial palm found on the wrench. This is a set of Martin's prints they made when he worked at the hospital. See here, it's exactly like this arch. See this swirl, just like this one." He kept moving the pencil back and forth. "Here like here. Here and here, and so on. Each place is a point of comparison."

Richards nodded.

"Ten points is really overkill. You know who it is with less than that. But ten satisfies everybody."

"Where's Martin now?"

"In jail in Gulf County. He was here in the city for the psychiatric convention last night. That's when he must've wired the Lincoln, sometime during the night. His attorneys are already fighting bringing him back here. They say his life would be in danger in a Davis County jail. No way he's gonna not come though; just take a couple of days to do the paperwork. And no way he's gonna beat this one. Gulf County Sheriff's department already seized his toolbox right out of his own workshop. Had a full set of everything in it except for one missing wrench, exact same size and same manufacturer as the one in Raymond's garage."

Richards's brow wrinkled with thought. "You said you can match up a couple of prints without ten points. How few can there be and you still know?"

"It varies according to where the points of comparison are, and, of course, what the technician who's going to testify is willing to go with. I've seen prints with three or four points that I knew were from the same person, but seven is about as few as a court's going to allow."

"Jerry, there were some footprints in Judith's bathroom. Raymond said they were too smudged to use. Could he have meant that there were some lines that could be compared, but not enough to go to trial with?"

"I don't know." He glanced toward the man eating at the desk. "Fred. You know anything about any footprints that were lifted out of the bathroom in the Salter case?"

"The ones of the victim were the only ones turned out. The bigger ones weren't any good. All smudged."

"Any lines at all you might could compare?"

"Prints were pretty well smudged. I really don't remember. Might've been a couple places you could guess at. Really don't remember."

"They been disposed of?"

Richards's brow furrowed.

"Raymond released them for disposal," Fred said. "Should've been thrown out already, but they were still around here a couple of days ago. I can check if you want, but you're not going to be able to tell anything."

Jerry looked at Richards.

"I'd like to see them anyway," Richards said.

Jerry turned back to the technician. "Fred, you mind seeing if you can rustle 'em up?"

The technician struggled upright in his chair and stood, flipping his sandwich wrapper in the waste can, then wiped his mouth with the corner of his lab coat. "Over here." He walked toward a door at the back of the lab. "At least I think they're in here."

Inside of what resembled a large walk-in closet, Fred scanned the evidence folders filling the shelves.

"Here they are," he said, reaching for a plastic envelope lying on the top shelf. "Should've been thrown out, we're running out of space."

Walking to one of the laboratory counters, he switched on an overhead lamp. Removing the prints from the plastic, he spread them on the counter and studied them for a moment.

"Yeah," he said. "I remember these now. There were some prints around the tub, all smudged, looked like they'd been wiped up. Then there were these two over by the sink. They hadn't been wiped at, but they were too smudged to use." He looked back down at the prints. "No, not even something you could risk an opinion on."

Richards's heart was knocking.

The prints were of a right and left foot. The left

foot, made when the killer stepped forward on the ball of his foot, showed nothing of the heel, just the partial print from the ball forward. In front of the ball, the big toe and the two outside toes were outlined perfectly, if smudged. The two toes in between the big toe and the others were missing. Richards reached down and placed his forefinger in the gap left by the missing toes. He looked into the laboratory technician's eyes.

"The way the guy stepped," Fred explained, "didn't have enough pressure for all the foot to show. See where the heel is missing? Same thing with the two toes. Just not enough pressure to leave a print."

Richards shook his head. "Not twice. He didn't step the same exact way twice. There's a sock print in the bedroom, the same two toes missing, and on the same foot. The killer only has three toes on his left foot."

CHAPTER

35

The exterior fixtures at the front of the Tidmore home were on, bathing the portico and its columns in bright light. The inside of the home was dark, no light to be seen through any of the windows, and there were no vehicles present.

Richards drove his Cadillac up the left side of the entrance way, not turning into the circular drive but proceeding on to the side. The Lincoln had already been towed away, but he saw the large charred circle where the explosion had occurred, and stopped.

Leaving the Cadillac's lights burning, he stepped out and moved around to its front.

The concrete was covered with soot, and cracked, the grass nearest each side of the drive shriveled and brown. With the wind increasing in advance of the new storm front moving up from the Gulf Coast, he at first thought the object skipping across the blackened concrete was a leaf, but then saw it wasn't. He reached down and took it in his hand. It was the charred half of a hundred-dollar bill. He stared at it a moment then let it flutter back to the pavement.

Glancing toward the house he saw where sections of cardboard had been inserted in the second-story windows in place of the blown-out panes.

Shaking his head, he walked back to the side of the Cadillac and reached through the window, extinguishing its lights, then walked to the front of the home and rang the doorbell.

Waiting a moment, he pushed the doorbell button once more, then stepped back and looked through the windows. He turned and walked around the side of the home toward the antique garage.

Its door was lowered and locked, so he walked around to the office entrance. That door was unlocked and he pushed it open and entered, turning on the lights and walking to the door connecting with the back of the garage.

Pausing there a moment, he looked at the faint traces of blue powder left when the investigators had dusted the knob and the sides of the door. He was beginning to hate blue powder.

Inside the garage everything was showroom immaculate; the 1939 Ford and the MG were sitting where he had last seen them, an empty spot indicated where the Lincoln should have been.

Standing in the eerie quiet, the bright lights reflecting off the polished surface of the antique automobiles, he was somehow reminded of a tomb. He lingered only a moment before turning and walking outside into the fresh air.

He looked at the moon. The clouds racing north on the winds were growing thicker, mottling the sky—just like the night Judith was murdered.

Lowering his gaze he noticed a light come on inside the first floor of the home. Its glow shown through the French doors of the family room and across the glassed-in exercise room extending from the back of the house. He glimpsed a figure at the glass door between the two rooms, and then the light went out again.

Walking to the house, he moved up the two steps to the exercise room's darkened entrance. Running his hand alongside the door frame, feeling for the doorbell buzzer, he noticed the flickering blue light inside. It was from a television set. He couldn't hear any sound.

Out of the corner of his eye he glimpsed movement in the center of the room—in the hot tub. A figure painted pale blue by the television's glow and another darker figure moved together at the back of the tub.

He backed down a step and as he did the larger figure suddenly sprang from the tub and lunged toward the door.

He was bathed in bright white light as the porch light came on.

"What in the hell . . . ?" a voice boomed.

The sheriff's form loomed large before him, wearing dripping swimming trunks.

"Brandon . . ."

"I rang the front doorbell," Richards said apologetically. "Didn't mean to startle you. I saw the light." His eyes were drawn past Tidmore's shoulder by the movement of the figure climbing from the tub.

Bathed in a mixture of the television's muted glow and the brighter light from the porch, dressed in the barest bikini, was Ruby, the Tidmore's maid.

He looked back to the sheriff.

Tidmore unlatched the screen door with a flick of his finger and turned away, speaking over his shoulder as he walked to the tub. "Come on in."

Richards hesitated a moment, then pushed the screen door open and stepped inside, avoiding eye contact with the brown-skinned woman who continued to stand staring at him.

The sheriff turned to the woman. "I'll see you in the morning, Ruby," he said.

She stooped and gathered a blouse and a pair of shorts from the floor, then moved with quick short steps through the sliding glass door to the family room, Richards's gaze following her.

"Catch the lights," the sheriff said, nodding toward the switchbox next to the back door, then turned and moved toward the television set, reaching down to switch it off.

The room went dark.

"The lights, Brandon!"

Richards stepped to the back door, fumbling for a moment before his fingers found the wall switch, then turned on the room's overhead lights.

The sheriff moved back across the room and stepped down into the tub, leaning back against its side. "Have a seat," he said. "Want a drink?" His tone was now normal, and not at all self-conscious.

Richards glanced toward the door to the family room and then shook his head. "No, thank you."

"I believe I do," Tidmore rose and stepped back out of the tub.

"Raymond, I'm sorry to have busted in on you like this. I just wanted you to know that I came as soon as I heard what happened. I didn't come earlier because the doctors had me knocked out."

"I heard. Glad you're doing better, and I appreciate

your coming by. Sit down." He absent-mindedly massaged his left thigh.

"No, I can't." Richards looked theatrically at his watch. "I have to go on back to the motel. Flora's waiting."

"Well, I certainly wish you'd stay awhile. But I appreciate you coming out anyway." The sheriff flexed his leg, then moved on toward the bar.

"One thing, Raymond. I went by the lab earlier."

"Uh-huh?"

And then Richards saw the trail of wet footprints the sheriff was leaving behind as he walked away from the tub. The prints made by the left foot were three toed.

"You sure you won't have one for the road?"

Richards raised his eyes from the prints to the sheriff. Tidmore dropped his gaze to where Richards had been staring, and then back up into Richards's eyes. He then turned and continued on toward the wet bar.

Richards glanced down again. The continuing prints were all five toed, including those now made by the left foot.

Richards realized the defect could be controlled with a conscious thought, the two arched and drawn toes exerting as much pressure as the others when a mental order was directed to them to do so. With more pressing thoughts flooding the mind, though, the effort was forgotten. An unthinking casual walk to the bar, and no control was present . . . or during a frenzied murderous attack!

"Brandon."

Tidmore was standing behind the bar, a smile on his face. Richards felt a chill settle over him. He glanced at the door.

"Brandon, I asked you whether you were sure you didn't want one for the road?"

Richards shook his head. He had to struggle against the urge to run. His stare had been noticed, but had his thoughts been understood, or dismissed as mere curiosity?

The sheriff placed an empty glass on the bar top and, his smile growing wider, his eyes remaining focused on Richards, reached down toward a lower shelf.

Richards lunged at the screen door, knocked it open, and hurdled down the steps, racing toward the Cadillac.

CHAPTER

36

Dashing wildly from the exercise room, Richards realized the hundred feet to the Cadillac was too far—the sheriff had only to cover the fifteen feet to the door and then down the steps to have a clear shot.

He swerved to the right and ran in among the heart-shaped shrubs surrounding the swimming pool, glancing back to see Tidmore emerging from the exercise room.

"Brandon!"

Richards stumbled and fell, feeling the stitches under his bandaged wrists pull loose as he skidded along the ground. Then he was scrambling to his feet and running out the end of the shrubbery surrounding the pool and across the twenty feet to a wooded area, diving headlong into a tangle of honeysuckle vines.

Tumbling, rolling, he sprang to his feet once again, tearing loose from the matted vines, ripping his trouser legs on the thorns intermingled with the vines. He dashed deeper into the woods—no shot yet fired at him.

Stopping to lean back against a thick-trunked oak, he tried to suppress his loud breathing, and listened.

Nothing.

Moving slowly, trying to make no noise, he continued deeper into the trees, when suddenly the patch of woods ended.

He stood at the edge of an open pasture, only seventy-five feet from where he had first entered the woods, and not much farther from the home.

Stepping out into the open field he looked to his right and then to his left. The patch of woods was barely two hundred feet wide. Tidmore could start at one end and with a mere two or three sweeps through the trees find and flush him from any place he hid.

He thought a moment. It was too dangerous to try and lie silently as the sheriff passed and then move in another direction. If he was discovered he would not be able to outrun a pistol shot.

He strained to hear back into the thicket of trees and bushes, but again heard only silence.

He glanced to the right and left once more. Tidmore could be coming around the edge of the woods to surprise him from either side.

He looked across the open pasture to the next block of timber left as a wildlife habitat. It was at least two hundred yards away. If he went madly dashing that way and the sheriff came around in his pickup he would have no chance. And the distant patch looked even smaller than the one he was presently in, even less cover.

To circle the woods back toward the house was his

only choice. But which way—and was Tidmore doing the same at that moment? His stomach was knotted so tightly it hurt.

He decided to move around the woods to the south. That direction would bring him out nearest his Cadillac with no more chance of meeting the sheriff than going north, the longer way around.

Staying just far enough from the edge of the timber to keep the quieter fescue under his feet, he started walking.

At the first corner he cut into the trees and crossed a ditch, taking a full five minutes in doing so to make sure he made no noise. He stopped on the far side.

Peering out around the base of an ancient cedar and looking down the line of trees he could see nothing, the thick clouds above him shutting out all the moon's reflected light. The sheriff would not easily see him, either.

Then he remembered the night-vision equipment Tidmore had borrowed to spot coyotes, or rustlers. A cold chill ran up his back. He strained to see out across the pasture . . . and wondered if there were eyes searching for him.

He hurried down the side of the trees.

Soon he was at the corner of the block, fifty feet from the back of the garage, and a hundred and fifty feet from his Cadillac and Flora's pistol.

He took in a deep breath as he stepped from the trees, then strode quickly on the balls of his feet to the back edge of the garage.

An opening in the clouds bathed the Cadillac in an eerie circle of light, a scene at once both tempting and frightening.

He had no other choice.

Moving partway down the side of the garage, he stopped.

Looking up, waiting for the gap in the clouds to close, he leaned back against the garage wall, trying to meld his shape into the straight lines of the building.

The telephone inside the office rang, startling him, its shrill sound crystal clear through the block walls.

It rang again.

A third time.

Halfway through its fourth ring it stopped.

He turned and moved back around the garage.

At the far corner of the building, only a few feet from the office door, he hesitated. His eyes scanned the back of the house, the heart-shaped shrubs surrounding the swimming pool, the edge of the block of timber. With a deep breath, his heart racing, he moved around the corner and to the door of the office.

Rushing to the desk, he lifted the telephone receiver and quickly punched in 911.

The answer came after the first ring. "Davis County Sheriff's Department."

He lowered the receiver, stared at it a moment, then placed it back on the cradle. His mind racing, he tried to think.

He remembered the gas ticket.

Fumbling in his pocket, he found the piece of paper Winstead had given him. Holding it close to his face he was able to read the number. He lifted the receiver and punched the digits in.

It rang three times and was beginning its fourth when Winstead answered.

"Hello." The simple word was slowly spoken. Winstead's voice was low and listless.

"J.J. The sheriff killed Judith. I'm out—"

"Brandon . . . ?"

"Listen, J.J. I'm at Raymond's. I'm in his garage office. He knows I know. I can only talk for a second. I was afraid to talk to the sheriff's department. You have to get out here. For God's sake, hurry."

"Brandon, what in the hell are you talking about?"

"For the love of God, J.J., I can't stand here and talk. He could walk in the door any minute. Please take my word for it. He killed Judith. I have proof. Call the city police or whoever you trust, but get out here as quick as you can. Please."

Richards replaced the receiver and hurried to the door.

Leaning outside, he looked back toward the house and gazed directly into the back of the sheriff's head. Not twenty feet away, Tidmore, his back turned, was moving his head slowly back and forth as his eyes searched the backyard.

Richards jerked his head inside the office and leaned back against the wall, his heart surging so rapidly he felt dizzy. He glanced around wildly.

The sheriff coughed—just outside the door.

Richards pressed his arms back hard against the concrete blocks, tensing his muscles, preparing to spring, and his left hand felt the piece of wood. He glanced down at the short lengths of two-by-fours leaning against the wall. He circled his fingers around one of them as the sheriff walked through the door, and then he swung.

Tidmore gasped and collapsed forward, his arms limp at his side, his chest and face slamming hard into the concrete floor.

Richards raised the two-by-four high over his head, but the limp form before him lay motionless.

Dropping the two-by-four, he dashed through the door and around the corner, sprinting to his Cadillac.

Yanking open the door, he pulled Flora's semiautomatic from the glove compartment and ran back toward the office.

Coming to a stop a few feet from the door, he clasped the pistol with both hands and raised it before him. He took a slow step toward the darkened entranceway, and then another, and finally to it. Leaning forward, he used one hand to reach around the corner to the light switch, found it, and flicked it on.

The form lying on the floor was still motionless. He stepped through the door and hurried toward the telephone.

"Brandon."

He whirled around, instinctively dropping into a crouch, holding the automatic out in front of him with trembling hands.

Tidmore, dazed and shaking his head, pulled his feet under him and stood. He reached a hand to his bleeding forehead and then looked at his blood-covered fingers.

Judith's blood! Richards felt hatred boiling up inside of him, washing his panic and need to summon help away.

He cocked Flora's pistol.

The sheriff raised his face at the metallic click.

"Brandon."

"SHUT UP."

The sheriff shook his head. "It was the footprint," he said resignedly. "You recognized the footprint. I knew you had when I saw you staring. I knew all along you were going to find out. I knew it."

Richards was now sure. His lips thin and tight, he lowered the barrel from Tidmore's face, down toward the sheriff's lower stomach. *He must suffer.* He lowered the barrel of the automatic farther, to the sheriff's kneecap . . . the injured leg? *A disability?* He raised his face. Tidmore was shaking his head in dismay.

Richards looked back to the leg. *The squirrel's dis-*

ability. "Minnefield was telling me it was you and I didn't listen." He shook his head. "Minnefield couldn't resist playing with me, seeing how far he could go, and I didn't listen. You're the crippled squirrel he spoke of, Raymond. The one who was a 'trifle slower' than the others. I've not noticed you limp. Did Minnefield? Or was it something else that he saw when you entered Judith's cottage which made him know that it was you?"

Fantasies. Richards's forehead wrinkled at the thought. "The costumes which Leeanne said you always wore. Your going-to-work costume, your working-on-a-farm costume. When you stripped naked, was that your killing costume? Your raping costume? God, it was all there before me, all the time. Minnefield's squirrel, Leeanne's talk of your costumes, your fantasies.

"And now I know why you have been so unusually accommodating. I've often wondered. You took me under your wing from the very beginning, let me go everywhere with you. Cops don't do that. But while I was with you, you were also with me; you were keeping an eye on me everyday, making sure you could control what I was to know. The lab . . . you never said anything about the lab. That's one place you didn't want me. Told the lab technicians to dispose of the footprints from the bathroom. Was I the only one that ever saw both the sock prints in the bedroom and the footprints from the bathroom? Yes, I was. The sheriff is the chief law enforcement officer in the county, isn't he? It was easy for you to direct who went where, who saw what." He licked his dry lips, clasping Flora's pistol tighter in his trembling hands. The perspiration running into his eyes was blurring his vision. Keeping the pistol level, he leaned his head over and wiped his face against his forearm.

"Brandon—"

"Shut up!"

Richards noticed the sheriff's face was even damper than his. Good.

"Brandon, I didn't do it. She was already dead when I got to the cottage."

"Shut up!"

"I swear to God, Brandon. She was already dead . . . Please!"

Richards felt a slight twinge in his stomach, but shook his head and reclasped the pistol.

"Listen, Brandon. Please listen. I was seeing Judith. She came to me when her husband carried the children off. I was the one who told her she needed to hire J.J. I went by to see her a couple of times after that, to see how things were coming along. One night it just happened. I've never done anything like that before in my life. I've always been faithful, I swear. But it just happened. Then it kept happening. I knew better. I wanted to stop. But I just couldn't.

"When she told me she was going to New Orleans, it almost killed me. I begged her not to. I even told her I would divorce Leeanne. She said I was crazy and laughed. But then she was sweet, Brandon. Your daughter was sweet to me. She said that she understood. Told me to keep what we had in the back of my mind, but to go away and not come back. She said she had to go to New Orleans. She was going to change her life. Said she had to, the twins would be growing up soon.

"Brandon, you know that she was leaving that next morning. I had to try and talk her out of it again—at least that's what I told myself. But I knew I was really going back for one last time. I'm sorry, but I was . . . going back for one last time.

"I had to be careful; Leeanne would have died if

she had ever found out. I parked my car on the old logging road that runs behind the cottages and came across the yards. The door was unlocked."

The sheriff swallowed, trying to force the increasing hoarseness from his voice. He licked his lips, slowly raising his arm and wiping it across his forehead.

The semiautomatic followed his movements, the barrel increasingly unsteady.

"I got excited. I liked the games, too. Her fantasies. She had me be rough before."

His eyes widened at the slitting of Richards's eyes.

"Not really do anything rough, Brandon, just act that way. I swear." His tongue snaked out to wet his lips again. "I was going to surprise her in bed, like a prowler coming in to . . . to rape her. I carried my shoes in my hand so that I wouldn't make any noise going across the floor."

He was having difficulty swallowing and moved his hand to his throat. "It was dark in the room and I went around to the side of the bed, and laid my shoes on the floor. . . ." He shook his head as tears began to mingle with the perspiration covering his cheeks.

"When I reached down she wasn't there. The bed was all sticky and wet. I didn't even know what it was. I should have known, but it didn't register. I only remembered thinking, what in the hell kind of game was she playing now? I stepped over to turn on the bedside lamp. When I did I felt her arm under my foot. My God!" He shuddered visibly.

Richards's eyes were two narrow slits. He was soaked in perspiration.

"I jumped back away from her. I felt my socks getting wet. It was a puddle of blood. I had stepped in it. I jumped away from it and yanked my socks off and ran in the bathroom. Hell, I was going crazy—I was going to wash them. Brandon, I had to get her blood out of my socks." He shook his head. "That's why my sock prints were in the bedroom, Brandon, and that's why my footprints were in the bathroom; I swear."

He nodded his head slightly, thrust his face forward. "Brandon, I was going to go back in there, call my office, and get somebody out there . . . but I couldn't make myself do it. She was dead. I wasn't hurting her by not calling. Nobody could help her. There wasn't any reason to destroy Leeanne, too. It would have, Brandon. It would have killed her." The tears were pouring down Tidmore's face.

Richards was shaking his head. He didn't believe it. Tidmore was lying. There couldn't be any doubt, though . . . and now there was some. He silently cursed his mind's confusion. He looked past his hand to the steel of the pistol barrel. He nodded his head at his own thought. There would be time later to do as he had promised Judith—when he was sure.

"Lie down on the floor, Raymond, on your face."

Tidmore shook his head. "Please."

"Now!"

Richards walked backward to the desk, leaning against it, waiting.

CHAPTER

37

When Richards heard the police arrive, he pushed himself away from the desk and walked around Tidmore's prostrate form to the open door.

There was only one vehicle, Winstead stepping out of it and walking to where the Cadillac was parked.

"Out here, J.J.!"

Richards glanced back at the sheriff and stepped to the side of the office, keeping Flora's automatic pointed.

"Brandon," Winstead said as he appeared in the doorway, "what . . . ?" He stared down at the sheriff who was looking back over his shoulder towards him.

"He killed Judith, J.J."

"No," the sheriff said. "J.J., it's not what it appears—"

"Shut up!"

"Brandon," Winstead said, "you'd better tell me 'bout this . . . quick!"

"I'm not wrong, J.J., he did it. We have to take him over to the city police. I don't want him back at the jail where his brother is. I don't want him walking around loose for even a minute. He did it!"

"Brandon, I want you to give me that pistol."

"No, J.J., not until you understand that he killed Judith."

"Then explain it to me, Brandon."

"He might have killed your wife, too."

"What . . . ?"

"Think about it, J.J. Just believe that he killed Judith and the rest falls into place. You'll see. I can prove he killed Judith."

The sheriff, slowly shaking his head, was looking back over his shoulder toward the big detective.

"Think about it, J.J., everybody's thinking Martin killed Judith. And he's threatened the sheriff. I'm sure that Raymond's told everyone about the tape he has. So the night after Martin's in the city for the psychiatric conference, Raymond's car is blown up. Obviously the explosion was meant for him. It was an accident that Leeanne and Kathy were in the car. Then the wrench is found lying out in the garage with Martin's fingerprints on it. It's from a set Martin owns, and the only wrench missing from the set. Now there is no doubt who did it."

Winstead glanced at the sheriff a moment, then back at Richards. "Go on."

"I walked in on Raymond making out with that Indian housekeeper of his—"

"No!" the sheriff exclaimed.

"Shut up, dammit, just shut up!!! Think a minute, J.J., you've been in law enforcement all your life.

What kind of cop has the money to have a place like this? He told me himself that the dairy has been losing money for years. Where is the money coming from for the way he lives? His wife? What did her father leave her? A million bucks, two million? Look at the home, the furniture, the diamonds she wore. I wouldn't doubt if he left more than that. Maybe there's a trust fund.

"You said yourself, J.J., an investigator needs to keep it simple, concentrate on what's plain to see. He's already admitted to being involved with Judith, even told her he'd divorce Leeanne for her. But then he would lose the money that way, right? His fancy lifestyle would be brought to a halt. If Leeanne was dead, though, he could play with whomever he wanted to, and have the money, too. J.J., Raymond has something wrong with his foot. He's the one who left the three-toed footprints in the bedroom and the bath. Trust me, J.J., he's the killer."

"Brandon, did you check to see if he had a gun?"

The detective's tone was suddenly businesslike, no longer exhibiting the uncertain tone it had displayed earlier—and Richards knew he had been understood. His shoulders slumped in relief.

"Did you check him for a gun?"

"No. I didn't think . . ."

Winstead moved to Tidmore and knelt, running his hands around and under the sheriff's chest and down to his waist. The sheriff's features twisted in dismay as he looked back over his shoulder to the detective.

Winstead stood and walked to the desk at the end of the office, searching through its drawers. When he moved back away from it he held a black .38 in his hand. He checked to see if it was loaded and then looked toward Richards.

"I've got an idea, Brandon. There were two men

who threatened your daughter, right? Raymond and that little brother of his run together, do everything together. I don't want to get into it now, but I've had him on my list ever since Judith was killed."

Tidmore's eyes widened.

"Hadn't said anything yet because it's a long shot—" He looked down at the sheriff. "—and because I damn sure wasn't going to be telling Raymond anything I had on my mind 'bout his brother."

"What?"

"Too complicated to explain right now, but I got an idea how to make it simple, find out tonight once and for all if Jerry is the second man your daughter was talking 'bout, whether maybe what she meant was the two men were together when they threatened her."

Richards looked down at Tidmore and then back to Winstead and shook his head. "Judith said that only one of the men who threatened her was in police work."

"She never said the second one wasn't. If it was Jerry and he gets a call from you saying that his brother killed Judith, what's he gonna do? He's gonna come out here and blow your ass away, get rid of you before you let anybody else know."

Tidmore was raising the top of his body from the floor again, and Richards pointed the automatic toward him, saying, "You're thinking if he's involved, then he'll come out here by himself?"

Winstead nodded. "A half a dozen cars pull up out there, we're wrong. If it's only one, we not only know that Jerry's the second man, but—" He glanced toward Tidmore then back again to Richards. "—we'll be sure that Raymond is the first."

"What do I say?"

"Make sure that you get ahold of Jerry first. Don't tell anyone else. If he's not there, get his home number. Tell him that Raymond's admitted to killing Judith. Tell him he needs to get out here quick. Go ahead and call."

Richards moved to the telephone and laid Flora's automatic on the desk. Lifting the receiver, he punched in the Sheriff Department's number.

Winstead walked up beside him, listening.

"This is Brandon Richards. I need to speak with Jerry Tidmore. Tell him it's an emergency."

He glanced back toward the sheriff, then at Winstead. The big detective nodded and smiled.

It was only a minute.

"Jerry, this is Brandon." He looked at Winstead, then wet his lips. "Jerry, Raymond has confessed to killing Judith. . . . No. . . . Jerry, Jerry, just listen. It was bothering him. He just told me. I'm at his office out at the dairy. Somebody needs to come out here and pick him up. I'll leave that up to you. . . . No, he's okay. He's just anxious to get it over with. We'll be waiting." Richards replaced the receiver and turned around, leaning back against the desk.

Winstead smiled and nodded again.

"What now?" Richards asked.

"Need to get everything tidied up before Jerry gets here." Winstead turned and walked back to the center of the office, staring at Raymond. "Stand up."

The sheriff came to his feet. "J.J.," he said, his voice a raspy whisper, "I can't believe you're listening to any of this."

"There are a lot of things you wouldn't be able to believe, Raymond." Still holding the revolver from the desk drawer, Winstead now held Flora's automatic in his other hand, and raised it to point at Tidmore.

BAM!
BAM!
BAM!

The sheriff was knocked backward against the wall, his body jumping as each slug tore into it. Eyes still wide, he slid down the wall and toppled sideways over onto his face.

Richards, mouth agape, stood frozen in shock.

"Tidmore already had everything," Winstead said, turning to face Richards. "It was me who was doing without and I just up and got sick of it."

Richards shook his head in disbelief.

"I did everything right all my life, Brandon. What did it get me? I hadn't got nothin'. My record, you say, my fine career in law enforcement. Shit, hadn't meant nothin'."

Richards felt his knees weakening and thought he was going to fall.

"I've never had a savings account, Brandon. Most of the time my checking account's not over a hundred bucks." He laughed sarcastically. "I didn't even get a gold watch when I left the department. Attorney general job was just paperwork.

"There was a federal marshal job open, good money. I was the best qualified. So the senator makes sure one of his supporters gets it, man never held a law-enforcement position in his life."

Winstead's face, cold and expressionless until then, suddenly twisted into a bitter scowl. "And I go home and what do I get? I don't mind not having sex, but it's 'spit your tobacco out before you come in here,' 'take those muddy shoes off,' 'don't sit in that chair, you're too big. You'll spring the back.' I'm listening to that shit one day and happened to be thinking 'bout what I haven't got at the same time and so I say, why not?

"So I got me a pair of half million dollar term policies, his and hers. I know every angle, know what the investigators look for. I really need to wait a couple of years before I snuff the bitch, but I don't have the money to pay the premiums that long. So I figure I needed someone else to keep the heat off me. With Raymond already having that tape where Salter threatened him, all I had to do was borrow one of the doc's little wrenches. Bingo, case closed.

"Only thing, though, I had to wait until I knew that Salter was gonna be in town." He smiled. "I couldn't let him be sitting down in his hometown playing poker all night with a couple a dozen witnesses, now could I? Knew he would be here for the convention. Just had to wait."

Winstead's face suddenly screwed back into a scowl. "Your daughter, though, that bitch, she screwed everything up."

Richards felt a wave of hate wash over him, mingling with his fear.

"She said that she was gonna tell my wife." The big detective shook his head, paused a moment, his features beginning to relax again. The smile returned to his face.

"Couldn't have that, could I? Couldn't have Kathy getting upset and screaming. That wouldn't look good. It'd put a new light on things if she got blown away after telling everyone I'd been steppin' out on her. Had to shut your little slutty daughter up . . . and I did."

Richards's mind fixated on the cold eyes and smiling face ten feet in front of him. He could see nothing else.

Winstead turned, pointing Flora's pistol back in the direction of the sheriff's body, and discharged the remaining five bullets into the wall above Tidmore's form.

Turning toward Richards, Winstead raised the sheriff's revolver level, at the same time inserting the empty gun in the waist band of his trousers. Reaching into a back pocket, he pulled forth a handkerchief and began casually wiping the butt of the semiautomatic where it protruded from his trousers, smiling all the time. Then he withdrew the gun, flipped it over in his handkerchief-covered hand, and held it against his chest, rubbing it some more.

"You were guessing too close, Brandon. Talking 'bout the sheriff killing his wife for money . . . Salter being framed. You might never get any closer, but then you might. And you might get others thinking, too. No need for me to take a chance now though, not with you putting yourself in the position you have. What is it 'bout your family, Brandon, always interfering? You and that slutty daughter of yours just can't stay out of other people's business, can you?" He laughed out loud, holding the gun out in his handkerchief-covered hand. "Here," he said, pitching it forward.

Richards caught the weapon in front of his face, and then dropped it to the floor.

A smile still on his face, the detective circled around Richards to where Tidmore's body lay. "That crazy Mr. Richards, they're gonna say, he done killed the sheriff. Just went crazy for no reason. Called Jerry and told him that the sheriff was the killer, had confessed. Then a few minutes later you called me and told me that you had decided to kill Raymond. Said you'd had a vision. I begged you not to. Called the sheriff's department to warn 'em. I'll do that in a minute.

"Of course, when the deputies got here you and Raymond had already had a gunfight, and you're not such a good shot. Semiautomatic gave you eight chances and you put five holes in the wall and only three in Raymond. He did better when he got a couple shots off right there at the end: one square between your eyes, the other one right over your head into the wall back there. Would be 'bout from this angle." He raised and aimed the revolver. "Well, bye. I hate to rush, but I need to be gettin' on out the back way before the deputies waltz in the front."

"Aiiieeeeee!"

Winstead glanced only an instant toward Ruby's scream, turning back and firing at Richards's hurdling form.

The slug furrowed a gash along Richards left side, unfelt. The second shot hit more solidly, ripping into Richards's side and angling down toward his buttock.

Richards's head slammed into Winstead's face, jolting it backward, his arms wrapping around the big detective's waist and lifting him bodily off the floor with the same strength a mother uses in tearing a door off a burning automobile to save her child.

It was Judith's killer!

Richards slammed Winstead's body back into the concrete block wall, then pulled him forward and slammed him back again . . . and again . . . and again . . .

CHAPTER

38

Another storm front was moving up from the Gulf Coast, heavy clouds racing north on the winds. On the highway below, a Cadillac turned onto the Interstate and headed southwest out of the city toward Lake Ponchartrain. Flora Todd was driving.

Brandon Richards leaned forward and looked up through the top of the tinted windshield, then settled back in the passenger seat.

Winstead had survived, surprisingly.

He had been in surgery for several hours and in intensive care for nearly a week. He was now handcuffed to a hospital bed and under guard, charged with the murders of Judith Salter, Eddie Hopper, Leeanne Tidmore, Raymond Tidmore, and his own wife, Kathy Winstead.

Richards was glad Ruby had brought him to his senses, screaming at him to stop and clawing at his back until he had finally released Winstead, letting the big detective collapse into a broken heap on the floor.

Judith would have wanted him to stop, too. He realized that now.

He glanced over at Flora and she smiled and reached out a hand to pat him on the shoulder, and then squeezed.

"I'm ready to talk about it now," he said.

"Baby, that's okay."

"No, I want to, and then I don't ever want to talk about it again."

"Okay," she said. "I keep wondering if he would have gotten away with murdering his wife if he had kept to his original plan."

"Probably. He had Martin set up perfectly. By waiting for the psychiatric convention when Martin would be in the city, Winstead was putting him in the area . . . and without an alibi. It would appear as if Martin slipped away from his hotel during the night and planted the bomb. Staying with Raymond that night, it was easy for Winstead to plant it and also disable Leeanne's car so that she was forced to use the Lincoln. Winstead had already stolen the wrench with Martin's fingerprints on it and that would be the clincher. Martin would be convicted and Winstead would be free to collect on the insurance policy on Kathy without anybody suspecting anything. But then he hurt Judith and she threatened to tell his wife.

"He didn't have any way to frame Martin for Judith's murder, but he decided that if he left enough circumstantial evidence, then, later, after Martin was arrested for killing Leeanne and Kathy, everybody would assume he had also killed Judith. The investigation into her death would be dropped.

"Winstead stayed outside the hooker's apartment until he saw Martin leave and then went to her cottage. He knew the coroner wouldn't be able to pin the time of death down close enough to prove Martin didn't do it, and that's all he cared about; just leave a possibility. He stole the AB blood from the emergency room in the city and planted it by the kitchen door where it would be easily noticed and typed. He was planting it when he saw Eddie Hopper staring in the window. He grabbed him and forced him into the bedroom.

"Knowing where she kept her .22, he used it to kill, or at least think he killed, Hopper. Then he fired another shot into the ceiling to indicate a struggle. Now he had the perfect scapegoat. He was no longer thinking about blaming her murder on Martin, but under the stress of the moment he forgot to clean up the three drops of blood.

"Security people at the hospital couldn't get Graff to say anymore, but the indications are he was standing at the fence and saw Winstead drag Hopper inside. Since Winstead grabbed Hopper around the neck and is a lot bigger than Hopper, I guess Graff thought he was seeing a monster tear his friend's head off. Hopper hid in the attic when he regained consciousness. I really feel sorry for him. He had to be terrified, not having any idea of what was happening. Atlene said that he was severely retarded. I don't guess we'll ever know what happened that night to cause him to go by Judith's after he escaped."

"Was Minnefield lying," Flora asked, "or did he really think Raymond was the killer?"

"Winstead came through the yards to Judith's cottage and left the same way. Minnefield didn't have a field of view in that direction. Later, Raymond came in the same way, but when he panicked he took the shortest route back to his car—dashing through Judith's backyard and across the field behind the cottage rather than take the time to retrace the longer route he entered by.

"Minnefield would have seen the sheriff leave, and this would be after he had seen Judith arrive and after Hopper had approached the cottage—maybe he even saw Hopper dragged inside. After learning of the murders the next day, Minnefield would have to believe Raymond was the killer—he was the only one Minnefield saw leave."

She nodded then looked at him. "What about Minnefield saying the killer was naked? No one else knew that until Winstead confessed."

He shook his head. "That's the biggest unanswered question left. He could have heard Judith was found naked. The security guards who found her were aware of that, and all the investigators. Maybe upon hearing that he made up the rest. That he was correct you have to lay to coincidence.

"The investigators say he couldn't possibly have seen that far through a gap of only eighteen inches in the curtains. They went up to the opening at night and tried. They said the only way they were able to see that clearly was by using binoculars. To believe that Minnefield did see that the killer was naked you would have to assume that his vision approached that of a man with binoculars."

Flora shook her head. "The poor man."

He looked at her. "Who?"

"Sheriff Tidmore. He lost his son, then his wife was killed, then . . . God, that's terrible."

"I'll never be able to forget hitting him. Then I called Winstead to execute him. God forgive me."

"You didn't know, baby."

"If I hadn't jumped to conclusions. He and Ruby in

that hot tub . . . She was working on his bad leg, had done it for years. Then I saw that footprint—"

"Baby, you thought what anybody else would, that's all. If the sheriff had just told what happened from the very beginning, not tried to cover up his being there— What's the line, 'What a tangled web we weave when at first we practice to deceive.' It wasn't your fault."

"A tangled web," he repeated. My God, he thought, all the pent-up hates releasing one after the other. It had been like a chain reaction, each of them trying to escape the confinements they themselves had fashioned: Hopper and Edginton, the dorms; Minnefield, the maximum-security unit; Winstead, his marriage and life; even Tidmore escaping to a younger woman who didn't own him. Richards took a deep breath, exhaling audibly.

"Let's quit talking about it," Flora said. "Let's think about something else now."

He nodded. "I'm going to have to if I mean to keep my sanity."

Flora patted his shoulder again, and then the rain started to pelt the windshield and she leaned forward and turned on the wipers. "Think about anything," she said. "See the rain? It's washing everything clean again."

Richards thought about the drops falling on the soft dirt above Judith's coffin and, next to it, the hard ground above where Stella lay.

He took a deep breath and then slowly exhaled, and stared ahead. In time, he hoped, in time.

And then out of the corner of his eye he glimpsed the station wagon in the next lane. In its backseat, a little blond-haired girl had her puppy sitting upright in her lap. She was holding one of its forelegs in her hand, waving the dog's paw at Richards. He nodded. The little girl frowned and waved the dog's paw harder, the puppy turning its head to lick the girl's face.

Richards waved and the little girl smiled a big smile, then touched the puppy's paw to its mouth and threw Richards a puppy kiss. She then threw one of her own and Richards laughed.

Flora reached over and placed one hand over his and smiled, and he smiled back.

BLACK RIVER FALLS
ED GORMAN

"Gorman's writing is strong, fast and sleek as a
bullet. He's one of the best."
—**Dean Koontz**

Who would want to kill a beautiful young woman like
Alison...and why? But whatever happens, nineteen-year-old
Ben Tyler swears that he will protect her. It hasn't been easy
for Ben–the boy the other kids always picked on. But then
Ben finds Alison and at last things are going his way...Until
one day he learns a secret so ugly that his entire life is
changed forever. A secret that threatens to destroy everyone
he loves. A secret as dark and dangerous as the tumbling
waters of Black River Falls.

"Gorman has a way of getting into his characters and
they have a way of getting into you."
—**Robert Block, author of *Psycho***

——4265-7 $4.99 US/$5.99 CAN

HOWL-O-WEEN
Gary L. Holleman

Evil lurks on Halloween night....

H ear the demons wail in the night,
O ut of terror and out of fright,
W erewolves, witch doctors, and zombies too
L urk in the dark and wait for you.
O ther scary creatures dwell
W here they can drag you off to hell.
E vil waits for black midnight
E nchanting with magic and dark voodoo,
N ow Halloween has cast its spell.

_4083-2 $4.99 US/$5.99 CAN